D0456872

FARRAR
STRAUS
GIROUX

Rules for Saying Goodbye

Rules for Saying Goodbye

KATHERINE TAYLOR

Farrar, Straus and Giroux

New York

Farrar, Straus and Giroux
19 Union Square West, New York 10003

Copyright © 2007 by Katherine Taylor
All rights reserved
Distributed in Canada by Douglas & McIntyre Ltd.
Printed in the United States of America
First edition, 2007

Library of Congress Cataloging-in-Publication Data
Taylor, Katherine, [date]
Rules for saying goodbye : a novel / Katherine Taylor. — 1st ed.
    p.   cm.
ISBN-13: 978-0-374-25271-7 (hardcover : alk. paper)
ISBN-10: 0-374-25271-8 (hardcover : alk. paper)
I. Title.
PS3620.A947R85 2007
813'.6—dc22

                                                    2006031198

Designed by Jonathan D. Lippincott

www.fsgbooks.com

1   3   5   7   9   10   8   6   4   2

for my parents

Part One

Preparing for Power

I knew how to listen in on the telephone extension without anyone hearing a click. Until I left home, my mother never, ever had
a private conversation. Eavesdropping was my hobby. I enjoyed it
more than kicking a soccer ball against the side of the garage to
see how much stucco I could knock off and more than stripping
bark from the oaks in our front yard with the claw of a hammer.

If I put just my thumb over the receiver, I could breathe as
loud as I wanted, even during the winter with a sinus infection,
and no one could hear.

"That is not the point. You are not getting the point."

"You should have never asked him. You should have just
taken the car."

"Last time I did that, I wrecked it. Do you remember?"

"Did you?"

"I dented the wheel well against the median."

"It's your car, too."

"Listen, I am coming to the point."

"The point is you love him."

"Yes," Mother said. "Yes, I adore him."

Other people's conversations were more reassuring than un-
raveling hand-knitted sweaters and more interesting than the

stack of old correspondence in my father's closet. Sitting in the dark of the phone closet off the entryway, with the receiver to my ear, when I was nine, ten, eleven, twelve, I learned the details of mutual funds and mortgage payments, how friendships disintegrate, and the common complaints of a marriage. I knew before anyone had mentioned the topic that my mother planned for me to go to boarding school.

"She can't go to school here in Fresno," she told Auntie Petra.

Auntie Petra was two hundred pounds overweight and taught second grade in Compton. The corners of her Venice Beach apartment were piled high with *Reader's Digest* and *Life*. She talked with food in her mouth. "What's wrong with school there?"

"Don't get me started on what's wrong. You don't have enough time for what's wrong."

"Give me one reason she can't go to school there."

"Because," my mother whispered, as if I might be outside her door and not downstairs listening from the phone closet, "this horrible little town is full of horrible little people."

That summer I was eleven my mother had a terminal argument with her best friend from college. Afterwards, she loathed our little town more than ever, so she and I drove to San Francisco for a weekend to buy autumn overcoats and to eat lunch and dinner in the high-ceilinged hotel restaurants that made my mother happy.

"Why did you argue with Alice?" I asked her. I had picked up that conversation in the middle, and I couldn't determine exactly what had caused the row.

"I'll tell you when you're older," she said.

"How much older?"

"Fifteen."

"Fifteen is too long to wait. I want to know now."

"I'm not telling you now."

"But I'll forget to ask when I'm fifteen."

"You never forget anything," she said.

We drove past the still windmills in the foothills before Berkeley. "Look at those," my mother said. "What a scam. Have we ever seen them moving?"

Our first day in San Francisco, the rain started. Mother and I parked the car at the hotel and walked together through the wet summer afternoon, under the department store awnings around Union Square. She was very slender then, and men turned their heads to stare at her. I was tall for eleven, so when my mother and I walked together, I imagined people might think we were sisters or intimate friends, leaning into each other and speaking close.

"Tell me about your argument," I whispered to her as we dodged animal rights activists outside Gump's.

"Fifteen is not so long to wait," she said. "It will give us something to talk about later."

"I hate later."

When the rain turned to a downpour, we shrieked as we ran from awning to awning. My new ballet slippers, which I insisted upon wearing at all times, were ruined. The city became a vibrant gray. We shook the rain off the ends of our fingertips. Our summer-weight overcoats were soaked straight through. We stopped, eventually, in a department store café, wet and cold and thinking the whole thing was a lot of fun, and I drank my first cappuccino.

"Listen," Mother said, taking off her coat, "what would you think about going away?"

"Away where?" I knew exactly away where.

"To school. In Massachusetts, if you'd like. Or Switzerland, if that's not too far away."

"When?"

"Whenever you like. Next year."

When I was eleven, I had a very hard time telling dreams

from reality. I didn't understand why other people couldn't re-member conversations I knew we had had the day before, or why one day my backyard was a landing strip for warplanes and the next day was just fig trees. I once broke my wrist jumping off the fireplace mantel. Sometimes I could fly and sometimes I couldn't. I had long daydreams about what came after the farms and the boredom of central California, and more than once I had packed a suitcase to seek my fortune, like the three little pigs who left home in the children's book. "I want to very much," I said.

"Really?" She seemed surprised and relieved.

"I want to very much."

"I want you to," she whispered in excitement. "I want you to go," she said. "You have more to offer than Fresno is prepared to accept."

"I am almost twelve," I whispered right back at her.

"Yes," she said. "I think you're ready. But your father won't like that at all." She smiled.

We left the café. The rain stopped and we walked along. She held my hand in her pocket. Her dark hair was curly from the damp. Men turned to get a good look at her.

In the fall, I applied to only one boarding school. "If you don't get into the best one, you don't want to go, do you?" If I did not get into the best one, my mother did not want me to go. Nothing but the absolute top was satisfactory for Mother.

At that time, The Claver School had one faculty member for every three and a quarter students. My mother had read various books on prep schools, books with titles like *Preparing for Power* and *Casualties of Privilege*, and had discerned that Claver was the best in the nation. The brochure for the school showed silky-haired girls in mahogany-paneled classrooms and relaxed young men in blue jackets coming out of the Gothic Revival chapel. There were photographs of students reading books beneath trees in the spring, and attractive, focused people on cross-country skis. There were exotic court sports to learn, like squash and fives. There was crew to row on the river through the forest and Oscar Wilde to be performed in the intimate auditorium of the school hall. The brochure included Claver's list of notable alumni, featuring two presidents and dozens of other important historical and political figures.

"What if I want to be a rock star?" I asked my mother.

"You can do anything you want to do," she assured me. "Just get out of this town first."

Over the next few months, my father ignored the process of applying and test-taking and the rounds of local and on-site interviews. It never crossed his mind that I might, in fact, get in. We had letters written by the soccer coach and the art teacher and, when my standardized test scores turned out very low, by the psychiatrist in Berkeley who had administered my IQ test. My mother sent off a box of newspaper clippings proclaiming my achievements in sports and the civic light opera, paintings I had done of my brothers eating breakfast, copies of my plays the local children's theater had performed. I didn't think much about what might happen if I was accepted. After my bad test scores, I stopped imagining what boarding school might be like. There was no fraught period of waiting for a response, as there was really no point in waiting for anything.

I spent afternoons silently listening in on telephone calls or throwing a tennis ball on the roof to see if I could displace any of the red Mexican tiles.

My brothers sensed something was going on. Richard, who normally threw tantrums but tended not to be downright destructive, smashed all my dollhouse furniture the weekend that our mother took me to Boston for interviews. My cheerful six-year-old brother, Ethan, started crying incessantly, and the weekend I took my SSATs he drank an entire bottle of Dimetapp.

"Why did you drink the Dimetapp?" my father asked gently, once Ethan had recovered from the stomach pump. From a very young age, my brothers and I knew all the brand names of every over-the-counter and prescription drug.

"It's good for sleeping," he said.

"Can't you sleep, Ethan?"

"I'm worried."

"Worried about what?"

"Kath is curious."

"You're right," my father said. "Kath is curious."

"Kath is going away."

In the spring, when I was accepted to Claver, everyone was surprised, and my father could not have been less pleased. "You're too young to go away," he said, and, "It's too far." Or, "The schools in California are equally as good." Or else, "You'll be homesick and miserable and you won't understand those people." His reasons varied each time he told me I couldn't go.

"It's his money," my mother would say in a calm and furious tone. "But you're mean," she told him. "Can't you see we got our hopes up?"

"No one had their hopes up," he said.

"I had my hopes up," Mother said.

"Then I'll send *you* to school in Boston," he told her.

"Send yourself to school!" she shouted.

"Look," I said, "if you don't want me to go because you don't think it's best for me, that I understand. But if you don't want me to go because you don't think it's best for you, that's not quite fair, is it."

My father raised his eyebrows. "You know what?" he said. "You're skating on thin ice." My father loved to say *You're skating on thin ice.* He also loved to say *There are two chances of that: slim and none.*

In the autumn, when I was twelve, my mother took me back to Massachusetts for school. She told me repeatedly on the plane to remember to stand up straight. At the hotel in Boston there was a fire. When it became clear this was not just a drill but an actual fire, I crouched in the hallway with the rest of the guests, waiting for the signal to descend the stairs, certain we were all dead. I shouted fiercely at my mother, "I knew it! I knew I would never make it out of Fresno!" She cupped her hand over my mouth, deliberately and with force. I could not tell if she was embarrassed because I had been shouting at her in front of other guests, or because I had revealed where we were from.

The fire was contained on the fourteenth floor and all the guests in their hotel robes and dress shoes made their way back to their rooms, weary but excited and chatty. I was a little ashamed of the way I had shouted in the hallway, but overall relieved that I might, in fact, make it out of Fresno.

School was a shock to my mother but everything I had anticipated from *Catcher in the Rye* and *A Separate Peace*: the dorm stark and quite a lot like a hospital, with beds in identical cubicles all in a row. There was no room to hang all the MoMA posters my mother and I had bought in San Francisco. There was barely enough room in the plywood closet for the new clothes we had bought at South Coast Plaza and the many, many winter coats my mother was certain I would need back East. Claver was an old boys' school which had just in the past twenty years begun admitting girls. There was no official soccer field for the girls. We played on a makeshift pitch between the dining hall and the schoolhouse, while the boys played separately, on their own acreage, with their own scoreboard and gardener. There were

Latin teachers who still believed girls were a scourge. Girls could get out of dissecting a pig, but boys were obliged: they had been doing it since 1886.

The day she moved me in, my mother showed no signs of hesitation or regret. She behaved as if sending her small-town California daughter to a very old New England prep school was the expected thing to do, as if, like the other families in the dorm that day, four generations of us had done this before we had. Of course, it seemed very normal to me. I was still jumping off couches, expecting to fly.

At the final school lunch, when the headmaster rose from his seat and said, "Parents, say goodbye to your children," my mother turned to me and said, "If you want to come home, just call me. Just come home."

"I don't want to come home."

The rest of the parents were leaving the dining hall. Every portrait of every headmaster for over a hundred years hung on the wall, admonishing the parents to go. Mommy hugged me goodbye for a long time. "I don't ever want you to feel trapped somewhere."

"I won't feel trapped."

She opened her purse and handed me an envelope filled with ten one-hundred-dollar bills. "That's for a taxi to Boston and a ticket home," she said.

I liked the weight of the money in that envelope. I was twelve, after all. I had never felt so much money all at once. I wanted her to leave.

She gave me a critical and tender look that told me I was probably slouching. "That money is just for an emergency," she said. She kissed me on the forehead. "Darling, don't forget to put your napkin on your lap." She turned and descended the dining hall staircase with the rest of the parents. Her red circle skirt billowed behind her. She did not look back to wave.

TWO

What Really Happened in the Eighties

"Aren't you ever going to kiss Westy Adams?" We were thirteen and Page Burns had boobs. Big boobs, like in the magazines. Page had Cindy Crawford–style boobs, pop-star-sized boobs, boobs that deserved an exclamation point. The type of boobs we thought we had to starve ourselves to grow—Page Burns had those. "Haven't you ever kissed a boy?" Page asked.

"I don't know."

"Shut up," she said. She daubed her nails Roller Derby Pink. After curfew in the dorm, Page would sit in the overstuffed chair at one end of our long corridor of cubicles and paint her nails a sophisticated, high-decibel color while everyone watched. My mother had described the dorm to my father as "a rather unpleasant Dickensian reality." There was no hiding odors or snoring or bad dreams. All twelve of us in the second form partook of one another's phone calls, fits of crying, and sore tummies. Page never cried or had a sore tummy. If Page ever got a bad grade, she certainly never discussed it over the phone with her parents. She knew how to buy whiskey in Boston and how to draw the shyest girls out of their cubicles when she wanted attention. We all adored the smell of Page's wet nails.

Westy Adams lived in the boys' dorm upstairs. He had flame-red hair and blue eyes that protruded from their sockets. Four months ago he had said, "Kate, will you go out with me?" and I had said, "Well, yes, okay," because I had been feeling homesick. Westy still had yet to hold my hand. I had begun to think Westy Adams was gay. Which was fine with me because I really had no interest in kissing him. I had interest in kissing Dexter Lennox, the prefect in Westy's dorm.

Page said, "You can't go through life without kissing boys."

"I'll kiss boys," I said.

She told me to shut up. She didn't look up as she spoke, applying thick, careful strokes to her outstretched fingertips. "I hope you don't think I'm going to teach you how to kiss, Kate. I have to do everything in this dorm."

One night Westy Adams took me to the science wing of the schoolhouse and said, "I think I had better kiss you."

I asked him why.

He said, "Because everyone will beat me up if I don't."

I said, "All right."

He leaned toward me, positioned his chin next to mine, and put his tongue in my mouth. He slipped it around a little bit and licked it back out. I smiled. I smelled formaldehyde from the pigs the fourth-formers had been dissecting. I heard the high-pitched hum from the lab's refrigerators. In the lounge in the science wing, all I could see of Westy was the dark outline of his profile. I thought if he ever tried to kiss me again I'd bite his tongue off and chew it, still alive, between my teeth. I'd mash it up like sauce so it couldn't be sewn back on.

"How was that?" he said.

"Fine," I told him. I thought his bug eyes were the ugliest things I had ever seen. I wanted to rip them out and leave them lying googly and surprised in the refrigerators of the science lab.

That night Page sat in her cubicle using the underside of a hair clip to separate two small lines of cocaine. She spoke to me across the hall. "Kate, you tell me right now. Tell me how you liked it."

"He's got a mouth like an old pear."

"What do you mean a pear."

"I mean it felt all slow and sloppy. Like an old pear."

"Oh, awful."

"I think I'm in love with his prefect."

Page kept small bags of cocaine in a pile beneath her underwear. She arranged substances and socks in such a rigid order that she knew if anything was missing by feeling for it. "Next you'll need to have sex."

I thought that sounded a little hasty. "I'm moving on from Westy Adams," I said.

"You do have so much to learn."

"I'm not kissing him again."

"You're so boring, Kate." She slammed her dresser drawer shut and whipped closed the curtain to her cubicle.

One of the boys in Westy's dorm told me "Adams is uncircumcised," which I felt embarrassed to know. Another boy told me, "I'll bet Westy's nipples are bigger than yours."

"That's fine with me," I told him.

"Westy's a fag," the boy said.

I thought probably they were all fags in that dorm. In fact, I thought probably they were all touching each other at night, Westy included, maybe kissing other boys with his fat mouth.

I began to have fantasies of what those boys were doing upstairs after curfew. Usually I imagined Dexter wildly involved. Usually the fantasies involved cutting or trying to choke each other. At night we heard the boys pounding around upstairs and shouting. There was no pounding or shouting in our dorm, but we had a lot of fights thick with silence. We had some stern talks when someone had read another's diary, and we had breakdowns when girls dropped one another as friends, which happened every two days or so.

That winter, the more I thought of those boys together in the dorm, the more I realized I had no desire for the childlike and inexperienced Westy Adams.

"You're a whore," Page said.

"I don't think so," I told her. We sat in chapel, whispered to one another beneath the hymns. "I just keep wanting to kiss everyone else."

"That's gross, Kate."

"Westy Adams makes me vomit."

"You're such a whore."

I said, "Maybe you're a whore, Page."

She turned to me, raised a calm eyebrow. "Don't talk to me like that."

Later I held my eyebrows between my bunched fingers in front of the mirror and practiced raising one at a time.

One afternoon Westy waited for me outside the gymnasium after squash practice. He caught me running from the courts to the separate building with the showers. I was sweaty and freezing, getting a stuffy nose, worried that I might catch pneumonia and angry that my pneumonia would be Westy's fault.

"Hello there, Kate," he said, catching me by the arm as I ran past.

"Hi, Westy."

"I haven't seen you in a while."

"Right." I ran in place.

"Is there a reason, do you think?"

I thought for a moment. I wiped my nose with the cuff of my sweatshirt. "You make me sick," I said.

"Oh."

"I mean, if you want to know."

"Like, I gave you a cold or I make you want to throw up?"

I stopped running in place. I shrugged. "Both." He didn't say anything. "I can't stand outside dressed like this."

"You look nice in that skirt." He put his hands in his pockets, his eyes wide and anxious.

"You're really annoying me, Westy."

"I'm sorry."

My nose began running uncontrollably, and though I wiped it with both cuffs, mucus ran over my lip. "Maybe it's not a good idea for us to see each other." I pursed my lips and expected him to collapse in devastation at the quick news.

"But we only ever see each other in Latin."

"Well then not go out."

He shrugged. "We don't go out."

"I don't think we have time to do things like kiss each other."

He thought about that. "Okay then," he said.

I stomped my foot and rolled my eyes and thrust my hips to one side. "God, you're boring. You are so boring. I don't have time for this." I walked away from him. I used the bottom of my sweatshirt to wipe my nose. He stood there a while and watched me.

At dinner that night I told Page, "I smashed Westy's heart today."

"I doubt you did that," she said.

"He cried," I told her.

"Maybe he was crying about something else." In the dining

hall, Page didn't listen to me when I talked. She looked around at boys and winked. Page liked the upper school boys, and the upper school boys liked her. She was from North Carolina and she knew the right words to use, words like "y'all" and "sugar"; she knew when to be kind and when to be ruthless. Every lunch and dinner in the cavernous dining hall, Page sat herself down at an empty table and waited for the rest of us to join her. We always joined her.

I said, "He's passive-aggressive psychotic."

She said, "Shut up, Kate."

Our friend Clarissa sat down at the table. Clarissa was smaller than the rest of us, a little mousey. She had a funny English accent and was much better at math.

I said to Page, "I'm not telling you anything."

Page said, "I'll hear it all eventually anyway."

The next morning I woke with a swollen jaw and couldn't hear out of my left ear. My nose had stopped running but my entire face felt plugged. The other girls left for classes. When other girls got upset or afraid and couldn't avoid things they wanted to avoid, like boys and best friends and perfecting their squash serve, they cried and cried in their cubicles or ate three packages of graham crackers or had their fathers prescribe Ritalin. Other girls talked things out, took exhausting walks, said an extra-long prayer in chapel. My immune system shut down. I pulled on my snow boots and checked myself into the infirmary.

"I have mono," I told the nurse.

"How do you know?" The nurse was short and fat and had a kind red face and I could see the split ends of her bleached hair from where I stood on the other side of the check-in desk.

"Because I know. I've been kissing boys and my throat is swollen and I'm exhausted."

"You could have postnasal drip."

"But my jaw is swelling up."

The nurse gave me licorice cough drops and put me to bed. "You have a broken heart," she said. "You'll feel better after a good sleep."

"No," I assured her, though I felt too dreadful to protest much, "no, I have mono."

The nurse took a vial of blood and stuck a cotton swab down my throat to make sure.

When I tried to sleep, everything in the room got bigger and bigger and smaller and smaller and bigger and bigger and smaller and smaller again.

That afternoon I woke to Page sitting on my bed, smoking a cigarette.

"Your face is swollen the size of a melon," she said as I opened my eyes. "You look awful. I hope nobody else comes to see you."

I tried to tell her to extinguish her cigarette, but opening my mouth sent a pain up through my ears and down my neck.

"I'm not putting it out. The infirmary is the only place on campus they won't bust you for smoking." She held the filter toward me to take a puff. I shook my head. "Ironically." She stubbed out the cigarette on the metal bed frame. "What do you have?" she asked.

I shrugged. I didn't have the energy to say mono.

"You don't have mono," she said. "Nobody at school has mono and you haven't been off campus in God knows how long, so I don't think there's any chance you're contaminated." She shook her head and reached into her pocket. "You are so predictable." She pulled nail polish out of her coat. "Give me your hand," she said. "I'll do your nails."

She held my thumb. I couldn't smell the polish.

"You were right about Westy," she said. "You did break his little geek heart."

Actually, that surprised me.

"All the boys think you're a real bitch."

That surprised me, too.

"Don't be surprised. Boys have no imagination."

With my free hand I touched my face. My jaw had swollen into my neck and disappeared.

Page said, "Now you have this terrific reputation."

"A whore," I managed to mumble.

"You should be so lucky." She stared at my hand as she painted, concentrating just as she would on her own. "No, now you're unavailable. You're discriminating. All those boring unimaginative fags upstairs are secretly going to want your approval. Thank God I'm around, Kate. You so desperately need advisement." She took my other hand. I held up the first one. She had painted my nails a shocking Orangina.

"So," she said, "you have got to do something about your face, because you have a very short window of opportunity to flirt with and conquer the appropriate boys. I don't want you to fuck this up."

I was surprised to hear Page use the word "conquer." Page was too cunning, I thought, to need such a violent verb.

Page came to visit the next afternoon.

"Your face looks better today, Kate."

"They gave me antibiotics."

"I thought you couldn't take antibiotics for mono."

"I don't have mono."

She reached into her coat pocket. "How disappointing."

"I have strep throat," I said. "If you look you can see the line at the back." I opened my mouth wide so she could see. She didn't look.

"Here." She produced shears. "We're going to cut bangs for you."

I had been growing my childhood bangs for two years and they had finally reached the same length as the rest of my hair. "Really?"

"I promise you'll look better."

"Really?"

She brushed the front of my hair in front of my face and I watched hair fall onto the stiff white infirmary blankets. I held my breath. I hoped my bangs would have time to grow out a little before I saw my mother again.

Dexter Lennox had the sort of face you wanted to tape back together. He had the sort of face that looked as if it had been built with parts from different busts. A thrift-store face, with an enormous nose, differently shaped eyes, a mouth too small for his jaw. I found him irresistibly unhandsome.

I had spent four days in the infirmary, enough time to have my presence around school considered a novelty when I returned.

"Dexter?" Not wanting to forfeit my valuable window of opportunity, I caught him alone in the common room of the boys' dorm, paying too much attention to his college applications. I knew he performed his prefect duties on watch in the dorm Wednesday nights, and so I had curled my eyelashes and brushed my bangs into a straight line and I had worn red shoes.

"Hello, Kate."

"Do you like my shoes?" I spoke in a low-pitched Lauren Bacall voice I had acquired as a result of the strep throat but which I thought was very sexy.

"I heard you were sick."

"I wasn't really sick. I just needed a little rest." The only time my mother had gone crazy and had to go to the hospital, Daddy had told us that she just needed a little rest. The phrase didn't sound familiar until after I'd used it. I touched my bangs, making sure they remained a straight line.

"Why is your voice funny?"

"My voice isn't funny."

"Yes it is, it's all gravelly."

"It's not funny. I always talk like this." I began to blush and get angry.

"If you've been drinking, don't talk to me. I'll have to bust you." He looked at his papers, didn't raise his eyes to me or my red, low-heeled slip-ons.

"I haven't been drinking."

"Good."

I paused. I stood in front of him but he continued to focus on the papers in front of him. "Dexter?" I said.

"Kate."

"There's something I think you ought to know."

"What's that."

"You make me want to do some very, very wild things, Dexter."

"Let me smell your breath," he said.

Delirious and thrilled, I put my mouth next to his.

"Don't come too close," he said. "I don't want to get sick."

I held my lungs still, wanting to stay there a while. I thought, *This is a man who will make things exciting.* He looked so ugly up close that he would always have to make things exciting. He had a limp jaw, I noticed, hesitating there for a moment: a jaw that meant he could never rely on his looks to keep people interested. Dexter's weak jaw was so exciting, I wanted to sink my teeth into it. Finally, suffocating, I exhaled in a whisper, "You could kiss me if you want."

He sniffed my freshly minty-fresh breath and said, "I get the feeling you kiss everyone."

I stood up and tisked at him. "I do not. Did Page tell you that?"

"Isn't your heart broken over Westy Adams?"

"No."

"You're a fickle woman. I'm not sure I find that attractive."

All at once he began to make me really angry. I wondered if fickle women were whores. I said, "Well I'm not sure I find you all that attractive, either."

"I'm not surprised." He looked back to his applications.

"I don't wear red shoes for just anyone," I told him. "Now you've really actually repulsed me, you've made me really disgusted." I turned and left. I was sorry I had bothered to wear a bra.

Later Page said, "You're an idiot." After curfew, we sat around in the dorm and ate cookies. No one else spoke when Page did.

Another girl said, "Kate, you're unbalanced."

"Imbalanced," said Clarissa.

"Unbalanced."

"Get a dictionary."

"Let's not talk about me anymore," I said. Lately it seemed everything I did became malignant gossip in the dorm: my kiss, my mono, my failed attempt with Dexter. At first I had appreciated the interest.

Page said, "You have wasted your new hair on acting like an idiot."

"It's the same as my old hair," I mumbled.

"What did you say?"

"I said it's the same haircut as I used to have."

"What is that supposed to mean?"

"Nothing."

Page's upper lip curled, an expression she used only to display the sincerest contempt. "If you had just had sex with Westy you would have never pounced on his prefect."

"I didn't pounce on him," I told her. "I talked to him like a rational person."

"I'm going to have to teach you about flirting."

"I don't want to flirt. I didn't like Westy in the first place."

Someone else said, "You're a big fake, then."

"You're a phony, Kate."

"Do you not like us, too?"

I told them, "You're all going to die of terrible diseases if you keep listening to Page's advice. You're all going to end up fucking hundreds of men." I looked around the dorm. Clarissa was the only one smiling. Her drab hair covered most of her face. There were not very many of the twelve of us who didn't want Page to cut our bangs.

Page sighed, raised a calm eyebrow, ignored me. After a while of thirteen-year-old-girl loud-filled silence, she turned and told me to shut up, Kate.

The other girls sighed at me, too. I pretended to be engrossed in Latin flashcards I had made during my stay in the infirmary. The other girls had conversations about drama club, the lesbian teaching Greek history, the approaching tennis season and whether or not Page would be captain of the JV team. The dorm phone rang, and I was relieved when it was not my mother. There was always a sense of distance that came over me in the evenings—distance from home, distance from the other girls, distance between what I wanted and what I was supposed to want. All that distance was made real when my mother would phone.

Page produced her nail polish. The girls tossed pieces of

cookie in the fishbowl and watched the goldfish come up to eat. I went to my cubicle and closed the curtain. Page said, "We ought to shampoo those boring fish to death." I got into bed, all the way under the covers so that I couldn't hear any more of what anyone said tonight. Snow piled against the window and the wind made a hushing sound through the windowpanes. I yawned, again and again, so that sounds came at me as if through a tunnel. Still, I heard the giggling and gossip in the hall. I heard Clarissa shuffling around in her cubicle next door. I heard the uncertain half-laughter that followed all of Page's ambiguous jokes. Wide awake, I held my breath and held my breath and hoped I would pass out.

THREE

The Education

In the spring, when it was still cold in Boston but warm in New York and Washington, we would take the train south on the weekends. Page's grandmother lived in New York, and she enjoyed having all the bedrooms of her apartment filled with girls. I was very interested in Page's grandmother. She was stiff and ungrandmotherly and she made gin and tonics for us in the afternoons. "If I am going to serve drinks to young ladies, I certainly am not going to do it before five p.m.," she told us. Her apartment had high, carved, dark-wood ceilings and deep wingbacked chairs and many-paned windows that looked into the many-paned windows across Park Avenue. Her library was equally as expansive as her living room, the library bar fully stocked with whatever liquor we desired and the kind of delicate crystal that made lovely musical noises when the ice knocked against it. There was a long hallway with several doors off it, and behind each door was an empty bedroom, always made up for us with crisp sheets and arrangements of tulips. In Page's grandmother's bedrooms, I learned how New York sounded: a constant echoing stream of traffic and shouting, of horns and the wind between buildings, life that went on all day and all night, muffled by the hum of the apartment's central air. I learned in that apartment that people did not necessarily shout from room to room when they wanted to find each other, that the cloth napkins at dinner could be reused for breakfast the next day provided they were not too soiled, and that old leather books were not just for decoration.

The diamond on Mrs. Burns's right hand covered half her ring finger, and she told anyone she caught staring at it, "I bought this myself."

"You bought everything yourself, Grandmother."

Mrs. Burns would smile. "Not everything," she would say conspiratorially. "Only the things I really needed." She was softly tanned and very slender, as if she were made of skin poured directly over bone. "And old ladies really need diamonds," she said.

Page shook her head.

"They do," Mrs. Burns said. "Once the last of your beauty is gone, it's important to replace it with diamonds." She smiled. She added, with emphasis, "Not before then. Never before then. You don't want to distract from your own looks with a diamond."

"I'll just wear your diamond, Grandmother," Page said. Page and her older brother were Mrs. Burns's only grandchildren, and Page was never bashful about what she would eventually inherit.

"Certainly not," Mrs. Burns said. "I expect you to be able to buy one yourself." She looked sideways at Page. "A diamond is much more beautiful when you buy it yourself."

Those weekends at Mrs. Burns's house, she gave us a lot of advice I tried to remember, certain I would need it later.

Like a parody of a Park Avenue grandmother, Mrs. Burns owned a small white dog called Bitsy, which had also been her sister's name. Unlike a parody of this sort of grandmother, Mrs. Burns had been a Wall Street lawyer during the 1930s, one of the only women in that game, and one of the only players not to have lost all her money in 1929.

I had never known a grandmother like Mrs. Burns. In Califor-

nia, my Polish grandmother and most of the grandmothers of my
friends wore aprons and had accents and cooked unpronounce-
able things. They were plump and unfashionable. The most sophisticated grandmothers in central California owned shopping centers
and had their nails done once a week, but not very many grandmothers were that sophisticated. Mrs. Burns insisted we call her
Lucille, which I found uncomfortable. She wore Chanel suits and
low heels and did not come out of her suite in the morning until
her makeup and hair were in perfect order. Her maid was called
Ruth. Ruth had been Page's father's nanny, and was nearly as old
as Lucille Burns.

Mrs. Burns was not stupid. We got away with a lot those
weekends in New York, but not because she didn't know what
we were up to. We poured vodka into cans of Coke and drank our
less sophisticated cocktails after dark, sitting in the island between the uptown and downtown lanes of Park Avenue. Page
phoned the local boys she knew from tennis camp or from Palm
Beach, and we met them on the Central Park side of Fifth Avenue beneath the budding fringe of maples or in the walnut-
paneled lobbies of their parents' buildings. Mrs. Burns told us
not to go over to Fifth Avenue. "It's not safe," she would say. She
warned us of the gangsters and drug dealers and muggers just a
block west of Park. "I'd never go down to Fifth Avenue myself,"
she said, "at night." Later, as an adult living on Second Avenue a
good walk from the park, I would remember this fear of Fifth and
wonder what Mrs. Burns would have said about my neighborhood, or if she would have even considered my neighborhood
at all.

Ruth made silver-dollar pancakes for us in the mornings,
which we did not eat but which we flipped out the tenth-story
window until the doorman called up and told us to stop.

"We're sorry, Joe," Page said into the building telephone.
"We were playing, and it was all my fault. I'm coming down

right now to clean it up." There was a pause. "Don't you clean it, Joe, I'm coming right down. Now don't you dare clean up my mess, Joe." There was a long pause. "Oh, Joe, y'all are so sweet." She hung up and turned to us. "He knows me," she said. "It's important to keep using their first names."

We never went to Broadway plays or to the museums or galleries. We went to Bergdorf's and bought red lipsticks. We ate lunch in faux-French bistros on Madison and drank tea at the Plaza and charged everything to Lucille, who told us always, "Charge it to Max." Max had been, Page said, Lucille's third husband. He had died four years ago and in his will had not left Lucille the money she thought she ought to have been left. Fortunately, he had died unexpectedly of a stroke, leaving open his accounts in all of New York's better and most established restaurants, accounts which were settled every month by his trust at the bank. Somehow these accounts had gone unnoticed by Max's lawyers and trust managers and children, and so Lucille rarely ate at home. She left generous tips at La Goulue, at Elaine's, at every restaurant in every hotel north of Fifty-seventh Street. Back at school, when ordering clothes from catalogues or sending for books, racquets, or groceries our parents would pay for, we would say we were "charging it to Max."

Page was not rigorous about who she invited to her grandmother's: anyone with family far away was probably welcome, if you could bring yourself to ask Page for an invitation. It took great courage and a certain kind of confidence to stay all weekend with Page. Her cruelty was legend; you never knew when you might be transformed from guest to victim, left suddenly alone under the maples on the edge of Central Park past midnight.

Clarissa's father lived in Washington, and Clarissa went to see him often, so she never came with the rest of us to New York. I was very fond of Clarissa: I liked that she never wore lipstick and didn't care that her hair was too brown and too long. She told funny jokes and was always prepared to help me in algebra and, later, in French translation. She was very good at soccer and never hogged the ball. She was quick and spritely and because she made them laugh and could beat them at squash, the boys in our class liked her very much. They called her over to eat with them at meals; they wrote vulgar notes in her anatomy textbook; they asked her upstairs during intervisitation hours for games of backgammon or gin rummy. Though Clarissa was nothing special to look at, we all saw her as Page's natural competition. Page didn't see Clarissa's charm and, worse, whatever Clarissa's strange appeal was, Page knew she couldn't develop it.

One weekend I normally might have gone to New York, Clarissa invited me down to Washington. I had no standing appointment or promise to Page, and I was flattered that Clarissa had singled me out for an invitation.

"That's really rude," Page said, "to invite you and not invite everyone else." There were only twelve girls in the second form, and three were day students. The nine of us who boarded were always, between ourselves, at one end of hatred or love.

"Everyone else isn't always nice to her."

"Well, you know," Page said, "she can be irritating."

"She thinks you can be irritating."

Page looked at me briefly and said nothing. I knew that challenging her would result in two days of silence. By the end of the spring, I challenged her on everything and Page was ignoring me nearly all the time. As much as I admired Page for her composure and for all the dangerous things she did and said and knew, she terrified me. When I didn't want to be exactly like her, I wished she would die of an overdose.

Clarissa's father's house was homey and comfortable in a way that Mrs. Burns's apartment was not. In New York, I had spent as much time in my room as possible, a little afraid of sitting on the elegant chairs or setting my drink someplace forbidden. Dr.

Cohen and his second wife had two small children and a spaniel, and the house was full of everyone's mess. Mrs. Cohen wore gardening gloves when she was cooking, because she was constantly forgetting to use a pot holder. She cooked exclusively from Julia Child but was both overly creative and inattentive; her inedible dinners were dark with nutmeg or wet with undercooked onions. Dr. Cohen appeared able to eat anything, and frequently it was Mrs. Cohen herself who would say, three bites into a meal that had taken her two days to prepare, "This is revolting! We're going to have to eat out tonight."

At Dr. Cohen's house, there were no cocktails, of course, and we had a bedtime, which, I imagine, was the same way we might have been treated if we were at my own parents' house. The refrigerator was stocked with a large variety of ice cream, which we were encouraged to finish over the weekend. The house smelled always of shortbread and baby powder. There was a relief in the comfort and guidelines of Dr. Cohen's house, a certain amount of love I never felt at Mrs. Burns's house, but never any of the excitement. When I was thirteen, ice cream and bedtime were hardly an adequate substitute for late nights and the islands on Park Avenue. That, at least, has not changed.

The snow had melted and Page showed off her endless legs. With her already full body and long, syrupy blond hair, there was no question she was striking. Even the teachers paid her special attention. When Page's cocaine use became so flagrant that our dorm prefect insisted she flush the whole lot of it down the toilet, the faculty dorm head and any teachers who must have noticed her copious tissues and obsessive lip-biting simply ignored it. To have paid any attention would have called for serious discipline, and Page was such an asset to the tennis team, and so lovely to look at, it was in no one's interest to discipline her.

I didn't mind Page's cocaine use, because it didn't seem to have any effect on her but improved friendliness. Her boyfriend in North Carolina, a sixteen-year-old football player whose family owned racehorses, found it alarming that Page might venture to buy drugs in Boston, so he sent her the best of what he could find in care packages disguised with granola bars and *W* magazine. He sent her small, perfect rectangles of cocaine so nice it looked pink. I knew how to tell the look of good cocaine before I learned the future tense in Italian.

Everyone in the dorm but Page, Clarissa, and I played lacrosse in the spring. The three of us played tennis on the red clay courts, and the backs of our legs and our socks and shoes were orange all season.

At tennis practice, Clarissa would make up songs as we rallied. Inside her brain she had a living rhyming dictionary, which she frequently used right in the middle of a return. *Praying Mantis, Agapanthus.* She could return a serve under one leg, and sometimes jumped over the net and into my arms when I hit a really good shot. She never called balls out that were in, and often called balls in that were out. Her strokes were lovely to watch, although occasionally her balls landed three courts down. I laughed all afternoon on the days I was matched with Clarissa.

After my third weekend at the Cohens' house in Washington, Page began to call Clarissa "Clari" and made an extra effort to catch up to her from the courts on our way back to the gym.

"Listen," she said to Clarissa one cool spring evening as the three of us walked from the showers to the dining hall, "why don't you and I be doubles partners?"

Clarissa's posture changed, became more erect. "You would make me look terrible."

"But I want to play with you."

I was silent. I wanted to go home. I was tired of the cold weather. I was tired of the constant, heightened sense of competition. I was tired of the school's isolation, two miles from the closest very small village, and I was weary and embarrassed from calling the locals "townies." I was my own sort of townie. I missed playing tennis at the Fig Garden Swim & Racquet Club, where you didn't have just one doubles partner and no one made fun of you for using an open stance on your forehand.

My mother wrote long letters in her loopy, girlish cursive, but it was clear to me she had no idea what sorts of things to write in a letter. *The neighbors have left their cereal box on the breakfast table and everyone can see it from the street*, she wrote. *We miss you and we left some oranges on the tree for you to pick when you get home. No one ever goes into your room*, she wrote, which made me feel dead. Her letters sounded much sadder than her voice on the phone.

By the end of the week, Page and Clarissa were doubles partners. Coach was giving Clarissa extra attention at practice, trying to improve her movement at the net and getting her more comfortable with aggressive players. Clarissa never jumped over the net to hug anyone on the varsity team, and she stopped singing at practice. She ate less. She stopped passing funny rhyming notes during study hall. No one was impressed with Clarissa at tennis, and she and Page were moved to the bottom of the varsity list.

"You can't flinch at the net like a pussy," Page shouted at her during dinner one night.

Clarissa didn't bother responding. She let her hair fall over her face. She chased peas around her plate with a spoon.

Just before the summer break, Clarissa and I both joined Page for a weekend at her grandmother's apartment. Clarissa wasn't overly keen on the idea, but I felt better in New York with Clarissa around, and I loved these educational trips to Mrs. Burns's, so I had convinced Clarissa to join us. Dr. Cohen had furnished us with tickets to a very obscure off-Broadway play about an old piano, and my parents had phoned Le Cirque to pay for dinner. I had not told my parents, of course, that we could have just as easily charged dinner to Max. There was a lot about school I had not told my parents. "You're talking awfully fast," my mother would say, and pause, her way of letting me know she knew I was leaving things out. "Slow down," she would say, "your voice sounds funny when you talk so fast." I was afraid that if I told my parents about things like Mrs. Burns and afternoon cocktails and the situation with dead Max's furtive restaurant accounts, my parents would have forced me to return to Fresno immediately. Even the times I wished to go home, I never wished to go home to Fresno, exactly. Once, in Fresno, I had referred to school as "home," and a pained expression spread across my mother's face. Now I was careful, no matter where I was, never to refer to "home" as anywhere specific. During my five years at school, home became less and less of a place, and more a general sense of wherever I felt most comfortable at the moment.

"Listen, there's something we have to do this weekend," Page told us on the train down to the city.

"There's a lot we have to do," I said.

"There's always a lot, from what I understand," Clarissa said.

Page braided and unbraided a small section of her hair. "Well," she said. She paused for a long time. I was next to the window, trying to focus on one spring blossom at a time, trying to make the ground look still as the train rushed past. Page paused for so long, I forgot we were having a conversation. No one said anything for nearly a half hour. We were all sleepy, we were all weary with one another. Finally, when Clarissa had started half-snoring, Page said, quietly, toward me, "So I have to have an abortion this weekend."

"What does that mean?" I said.

She looked at me.

"How?" I said.

She raised her eyebrow, rolled her eyes, shook her head. She loosened the braid by her ear. "Don't ask me questions," she said. "Just come with me."

I suppose I had assumed Page would have been having sex with her older boyfriend. He came to Boston occasionally, and took her away on overnight stays, but we were thirteen, and there were still things I thought were impossible for people our age.

"You can take a breath now," Page said.

I exhaled.

Page's boyfriend had set up an appointment with a doctor in New York who apparently believed Page to be over eighteen. Clarissa and I told the doctor we were her sisters. The doctor ignored Clarissa's English accent. Nothing was extraordinary. After Ruth's silver-dollar pancakes and before Mrs. Burns's late-afternoon cocktails, we three girls walked to Ninety-first and Madison, Clarissa and I sat in the doctor's empty Saturday waiting room for not more than forty-five minutes, and Page was delivered to us just exactly the same as when we'd arrived.

"So what was that about," Clarissa said afterwards, wanting more than just the immediate details.

"You can't always believe everything everyone says," Page said, lighting a cigarette. We walked down Madison. For all the drugs and drink, somehow a cigarette seemed like the most forbidden of all the dangerous vices. When we were at school, cocaine was one thing; cigarettes were quite another, and much more difficult to conceal. Clarissa and I looked at her in disapproval.

"Oh, don't," Page said. "Quit your parenting for just today. Stupid girls."

Clarissa took a cigarette, her first ever.

I couldn't bring myself to try one.

"How is it all this happened without our knowing about it?" Clarissa asked. I had wondered the same thing but had been afraid to ask.

"I'm very good at having a secret," Page said. "You grow up with my sort of family, you develop a talent for it." I wondered what sort of family could make you that good at secrets.

We dropped off a prescription for painkillers and sat in an island on Park. "I am bleeding like you wouldn't believe," Page said.

Clarissa smoked cigarette after cigarette. "This is easy," she said. "And airy."

Page grimaced. Clarissa smoked her entire pack of cigarettes.

For the rest of the weekend, I felt carsick. Page mostly stayed in bed. "You just wouldn't believe how much blood there is," she said again and again. We told Mrs. Burns there had been a lot of stomach flu at school. Ruth made chicken broth and put Page on a diet of clear soda and saltines. Clarissa and I went to the play and to Le Cirque alone. We never got any of those details out of Page, but we didn't press very hard. There were some things you didn't want your friends to have to tell you.

"They must think we're very silly," Clarissa told me at Le Cirque after the waiter had taken our order.

"Who?"

"The waiter. The people here."

"Why's that?" I said. It never occurred to me that people who looked at me saw a thirteen-year-old girl acting out elaborate fantasies of who she thought she should be. I was acting like myself, like the self I had become.

"He thinks we're spoiled, he thinks we're silly." She looked toward the waiter. "Hanging out at Le Cirque on a Saturday night. It's ridiculous, really. Come on." Clarissa sank down into her chair, looking bashful. Clarissa knew enough about everything to feel a little self-conscious being by ourselves at the nicest restaurant in New York on a Saturday night.

"We're not spoiled," I said. I was much too homesick most of the time to consider myself spoiled. Le Cirque was a consolation for missing my parents and my brothers and my old bedroom. All of New York was a sort of comfort, a part of what made *going away* tolerable. I sat up straight, remembering what my mother had told me. I had my napkin on my lap.

We shared a roasted wood pigeon and were careful to chew well and not swallow the shot. Clarissa had been advised by her father to order their best entrée but to not swallow the pellet. For dessert, we shared three crème brûlées. We ate the first crème brûlée, and ordered another, then ordered another. Afterwards, we were hungry for something savory again, so we shared a bowl of lobster bisque and some walnut bread.

If my parents had forgotten to phone in their credit card number, we would just charge dinner to Max.

Before the major matches of the season, Coach moved Clarissa back down the ladder to play doubles with me. We encouraged each other to serve our strongest serve every time, because the first serve is the most gratifying, and it's no fun to tap the second serve predictably over the net. This resulted in many losses due to double faults. She spent a lot of time singing and making up dances. She pinned men's underwear ads to the back of her tennis shirts. She could do headstands and her skirt would fall down to her stomach, revealing her white, grandmotherly underpants. "Who cares about this silly game?" she said all the time.

"We have to win once in a while."

"We do win once in a while."

"No, no, we have to win half the time. We're good enough to win half the time, Clarissa."

"Why?" she said. "You want Dave Fish to scout you out?"

"No," I said. "I like to win just once in a while. We can concentrate just half the time."

"It's more fun to be funny," she said.

"You're already funny."

"You're funny in the face," she said. She leaped across the court and hugged me. I bit her shoulder. She bit me back. We served our strong, double-fault serves. Clarissa gave me that comfortable feeling I had started to think of as *home*.

FOUR

A Topic for Conversation

There was nothing my mother loved much more than television, particularly when she was depressed.

The second summer I was home from school, Mother was lower than I had seen her in a long time. She said to me one night, after Richard had been expelled from the Swim & Racquet Club for swearing on the court and my father stayed at the golf course drinking cocktails past dark, "I would like to take a gun to my head." She said it calmly, as if she meant to say, "I think we should stop eating red meat." My mother, as a habit, did not speak in hyperbole. Several years previous, she had told my father she felt like taking a bottle of Valium. He soothed her a bit, stroked her hair, told her not to let a little bad mood get hysterical. When he went out to play golf, she swallowed every pill she could find in the house.

I didn't respond to the gun comment.

She watched the television intently. "I think I should get a better psychiatrist," she said toward the television, though I assumed she was speaking to me.

"I hope you do it before I go back to school."

She looked toward me. She was smiling, but the tears were all over her face, and she didn't bother wiping them away. I wondered if she was so used to the sensation she didn't realize anymore when she was crying. "Don't worry," she said. "I shouldn't have said that to you."

I did not leave her alone very much that summer. We would sit together in the den day after day, watching *The Thin Man* or *North by Northwest* on cable, or reruns of *Three's Company*. There were things she wouldn't watch: daytime talk shows, for example, or entertainment news. Nothing with fat people in shorts, and nothing where interviewees started weeping. She liked detective shows and business news, and she loved the soap opera *All My Children*, which she called "my program." That summer I learned the names of all the *All My Children* characters and their complicated histories. The longer the television stayed on in our house, the more I knew I ought to fear leaving my mother alone.

My father referred to these weeks or months my mother spent watching television as "her spells." If I was at school and my mother did not phone every day, I called my father at the office so he could confirm: "She's having a spell."

"Why is she depressed?" I would ask.

"Your mother has been depressed a long time," he would try to explain. He never explained where it came from, or why it had stayed with her so long. Probably, he had many of the same questions I did.

After a spell had passed, Mother would refuse to admit anything had ever been wrong.

"How are you?"

"Just fine. Just the same."

"Where have you been?"

"Here."

"You haven't been answering the phone."

"I'm busy, too, you know."

"You haven't called me every day like you usually do."

"Katherine," she would say softly, "you shouldn't be dependent on me."

FIVE

Upper School

Clarissa's mother lived in London, where Clarissa had grown up and now spent holidays. "I can gauge how depressed she is by the number of empty cigarette packs in the garbage," Clarissa told me when we were back at school after that television summer. That year, Clarissa had bobbed her hair and grown taller by two inches. Her wisdom teeth had been extracted and her cheekbones were wide and high. She was, suddenly, very pleasant to look at. We were fifteen and had moved into the upper school, which meant we had actual rooms with real doors and windows that looked out to the forest and hills or onto the broad lawn, called The Circle, within all the main school buildings.

"Does she hide her peanut butter and chocolate chips underneath the sofa?" I asked.

Clarissa shook her head. "Once she set the sofa on fire, though. Once she set her hair on fire. Set the rubbish on fire countless times." Smoking was illegal anywhere on campus, and smoking in one's room was particularly risky, as the smell could be detected for days, but Clarissa's single looked onto a thick part of the forest with no buildings anywhere and no paths for walking, so she did not hesitate to sit on her windowsill with a lit cigarette, exhaling the evidence into the woods. She wrapped the butts carefully in tissues and threw them out later in the trash cans by the schoolhouse.

The double Page and I shared that year, the year we were in the fourth form, looked right out to the chapel and dining hall, so Page's smoking was done furtively at the river or beyond the farthest lacrosse field. I wanted very much to smoke. I liked the way cigarettes looked in profile, and how calm my friends seemed smoking them. But I had started studying voice with an instructor who came to the school twice a week, and I wasn't sure yet whether I intended to become an opera star. I didn't want to damage my potentially lucrative vocal cords.

"When we lived in the country, my mother thought matchbooks made very nice toys," Clarissa continued. "They were free, after all, and the divorce had devastated her. She would give us her extras and tell us to go into the woods and play. Go play with the matches, children. My next-door neighbors and I burnt every living thing smaller than we were. Snails, bunnies. Trapped field mice." She picked dead leaves from the fern on her bookshelf. "She's a good girl, my mother." She poured flat cola into the plant. "But after a couple of dead bunnies, I started spending summers with my father," she said.

The first snow of the winter was slush. Page and I put on our rain boots and went down to the boathouse while we could still sit on the bank of the river. There was a silence there that helped us navigate, later, the noise of the schoolhouse, the dining hall, the dorm. At the river, Page and I didn't speak much. We had lived side by side for two and a half years and there was not a lot left we had to say to each other. We were caught up on gossip by the time we got from our dorm room to the woods.

"Is it weird if I ask you to shave my legs?" she said.

"No." I watched her smoke. "Why do you need me to shave your legs?"

"There's a patch I always miss behind my ankle, kind of up on the calf."

Page was the sort of girl who shaved her legs in the winter in case a boy might take off her pants. I was the sort of girl who shaved my legs in the winter because I wore a short skirt to play squash. "We can do it when we get back."

She smoked slowly, with the confidence it takes to know no one is going to come upon you and report you to the dean.

We walked the mile and a half back through the woods to campus. The night was cold with that slushy snow, and big wet flakes fell onto the lamps and into the necks of our overcoats. The lights were on in all the dorms and we saw different friends and people who were not our friends hunched over their desks at work.

Back at our room, Page got a bowl from the dorm kitchen and filled it with hot water and soap and I shaved her legs in careful, long strokes.

"Do you want me to shave yours?" she asked.

"I don't miss a spot," I said.

"But it's fun. It tickles."

Afterwards, at our desks, Page copied out her French translations and I read *On the Road,* which I had not been assigned. I was constantly reading books I had not been assigned. This was very bad for my grades, but very good for my education, I reasoned.

My mother phoned and was cheerful. She was going to have a Christmas party. "There will be the neighbors, of course, and your father's friends." She always said *your father's friends* with disdain, as if they were a group of hoodlums up to no good, though they were mostly simple doctors and farmers up to nothing aside from drinking bourbon and playing golf. My father's closest friend had the largest privately owned garbage-collection service in the state of California. When asked how things were going, this friend of my father's would answer, "Oh, you know, just trying to make a living collecting trash." My mother referred to him as "The Trash Man."

"The Trash Man and Beatrice will be there." Beatrice was The Trash Man's wife. She drank so much she smelled of gin, as if gin were her perfume. "We'll have such a nice party and you'll be home and it will be like you never went away to school."

"But I am away at school." Page pressed her face against the glass of the dorm phone booth and laughed and laughed. She spread her tongue out on the window and smashed her nostrils against the glass.

"Yes, but when you're home we can pretend you're always home." I didn't understand why my mother wanted to pretend. She had fought and planned and pleaded to get me into school three years ago.

"All right," I said.

"I miss you, that's all."

"I miss you, too. But we don't have to pretend when I come home at Christmas." It was always difficult to talk to my mother while I was trying not to laugh at Page. My mother took everything personally. "Look," I said, "I have to go."

"Oh. All right."

I hung up the phone and pounded Page on the shoulder hard to punish her.

"Don't hit me!" she shouted. "You'll leave a bruise!" She was serious. "God," she said, "haven't you ever heard it's nice to have milky shoulders?"

The winter in Fresno smells like damp soil and citrus, chimneys and the rotting of autumn leaves. At school I began to crave these things, an unexpected development I kept secret from my mother. In the dorms during winter, we had to open the windows against the forced heat. School smelled like steam and metal, like endless snow and the concentrated sweat of squash courts and the gymnasium locker room. Chlorine indoors, onion soup, cigarettes in the cedar forest, and the sharp chill off the river. Landing in Fresno after the flight from Boston, I was horrified to find myself comforted by the wet winter-agriculture smell particular to the Central Valley: fertilizer and controlled burns and all the smells of Fresno I recognized.

"Show me the new pictures," Ethan pleaded. It was Ethan's favorite pastime, when I returned from school, to look at photographs of my friends and remark on how happy we all did or did not seem, how our haircuts had changed, who looked friendly in their cable-knit sweaters and who looked frightening. "There are never any pictures of you," he said.

"I'm the one with the camera."

He nodded, but it was clear my answer didn't entirely appease him.

"I'm in other people's pictures," I said, though I wasn't sure that was true.

"I wish you could get photos with you in them." Clearly, Ethan was afraid his older sister simply wasn't in the picture. I knew this with certainty, because it was how I felt nearly all the time.

"I like all the snow," Ethan said. "And I like Clarissa's double-breasted overcoat."

The guests at my parents' Christmas party dressed in red-velvet pantsuits and had red-and-green lightbulb earrings and wore gold-sequined mules. Beatrice was drunk by the time she got there. She stuck her hand in the chocolate log cake. The Trash Man ignored her, or pretended not to notice. He was bald with large tufts of curly hair over his ears, which he absentmindedly twirled. "Look at that old guy there," he said to me, pointing out a retired doctor dancing with one of our young married neighbors on the porch outside the living room. "There's hope for me yet," he said, working a curl at the back of his head. "You want to come out to the porch and dance?"

I pretended not to hear him.

All the guests seemed to talk too loud. Beatrice tipped over the shrimp bowl. I felt equally as out of place at my parents' Christmas party as I did in Mrs. Burns's apartment, or in the dining hall when older boys would come to sit with us. While my parents were well engaged with their guests and my brothers were sitting on the bench next to the pianist, singing carols, I escaped to my room. I changed out of the long purple corduroy dress my mother had bought for me at Laura Ashley in San Francisco and I hid for a while in my closet with the lights off. Ethan came up to find me, but when he called my name I was silent. My mother came looking and I remained crouched in the closet as still as I could. I heard her continue to call my name down the hall. Later, when I heard the party quiet down and the last few conversations turned into goodbyes, I got into bed. When my parents came looking for me one last time, I pretended I was asleep. I pretended I had been asleep the whole time. Jet lag, I would tell them. I would not tell them I felt like an intruder everywhere but in the back corner of the closet, hiding with the lights out.

SIX

Harness Your Hopes

My brother Richard was fourteen and had been suspended from the local high school for arguing with the debate coach. He was recovering from a fractured eye socket suffered after provoking one of the neighborhood bullies on the basketball court. He was on the outs with our cousin Doris since he had stopped by her pool party to throw firecrackers over the gate. My mother said, "Richard is going through a phase," but Richard had been going through a phase since he was seven.

Richard hadn't applied to prep schools because he didn't like to be away from Fresno, and our parents were afraid of the trouble he might get into if they were not close by to deflect it. Unlike Ethan, Richard didn't like the look of my friends in the photographs, placid and smug in their oversized khakis and rope belts. "You people dress like slobs on purpose," he said once, disgusted. "Why don't you have some self-respect?" Richard always tucked in his button-down shirts and wore his jeans well fitted to his waist. He would not have fit in comfortably at school, not only for his rigid dress, but mostly because he was entirely incapable of hiding his bad behavior, something we at Claver took very seriously.

Richard went to see his shrink three afternoons a week, but

confided to me during summer vacation that the shrink always made him angry.

"They ask you trick questions," he said. "What they're asking you is never what they really want to know."

"That's not just shrinks," I told him, my slippered feet propped up against the leaded-glass window in the breakfast nook. "That's people."

"He tries to come up with all these ways I really feel about school or the club or Doris, and I keep telling him she's just a bitch."

"You didn't have to ride your bicycle over there to light fire-crackers, though."

"It's only a mile away," he said.

When I was eight, Doris told me there was no Santa. We were in the back of her mother's Mercedes, on our way to swimming lessons after Doris's speech therapy. When we were eight, Doris made a lisp sound like a sophisticated affectation. "Your dad ith Thanta," she said.

"How do you know?"

"Don't be thuch a thtupid idiot," she hissed. Doris had an exotic Basque mother and four older brothers who played football. She had access to information that I didn't. When she advised me not to be an idiot, I tried to listen.

Later on, Doris taught me to read *Cosmopolitan*. "*Cosmo* tells all," she said. I flipped through her magazines but never knew exactly what *Cosmo* was telling me. "Haven't you read *Lolita*?" Doris asked.

"Who?"

"*Lolita*," she said. "I don't even know where to begin with you. You know, it's in that Police song."

"I don't know."

"You don't know anything."

At the dentist or at the hairdresser or any time I had access to *Cosmopolitan*, I would flip through as many issues as possible, scanning for information about Lolita or other things to instruct me in knowing a little bit of something, which I came to assume was figuring out the meaning of the word "orgasm."

Doris had fashion photographs torn from magazines arranged in a collage covering an entire wall of her bedroom. In these photographs, women in wraparound, see-through tunics pouted at the camera with very sad expressions. Emaciated girls almost our age slouched in two-piece bathing suits wearing oversized jewelry and fake diamonds as big as knuckles. Their makeup made deep, dark circles in the wells of their eyes. Little black dresses of Lycra and chiffon revealed the intimate outlines of their breasts and every defined wrinkle of their tummies and armpits.

"Would you ever wear something like this?" I said, laughing at a woman's water-soaked cocktail dress transparent over everything erect on her body.

Doris looked at me, confused. "Of course," she said, "if I were thin enough."

When I went away to school, I realized there were other people in the world who knew as much as Doris. For example, the girls at school taught me that being thin was much more attractive when concealed with chunky sweaters and oversized jeans left to hang at the hips. Other girls' mothers knew the importance of pronounced jawlines and skinny wrists and wedding rings that slipped off when you reached for your drink. At school, girls bought their loafers one size too large so even their feet looked skinny.

Doris came to visit during my fourth-form year. She slept in a sleeping bag on top of a pile of clothes in the room I shared with Page. I was very proud of Doris but surprised at myself for being embarrassed by her short skirt and blue eyeliner. In New England, the sun-streaked hair and leopard-print mules that had seemed so worldly in California suddenly seemed to me like a social liability. Still, Doris was beautiful. There was a square-jawed ice hockey player called Mark Speight in the class ahead of me. He was well built and gorgeous, but we all disdained him a little bit for his thick Boston accent and even for how good he was at ice hockey. As I walked with Doris one Saturday morning from my dorm to the schoolhouse, he stopped in the middle of the path and stood there, dumbstruck, with a gaping hole for a mouth, and then turned around to follow us. "Don't break your neck," I said to him, which was a very good line I had just read in a story.

Page and Doris disliked each other immediately.

"Your typical suburban slut," I heard Page say from behind me in the dining hall. I could imagine her shrug, her dismissive smirk, as if Doris were a topic not even important enough to discuss. Doris sat right next to me, unaware that she was the subject of any conversation. Doris maneuvered taupe eggplant around her plate without interest. Page leaned back in her dining hall chair to shove me, her shoulder against mine. "Small skirt, and even smaller vocab," she said. I was caught between agreeing with Page and wanting to kill her. In class, in study hall, at dinner, we often played this game: shoving our shoulders hard against each other, to see who would give first. Almost always, neither of us gave first. We kept our shoulders connected all through chapel, all through class, all through dinner. We thought this was hilarious.

That visit to school when we were fifteen, Doris showed me the hair that had grown in thick on different places on her body. "My mother put this bruise on my arm," she said and displayed a mark the size of a peach on her biceps.

"How?"

Doris shrugged. "Accident, I guess."

"Big accident."

Doris nodded, and punched the bruise twice with her opposite fist. "I like it, though. It looks mean."

I had seen Aunt Lou drag Doris by the hair from room to room when we were younger. I had seen Aunt Lou, one Christmas Eve, smack my brother Richard so hard against the side of his head that he toppled to the other side of the kitchen. There were many other bruises I noticed on Doris's body, behind her knee and on her shoulder blades, but she didn't mention them, so neither did I. That trip, Doris ate nothing. Shortly after she returned to California, she had to be put in the hospital and fed through a tube.

"Doris escaped from the hospital and went to aerobics," my mother told me over the phone.

"She needed exercise," I said. "She was stir crazy in that place. Anyone can understand that."

"I guess so," said my mother. "But Aunt Lou was angry."

Having seen the scope of Doris's bruises, the idea of an angry Aunt Lou was more alarming to me than Doris escaping from the hospital.

Doris's effort to not eat and be hospitalized was entirely unsurprising. Her father was a general practitioner, and being sick was the best way to get his attention. My father was an orthopedist, and between the ages of seven and twelve I had to be taken to his clinic for two broken wrists, a torn ligament in my knee, a severely sprained ankle, and, to my enormous delight, scoliosis.

Richard was impatient with Doris. "She's a nut and she's a blight on our family," he would say, his hands on his hips, his chin high.

"Richard," I said, "you're the one expelled from the tennis club." I was home for the summer and a little embarrassed to show my face at the club.

"That's their fault!" he shouted. He pounded his fists on his legs. "They were spying on me!"

"It's true," my mother said. "What kind of club manager waits and waits by the court door for a little boy to use the F-word?"

"I am not a little boy," Richard shouted again, "and I meant to use the F-word!"

Richard spent hours every day that summer hitting a tennis ball against the back of the garage and talking to himself, oblivious to the dust and the heat that permeates and debilitates the Central Valley from June through September. "I am not waiting for any of you to understand the things I do," he announced one day in August, drenched in sweat from hours of hitting the ball by himself. "I don't understand the first thing about you people."

"Who people?" my mother said.

"You people!" Richard shouted from the kitchen. We could hear him drink directly from the pitcher of lemonade in the refrigerator.

"Don't, Richard," she called.

"You don't, Mom."

"How can he stand it out there?" I asked my mother. By four p.m. the summer heat in Fresno had reached 115 degrees.

She reclined on the sofa, dressed in her cotton nightshirt, directly beneath an air vent. "Richard is, you know." She paused. "Different. From us."

Richard had the blender going, shoving ice at the blade with a wooden spoon.

"Just let him do whatever it is he wants to do," she said.

"Damn!" he shouted. "Damn it to hell!"

"Don't tell me what he's doing," my mother said.

I peeked into the kitchen.

"He's blended a wooden spoon into his lemonade," I said.

She nodded. The direct vent of the air conditioner blew long, dark curls away from her face. Ethan was away at space camp, and would fly from space camp directly to deep-sea-diving camp. Ethan knew all the easy and respectable ways to escape a summer in Fresno, and Ethan was not even eleven. I begrudged his leaving me alone with everyone else, for being clever enough to get out.

Richard came in with a tall glass of lemon slush. "That damn blender caught on the wooden spoon," he said.

"Don't swear," my mother told him.

"That damn fucking blender," he said. He drank the slush, splinters and all.

We sat in the den together, and the heat, mercifully, for a moment, kept us from speaking. After a while Richard said, "I heard you tattle on me, Kath."

Much too overheated to argue, I nodded. "I did," I said. I sidled up next to him and shoved him with my shoulder. He stood up quickly and jumped away from me.

"Don't touch me!" he shouted. "I know you tattled! Is that all you can do? I don't see you practicing any tennis!" I let him go on shouting by himself. "All you do is sit here with Mommy, and talk and tattle. You are a waste!" He was right, to a degree. I would be sixteen soon and should have spent that summer learning to drive. Instead, I kept an eye on my sad mother and filled notebooks with stories about bored girls in a dorm. I would go back to school in the fall, so what was the point of learning to drive?

"She never practices her vocal scales, either," my mother said. "How are you going to be a Broadway star if you don't practice your scales?"

I looked at her. Neither of her shoulders was available for shoving; she was flat against the sofa beneath the vent. She turned her head from side to side, enjoying the air blowing the curls from her forehead and face.

It seemed as though my father would never come home. My father came home from work late, after the night and the air conditioner had harnessed the heat. By the time my father came home, no one ever had the energy or courage to tell him all the ways we resented each other.

SEVEN

Associated Features

The winter we were seventeen, Doris had a nervous breakdown. She saw it as the logical progression in her career.

"Bulimia is no fun, and really, no one is sympathetic to people purging up good food. People just think it's vile," she said. We drove the 99 between Bakersfield and Fresno from L.A. in her white Acura with no bumpers. The car was new, a birthday present, but someone had stolen the bumpers one night when Doris had left the car in a vineyard after a keg party. "And now my doctor says I'm agoraphobic, but that's inaccurate because I'm obviously not afraid to leave my house. I've read the *DSM* and what I think I have is a moderate panic disorder." She smoked cigarettes and spat phlegm out the window. "I thought it might be organic delusional syndrome, but that's actually much more serious than it sounds. So." She inhaled deeply on the cigarette several times.

"You've done your research."

"My doctor's put me on some sort of drug, but they're like vitamins, you know, like B-complex vitamins. Those make you feel really good but they tear out your insides if you eat too many."

"Right."

"Or like vitamin C. Too much vitamin C will corrode your rectum."

"I thought you just processed out the extra."

"That's drugs. You see: drugs, you just process out the extra. But too much vitamin C will actually tear out your insides. All that acid just eats the flesh away."

"I see."

"I mean, I know what I'm talking about when I tell you about how to handle a moderate panic disorder."

The summer before my sixth-form year, I had faked a sleeping disorder and ended up in the sleep unit at St. Agnes Hospital. I didn't want to go back to school, and not sleeping seemed the easiest affliction to fake. A combination of coffee and NoDoz and old English sitcoms on TV kept me awake. After the first three nights, not sleeping came naturally. By two weeks, the wells beneath my eyes turned a deep plum. The rest of my complexion developed a papery hue, with tiny veins apparent in my cheeks and forehead. I was enormously pleased with myself and hoped I might be able to spend the entire year of standardized tests and college applications in a quiet beach town, recovering.

Nothing came of my ruse. The sleep-unit doctors gave me small blue pills and told my parents I could be suicidal. "We'll wait and see," my parents said.

Ethan started in the second form at Claver my last year there, and having him at school was far more comforting than any beach town could have been.

"Wear socks with your loafers in the winter," he said one morning, running into me on our way to chapel. "God, Kath, I'd hate the cold, too, if I were barefoot." He shook his head in disbelief. No one else had ever noticed I didn't wear socks in the winter. Socks made me claustrophobic, and I liked to see how much of the cold I could take. "February in Massachusetts is not the time to make your fashion statements," he added, taking his seat in the back of the chapel with two other slender, sartorially conscious boys from his form. I noticed, at Claver, that Ethan made the most broodingly attractive young men his friends. The three of them shook their heads at me.

"Wait and see how crazy you guys feel by sixth form," I said.

Clarissa was the chapel prefect. Standing by the door in her long double-breasted overcoat, she checked all four of us off on her attendance sheet. "Look," she whispered, "at my clever fashion statement," and hiked up her pink wool trousers to show me that she, too, was wearing nothing but skin inside her loafers. I tipped my foot upward to show her that my loafers had holes in the bottom. At school, suffering was a sort of competition. "Minx!" she whispered.

After five years at Claver, I never wanted to see snow again. I never wanted to see tricolor scarves or loafers without socks or quilted down parkas. Never again would my wet hair freeze. Never again, I vowed, would I remove three layers upon entering a building, or lose three scarves a season, or need separate pairs of boots for snow, ice, rain, and sit-down dinner. I had no affection for autumn leaves or the fresh smell of a spring thaw.

Page went on to Duke, close to home, where her ex-boyfriend was a senior. She missed horse farms like I missed peach orchards: reluctantly, but badly. Clarissa went back to England and took a year off to read as many French novels as she could before going on to study them at university.

"Actually, I want to spend a year in London just talking to my mother," she said. The funny accent Clarissa had in the second form had disappeared entirely by the time we graduated. "Every time I see her, I'm surprised how I barely remember what she looks like." Clarissa wanted to get as far away as possible from the United States. To her, America had been little but a country of unhappy teenagers.

I chose a small college in northern California. In California I would enjoy lemons year-round and never bother with mittens. I would take long runs at the beach or in the always-green hills. I would ski in the sun, and wear light cotton clothing until December, and I would have one pair of shoes for everything from classes to dinner to long nights in California cafés, where the windows are always open.

In fact, college in California was not like college at all. It was like reading books at a country club. My theater major was an ongoing talent show. After Claver, college was—intellectually and socially—no challenge. I practiced my vocal scales for an hour every day, and I met Doris much too often at cafés or pizza places or the dark bars she liked very much near her apartment on Haight Street. Doris was a communications major at Berkeley, but seemed to want nothing to do at all with Berkeley.

"I'm skipping class again," I would tell her, delighted.

"Ha. I don't bother registering for classes anymore."

"What do you do with your tuition money?"

She smiled. "Real estate," she said. "My studio is worth way more than a degree, and I'm buying a one-bedroom near school to rent out to idiots." Afternoons with Doris were equally as educational as sitting in class.

"What will you do when your parents find out you've spent your tuition on apartments?"

"How will they find out?" She stared at me hard. Her question was also a warning.

"When you don't graduate, I guess."

Doris smiled. "You're so funny," she said. "Do I seem like the kind of girl who would go to her own graduation ceremony?"

I thought we were very good friends for a while. I told her things I could have never said to men or my mother or to any of my new college friends who didn't know what it meant to live inside our peculiar species of family. There was no need to discuss why neither of us wanted to go home at the holidays. There was no need to explain to Doris things like why my last day at Claver was one of the last days I would ever speak to Page. Doris understood the tight knot of hatred and overbearing love between our parents and their siblings, between our own siblings and ourselves, and Doris understood how those relationships formed a map of how we felt about everyone else.

Richard remained unimpressed with Doris. They shared no love for one another whatsoever.

"How long are you going to hold a grudge?" I said. Richard had despised Doris since long before the firecracker incident. His grudge began when she'd nicknamed him "Thtupid" at age six.

"This isn't about a grudge." He shook his head. "This is about the sort of person she is."

"What sort of a person is that?"

"A person with no value system," he said, "an attention-hungry freak with loose morals," and he turned up his chin the same way he always had.

"I got a tattoo," Doris said one afternoon in a café near Golden Gate Park, and pulled down her collar so I could see the swollen outline of a fox drawn just below her clavicle.

"Why?" I asked.

She thought for a second. "I wanted to see if I could feel the pain," she said.

"Did you?"

She nodded and smiled and bit my forearm, hard. "Did you feel that?"

"Yes. Christ, yes."

"You see. Sometimes you need to make sure you're feeling enough pain." She bit me hard and I ripped my arm out of her mouth. It stung and throbbed, but in a very fundamental way, something that resulted in a kind of relief.

A couple years later, after I had graduated college and moved to New York, I would meet a sadist whose father had been the ambassador to Venezuela and who pulled my hair so hard one night as we made out on his sofa a clump of it came away in his hand.

"Did that hurt?" he asked, his face alight with pleasure.

"Yes," I said, rubbing my head.

"Do you know that it's painful, too, to be the one wielding the whip?" he asked.

I understood, and I nodded. "For the time being," I said, "don't pull so hard when we kiss."

"A little pain reminds you how nice the kiss is."

I agreed. "But just a little." Unfortunately, the sadist and I had different ideas of how much pain was "a little." Our association didn't last very long. I liked that his walls were lined with books, that he never ate in, and that his unplugged refrigerator was filled with nice zinfandel, but he enjoyed hurting me much more than I enjoyed being hurt.

"My mother's going to die," Doris said, sitting in our favorite café, drinking glasses of white wine with ice on the side.

"Everyone's mother is going to die."

"Well. Soon. Sooner than yours," she said, and chuckled, and looked at me sideways in that way she used to look at me when she was talking about sex.

"She is not," I said.

Doris shrugged. She smoked a cigarette. She was better than anyone else I knew at smoking cigarettes, which was saying something. "She's dying," Doris said. "She has a tumor in her uterus. A tumor," she enunciated slowly, as if she were spelling it out.

"She's not going to die," I said.

Doris smoked and nodded, smoked and nodded. Denial is not the response a girl in her twenties wants at the news her mother is dying. I knew at once I had reacted badly, but I didn't know how to make it right. "She's not going to die," I said again.

Doris exhaled, a long exhale as if she were exhaling the contents of an entire year. "Okay, smarty-pants," she said. "My mother is not dying." She inhaled again with a sneer. In that sneer, I knew things between us had changed. In that sneer in the middle of her cigarette, I knew things were almost over between us. "You are the cleverest girl I know," she said.

Aunt Lou didn't die. Aunt Lou had a hysterectomy and a facelift and was as good as new. People that mean don't let cancer kill them.

"Why can't you just be a friend?" Doris said that afternoon we tried to talk but did not talk about her mother's cancer.

"I'm not your friend," I said. "I'm your cousin."

It was one of those afternoons I wished I smoked cigarettes.

Later, it occurred to me, when I thought about things too much, that Doris took a lot of pleasure in discussing her mother's illness. Doris, I thought, enjoyed her mother's cancer. I tried very hard not to mention this possibility to anyone, just as I had tried not to mention how Doris spent her tuition money, just as I had never mentioned to anyone the bruises covering Doris's body. Cousins can be even more dangerous to each other than friends.

Doris missed my twenty-first birthday party and my college graduation, six months apart, because on both occasions she was in the hospital.

"But you were just there," I said the second time.

"Things happen. My shrink is an asshole. From now on, I have to make sure I get sick on the weekends, or when he's out of town."

Doris made mental institutions sound glamorous. By then she led a fast life, a fabulous life, a life full of handsome boys with scars. She lived in a dangerous part of San Francisco and sold advertising for the *Chronicle*. She was nearly six feet tall and aggressively gorgeous. In Fresno, she was still famous for her slender big-city beauty and her reckless behavior with men; at a party last summer I'd overheard a stranger in overalls say, "Doris Jablonski? That girl had sex with me just for the exercise."

Some people would have said Doris was a slut. I didn't. I admired her. I admired the way she unapologetically used sex to get in shape.

I graduated and, wanting my days free to audition for musicals and write my own plays, got a job bartending at one of the cafés where Doris and I had spent much of our time over the past four years. I looked forward to seeing her there, but she never came in. She had an office job, and it was likely she just didn't have the time to stop by. I suspected she felt betrayed that I'd commandeered one of the places she had considered *ours*.

That bar was full of Central Valley people—the grown children of my parents' friends or people I had known in grade school, girls from the Fresno Public Children's Theater, girls from rival soccer teams, boys I had played tennis with at the club, people from a place I'd done everything I could to leave behind. Often, I pretended not to recognize them. San Francisco seemed to be populated by every person from Fresno who thought they were moving to The Big City. "You played center forward against me in the city cup when we were, like, ten," a curly-haired fat girl said to me one night, before her first beer. "I tripped you and got a red card," she said.

"Did you?"

"You don't remember? They put your arm in a sling."

"It was a long time ago, I guess." Of course I remembered everything, including this fat girl's ten-year-old freckle-face, and especially the sling, which my father had in the back of his car. A possibly sprained elbow had made me deliriously happy at the time.

"Didn't you go away to boarding school?" she asked. It was the last question everyone asked, before I turned and ignored them.

I learned not to wear my glasses, so I couldn't see more than what was right in front of me.

"I'm homesick," I told my mother.

"For where?"

"I'm not homesick for anywhere specific, I'm just homesick."

Clarissa understood what I meant. You don't have to know what you're missing to get a longing for something, a craving that nothing quite satisfies. Clarissa and I exchanged long, eight-page letters two or three times a week. I had written to her about my kind boyfriend whom I didn't love back, about how I didn't see Doris anymore, how there wasn't time to rehearse for plays while I was working at night.

MOVE TO NEW YORK, she wrote on a postcard, in block letters, without signing it.

A neighbor of Auntie Petra in Venice Beach had a rent-controlled apartment on the Upper East Side of Manhattan.

"She'll put you on the lease as her roommate, so long as you pay all the rent," Auntie Petra told me.

"I ought to see the place first."

"That's not how these things work," Auntie Petra informed me. She had rarely left her apartment in the past thirty years except to drive to South Central Los Angeles, where she had presided over two generations of second-graders, yet Auntie Petra would have you believe she knew all the details of important worldly things, things like the best month to climb Machu Picchu and how to acquire a rent-controlled apartment in New York. "You just say yes," she said. "You don't think about these things twice, darling. Not when you're waffling in San Francisco, tending a bar full of displaced farmers. Just go, and go now."

I quit my job at the bar. I broke up with my strong-jawed, adorable, comic-book-reading boyfriend. I packed my books and all my old winter clothes from prep school. Within the week I had left everything behind for something more interesting. I was getting good at that.

In families, a lot of time can pass without anyone realizing any time has passed. What seems like last Christmas or the Christmas before may have actually been a Christmas from twelve years ago. Hurt feelings and forgettable spats can go on for decades in families. It wasn't until a mutual friend came through New York that I realized it had, suddenly, been two years since I had spoken to Doris. Somehow, Doris and I had fallen out without ever having fallen out.

"It's been a few months, I guess." It was embarrassing to admit how long it had been since I'd thought about contacting Doris.

"It must have been longer than that," our friend said. "You've missed all the best parts."

"Are they really the best parts?"

"Better even than when she had the mirrors stolen off her new car."

"It was the fenders."

"The fenders."

I chose New York for the musical-theater auditions and to get as far away as possible from people like this: people who had known me too long, who knew my cousins, who knew that Doris got her fenders stolen from her new car when she got drunk and left it in a vineyard. I had moved to New York to get as far away as I could once again from vineyards.

"It's not like I'm telling you anything everyone doesn't already know," our friend said.

Doris sold all her real estate, purchased herself a townhouse in the Heights, and went on an extended coke binge that landed her in three kinds of hospitals. I knew Doris, though. Townhouses can be frightening. No one wants to be alone with a townhouse. I knew Doris felt safest in hospitals.

Pedestrians knocked oranges from the fruit stands on Second Avenue and the fruit rolled across the pavement and into the street. Second Avenue was always full of squashed fruit. I walked home as fast as I could. It had been ten years since I left home for boarding school. Through high school and college I had returned only for family holidays and an occasional summer vacation. Still, I continued to flee as if Fresno were gaining on me.

I was counting oranges at the side of the street and almost running when I heard a car screech to a stop and pedestrians shouting. I looked up to see what had happened and realized I had almost been hit by a van. Others yelled at the driver on my behalf. A woman in a fox-trimmed suit trotted up beside me to make sure I was all right. I was all right, I said. Anywhere else I would have been embarrassed to have walked out into the middle of the street like that, but New York was populated by eight million strangers. Every stranger I passed was a comfort. I ran the rest of the way home. Anything could happen to you in New York and you would not be a headline.

EIGHT

Sunday, 4:45 P.M.

"Your mother is insane."

My first year in New York, I came home after a particularly violent snowstorm. My father was giving me the family updates.

"She's schizophrenic, Katherine. She's a lunatic. You know how she can turn on you. You say one thing wrong somehow, and she turns."

When he wants to talk to me he takes me shopping. "I'm telling you," he said, "this is it. I'm worn out."

We drove in his midlife-crisis sports car. "Daddy, can't we listen to disco?"

"I try to do everything she says. I try to be understanding." He frowned behind his wire-rimmed glasses. His golf shirts were reliably awful, but today's was remarkably so. "Do you think it's menopause? For ten years I've been hoping it's menopause."

"Go faster. You drive like an old man in this car." When I'm with my father I chew bubble gum and put my feet on the seats.

"She just eats and eats and eats," he said.

"Let's buy some rain boots."

"You don't have rain boots?"

I found the Pet Shop Boys on the radio. "Gay eighties disco," I said, pleased. I bobbed my head and bounced in my seat.

"And when she's not eating, she's crying or screaming at me."

I sang: "*I love youuou, you pay my rent.*"

"I think Ethan is gay."

"He is. I told you."

"He is not."

"Yes he is too."

My father sighed.

I said, "And thank God. That's one less sister-in-law."

"Change this station."

"Go faster, Daddy. What's the point of having this car? Let me drive."

He came to a stop at a yellow light. I unlatched the roof and put the top down. "I have the air-conditioning on," he said.

"What's the point of having this car?"

He accelerated and I put my hands up and let them flap against the air. My parents live in a small town. People thought I was waving hello.

"What makes you tell me Ethan's gay? Keep your hands in the car, Katherine."

"Let me drive."

"I'm driving."

"Your other son makes up for Ethan in heterosexual behavior," I assured him.

"Don't talk to me about that."

"Fuck fuck fuck all day long."

"I don't like that language."

"He's the one you should be concerned about."

"Take your feet off the seat."

"You have X-rays on the floor." My father drives his work with him everywhere. "Do you want my footprints all over someone's hip replacement?"

"Where does one buy rain boots?"

"Not rain boots," I said. "Let's buy something fancy."

"Why do you need something fancy?"

I changed my mind. "I don't want anything. Let's get some caffeine."

"I must be boring."

"Let's get some martinis." I smiled toward him, raised my eyebrows. I was trying to be cute. I was too old to be trying this hard to be cute.

"I don't know what to do." He sighed and pouted. I thought, Pathetic to see him pout. I stuck my tongue out, wagged it at him. He said, "That's unbecoming."

We stopped to buy flowers for my mother. Patients said hello to him in the shop. "This is my daughter," he told them. I smiled, shook their hands. They adored him, doted on him. They told me immediately about his care, his kind surgeon hands, his steady, swift operations. They were fans and behaved like people in love. We bought red orchids in a woven pot.

In the car I said, "Have you seen those people naked?"

"Move those X-rays to the back," he said.

"Perfect life," I told him. "I want to drive around in this car. I want my wifey-pie to have dinner ready when I come home. I want to take sunny vacations and golf on Wednesdays."

He said, "When I die I want to come back as my daughter."

At home, we found my mother in her nightgown, facedown on the sofa, the television going. "We have surprises," my father said tenderly, happily, as if he were speaking to a puppy.

"Surprises?" my mother said, looking up, hesitating.

"Look," he said, presenting her with the orchids. My mother has always been unreasonably taken with orchids, particularly orchids of rare color.

"You love me," she said, surprised, rising to take the flowers from him.

He kissed her, and reached to turn off the television. "I heart you," he said. "I liver you."

"I got mad at Daddy," she said to me.

I nodded.

Later, on our way to pick up dinner, Dad told me, "Mommy doesn't need antidepressants, you see. She needs flowers and sometimes she needs antiques."

When I left for prep school the first time, Dad cried at the airport.

He cried again five years later when his brother died.

Since then, I've been waiting.

Part Two

NINE

Traveling with Mother

There are no female gynecologists on my family's medical plan. I didn't see a doctor for six years because I refused to be examined by one of my father's golf partners. When the dog had cancer, Daddy flew it from Fresno to UC Davis for special treatment. When my hair was falling out, he sent me to see a man who told me, "Eat more protein. See a psychiatrist. Your father has a fine swing."

My mother didn't think either of us needed a psychiatrist. She thought we needed a leisurely mother-daughter drive across America.

That summer people in the Midwest were dying from the heat. I had never thought about the Midwest except as space on the map between California and New York. That summer Richard ran an unmarked cop car off the road on the 99 between Stockton and Sacramento and was charged with assault with a deadly weapon. My grandmother was moved out of her house and into The Home. My obese Auntie Petra lost seventy-five pounds by having a shake for breakfast, a shake for lunch, and a sensible dinner.

My hair came out in clumps. It clogged the drains in my bathroom and kitchen. There was so much of it, I couldn't wash it all off my sheets. An enormous bald spot had appeared at the back of my head. In New York I was worried and nervous and couldn't concentrate. I had moved there the previous autumn to audition and write, but found myself too homesick to do anything but cry and socialize. I threw enormous parties to make myself feel less lonesome, and my neighbors left nasty notes threatening to tear me asunder. A man wearing Rollerblades molested me on Sixty-eighth Street. I had the screens removed from my windows in case I decided to jump out. Instead I decided to fly home to California.

In Los Angeles I called my hairdresser. His name is Alfredo and I roll the "r." I said, "I don't care how busy you are. I have an emergency. My hair is falling out." He said, "First you come, we cut it all off. Then you stop worrying about whatever you worry." He rolls his "r's" too. Alfredo knows all my secrets.

In Los Angeles I met with a producer who had written a part for me in a musical financed by rich Germans. I told him, "I'm not an actress anymore. I won't prostitute my emotions." Afterwards I felt ridiculous. Afterwards I wondered why I seemed to have no control over the things that came out of my mouth.

The dog died the day I arrived at my parents' house in Fresno. The bionic dog, the three-thousand-dollar chemotherapy dog. Cancer ate his ears off. Daddy had brought that mutt dog home after he ran over my Dalmatian with his truck on my tenth birthday. My brothers and I had marked the Dalmatian's grave in the backyard with a cross and stones. After the mutt dog died of cancer, I suggested we bury it in the pet cemetery outside. Daddy said, "What cemetery?"

I said, "Where you buried Buttons after you smashed her."

He said, "Katherine, I scraped that dog off the driveway and threw it in the garbage."

I said, "That's against sanitation laws."

My mother agreed. She got wild-eyed and said, "Your father yells at me when I break the speed limit."

In Fresno the internist I saw for my hair asked if I was anorexic. I told him no. He told me I was probably anorexic whether I realized it or not. His nurse took my blood and stuck me with a needle three or four times before she found my vein.

The dermatologist looked at my scalp and told me I could be having a nervous breakdown. I told him I felt too bored to be having a nervous breakdown. He told me my hair would grow back.

The gynecologist was a family friend. He said, "Your father has a full head of hair. Your reproductive organs are all in order. I'll see you at brunch on Sunday."

My mother waited for me outside each doctor's office in her car, listening to news on the radio. When I returned after an unenlightening examination she would say, "Those doctors don't know what they're talking about. You and I need to go see Mount Rushmore." I told her I had no interest in Mount Rushmore. I told her I could not possibly enjoy Mount Rushmore while I was dealing with the trauma of hair loss. I said, "Mother, I have no time in my life to go driving about with you all summer." She said, "You'll be sorry when I'm dead."

She called Triple A to map out our trip. Mother began to see Mount Rushmore as the promised land, the solution to our suffering. We packed the car full of bottled water and rice cakes. We bought packages of red licorice and vitamin C. Mother bought dozens of Peppermint Patties and locked them in the glove compartment. She told me, "These are for me and you can't eat them.

Let me have only one a day." My father bought me books on tape: *The Prince*, Oliver Sacks, the complete works of Kant. I brought along language tapes and thought I might spend the trip learning to speak Italian.

The first day, we drove from Fresno to Portland, where Mother was upset with the hotel accommodations. She refused to get out of the car at the Holiday Inn. "I don't like the looks of this place," she said. "There's no one out here to help us with our luggage."

I told her, "Mother, this is a road trip. You cannot have fancy room service and concierge on a road trip."

In our room she found a toothpick on the carpet and refused to take off her shoes. She wouldn't use the bathroom or touch the phone without a tissue. In the morning we drove seven miles out of Portland to find an IHOP because Mother craved Cream of Wheat pancakes. She complained about the service. We found downtown Portland uninteresting and left early for Washington State.

We stopped at a gas station where Mother bought an aerosol can full of bleach. "For the toilets," she said.

"You never sit on the toilets anyway," I said.

"You never know what could happen," she warned me.

I didn't know you could buy aerosol cans full of bleach.

At the Seattle Sheraton we changed rooms four times. The first room had an acceptable view but construction eight floors down, which Mother thought might disturb her napping. The second room was quiet but hadn't as nice a view as the first. The third room was quiet and had a nice view but wasn't as large as the first or second. When we arrived at the fourth room, Mother told the bellhop, "This will be fine. Leave our bags here and thank you very much." The bellhop refused to leave, suggesting we sit in the room a while and try it out before we made our final decision. Mother waited a moment. We all stood still without speaking. Eventually she said, "No, this room won't do either. I hear a buzzing sound." I heard no buzzing sound. The woman at the desk said it might have been the air conditioner. The hotel moved us once more and sent up a bottle of champagne.

We ate dinner at a fish restaurant on the pier. Mother disapproved of where we had been seated. "I don't understand why we cannot sit by the window," she said. She protested to the hostess, the waitress, the busboy, and finally the manager, who brought us free oysters and told us the window seats were all reserved. I had a martini.

Mother tired quickly of Seattle, of latte, and of people in combat boots. We took a ferry to British Columbia—we thought we might see the gardens in Victoria—but Mother tired of that, too, after we bought rotten sandwiches from a refrigerator in a café and Mother engaged in a quick argument with the people at the desk of the Empress Hotel. Less than twenty-four hours after our arrival in Seattle, we began heading east.

In the car Mother insisted on listening to Christmas music. Through Washington and half of Idaho I slept and Mother sang along to "Feliz Navidad." She drove a hundred miles per hour.

At dawn in small-town Idaho she turned off the freeway. We had driven all night, unable to find a hotel to suit Mother's standards. Idaho smelled like pine trees and wet dirt. I needed to brush my teeth.

"Would you like me to drive?" I asked.

She pulled into an empty IHOP parking lot. "I'm stopping here."

"I'll drive."

"No, we're going to eat here," she said.

"I think they're closed."

"I want my Cream of Wheat pancakes."

"Mother, they're not open."

"We'll just wait here until it's time."

We waited two hours. At precisely seven-thirty, when the doors to the pancake house should have opened, Mother banged on the locked front door. "Let us in! You have hungry travelers waiting!"

"Don't be so disagreeable," I told her.

"I'm not disagreeable," she said. "They're late opening." She banged again until an ordinary blond girl in braids and white nurse shoes unlocked the door. "I'm terribly hungry," Mother said to her. "I don't mean to be disagreeable." The blond girl seated us by the window.

I smiled to cheer myself up and drank a pot of coffee.

Through Montana, Mother slept and I learned Italian from tapes. She snored and yelled at me even while dreaming if she sensed I was driving faster than eighty miles per hour. Outside of Bozeman she woke up. "I need a shower," she said. "I need some room service and a bed and toothpaste."

"There's a Best Western in Bozeman."

"No! I cannot tolerate Best Western! No Holiday Inns, no Quality Inns, no motor-home places. Let's listen to Rush Limbaugh."

"No," I told her. "Don't you want your daughter to be bilingual?"

"I need some soap." She picked up the cell phone and dialed the American Express travel office. "Hello, this is Elizabeth Taylor. Not *that* Elizabeth Taylor. I'm in the middle of Montana and where is the closest Four Seasons?"

"You're making my hair fall out."

"How far is that from Montana?" She turned to me. "The closest Four Seasons is in Minnesota." She spoke into the phone: "Well, I can't drive that far! I need something immediately. Thank you very much." She hung up.

"You're *pazza*," I told her. I had learned that from my tape. It meant "crazy" and I was excited to say it.

"There's a hotel inside Yellowstone Park," she said. "We can turn around and drive there." She navigated from a Triple A map.

We arrived at Yellowstone early in the evening. The woman at the entrance booth told us all accommodations within the park were booked and in order to exit the park before it closed we would have to drive through without stopping. Mother looked as if the news quite devastated her. I told her not to worry.

We drove through the park slowly, stopping frequently to look at deer, buffalo, hot springs. Mother wasn't impressed. "We've been here fifteen minutes and I haven't seen one bar yet!" she exclaimed. "I'm going to get our money back."

"There are not supposed to be bars in national parks, Mother."

"There are too. What do *you* know? Davey Crockett killed him a bar when he was only three."

The parking lot was full at the Old Faithful Inn. I told Mother to wait outside. I took her credit card and went in to the desk. "Do you have a room available for Elizabeth Taylor?" I imagined myself quite together and beautiful and tried to forget my patchy hair and that I hadn't showered in two days.

"Pardon?" The receptionist was a college boy whose name tag said, "BOB Oregon."

"Elizabeth Taylor would like to stay at the hotel tonight." I spoke quietly and in my best Hollywood lockjaw.

"Elizabeth Taylor?"

"Yes, thank you." I handed him my mother's credit card.

He read the name on the card and smiled excitedly. "Just a moment." He left and came back a moment later with the manager and a key. "The hotel would be honored to have Ms. Taylor stay with us," the manager said.

"Oh, she'll be very pleased."

I collected my mother outside and shuffled her in past the desk beneath a hooded raincoat.

That night we ate grilled-cheese sandwiches I bought at the Old Faithful Diner and drank bottled iced tea from the Old Faithful Market. We tried to sleep early, but the beds were hard. We tossed about, each pretending to be asleep to the other.

In the dark, Mother said, "Is your hair falling out?"

"Not so much anymore," I told her. We listened to the awake people in rooms around us. "I'm sleeping," I told her.

She paused a moment, sighing. "Are you sad, really?"

"I'm not sad." I said it as if she had asked a ridiculous question.

"Are you?" She was whispering now.

"Yes, Mother. I am sad. My hair is falling out."

She lingered a moment in the space between speaking and not. "Daddy's friends think you need a psychiatrist."

"They're all bored Fresno doctors. They're afraid of me." I whispered, too, now. "I don't want to be on those drugs."

"I don't either," she said. "I want your hair to stop falling out."

"Me too."

"Maybe if you were happy."

"I don't have to always feel like being happy, Mother." I turned to the wall, away from her.

"Neither do I," she whispered, still facing me.

"Those doctors are *pazza*."

"Daddy's friends are idiots."

"Be quiet, I'm sleeping."

The next day we drove about Yellowstone. We saw buffalo and moose, deer and volcanic activity. We walked off the paths and park rangers yelled at us. We were too impatient to wait around for Old Faithful to erupt.

We missed the heat in South Dakota. The day we found Mount Rushmore the rain came down in hurricane volume. Tourists took refuge in the gift shop or snack bar. Mother and I stood outside amid the lightning, drenched but not cold, staring at the carved faces.

I said, "This isn't as climactic as it was supposed to be."

"I should have seen this a long time ago," she said.

We had an argument just outside of South Dakota. I didn't give her enough warning for a turnoff and we had to drive an extra thirty-two miles to get back on our route. She shouted at me with all her might. Neither of us apologized. By the time we arrived in Minneapolis that night, we had not exchanged a word all day. She finally said, "If you don't want to travel with me, I'll leave you off at the airport and you can just fly back to New York by yourself."

"That's fine," I said.

"Roll down the window and ask someone where the airport is."

"Find a gas station."

"Just roll down the window!"

"I hear you, Mother, don't shout."

"I'm taking you to the airport."

"Fine."

"I don't know how we're going to find the airport."

"I'm sure there will be a sign."

We never saw a sign. Instead we found the Four Seasons and stayed there overnight. Mother's mood improved considerably. We did not change rooms. Still, she refused to take off her socks and told me twice not to sit on the bedspreads. "People have sat on those with their dirty bottoms," she warned me. We ordered hot chocolate and grilled-cheese sandwiches from room service.

My hair had stopped falling out by the time my mother left me in New York. I noticed once we got back that there were no nests of it left on my pillows in the morning. Clumps no longer came off in my hands while I showered.

The doormen were happy to see their friend Mrs. Taylor. She tipped them every time they opened the door. Normally she liked to visit for weeks on end, but this time she didn't stay long.

"I have to go to your little brother's felony hearing."

"He'll be happy to see you there."

She bought me new towels, dusted the bookshelves, and put all my books in alphabetical order.

She continued down the southern route, alone, back to California. My apartment seemed hollow after she left, as if all the furniture had gone missing. I rearranged my books the way I liked, with my favorites in the middle and the boring ones on the very top and bottom shelves. Despite hosting all those noisy parties, there was no one I could phone for company. I didn't know the names of most of the people who had come to those parties, much less their phone numbers. I had to fill up all my space with something that would not upset my neighbors, so I sent for applications to graduate school. Getting a job seemed out of the question. My theater major had qualified me for nothing, and prepared me for less. Perhaps, I thought, if I had not skipped all those classes, I could have learned the mechanics of an interview, or What To Do When Acting Does Not Work Out. All I was equipped to do was sit in a room by myself, thinking up stories, reciting passages, reading books.

TEN

The Family Home

"I love you, Katherine, but I hope we don't have to live together for the rest of our lives."

Ethan was standing in the doorway that separated the kitchen from his bedroom in New York. He had come home from work at the nightclub three hours before and I'd roused him with the coffee grinder and the kettle. "I get lonesome in the morning," I said.

"But I have to sleep."

I wanted someone to talk to.

"You can sleep in the afternoon," I told him. Ethan took the subway home every morning at seven, crammed between people in suits on their way to early conference calls with London.

"Do you know what time I have to work in the afternoon?" he said. His lovely broad brow was furrowed with anger and patience. Ethan would be at work again by four p.m. I knew I was waking him up after only three hours of sleep, but I thought conversation was important.

"Ethan," I said, "if you come out here, I will tell you a lot of really good jokes."

My graduate school friends knew a lot of very fine, filthy

jokes, and in the mornings when I was lonely, I wanted to share my punch lines with Ethan.

"I love you, Kath," he said mostly to himself but partly for me. "But I hope you sell a book soon and move away and give me your apartment."

Just as I was finishing my master's degree in writing and after Ethan graduated from college, he moved into my rent-controlled apartment on Seventy-fifth Street in New York. I firmly believe rent-control laws prohibit gainfully employed art gallery assistants and copy editors and salesgirls at Banana Republic from living in Manhattan by perversely skewing the market, causing prices of unregulated apartments to artificially skyrocket. This did not stop me from taking advantage of a good situation. For the ten years I lived in New York, I was a graduate student and then a production assistant and then a one-night-a-week bartender living in a fashionable part of Manhattan for practically free. The only people with any right to the sort of apartment I was living in were corporate contract lawyers or post-Wharton bankers who were instead sleeping in their offices, too tired to take the subway back to their walkups in Queens. My swanky apartment gave visitors the misguided impression that freelance writers and bartenders tending completely empty bars must make quite a decent living in Manhattan.

Technically, that apartment on Seventy-fifth Street was a two-bedroom, but its description as a two-bedroom always amused me. What in New York was described as a second bedroom in any other city would have been called a pantry, or, most generously, a breakfast nook. When Ethan moved in, I hired my carpenter friend Albert to build a door separating Ethan's room from the kitchen. Albert was the super at a tenement on the Lower East Side and ran a small publishing company in his basement. He had started the press in college, working in a copy shop near NYU, printing books of his friends' poetry during the overnight shift. Albert had a genius ear for poetry, and these days his authors' books won prizes and were occasionally reviewed in the *New York Times*. He had been a guest on *Charlie Rose* and profiled by *20/20*. Still, when you phoned his apartment, his answering machine said, "You have reached the super. Please leave a message." I wanted to do all I could to support Albert, and I needed a door. Albert thought a regular door would look awkward and skinny in the narrow passage from the kitchen to Ethan's room, so instead he built a three-paneled slatted, fold-up door, and he said the slats would give Ethan increased ventilation. The slats may or may not have given Ethan increased ventilation, but there is no question they gave him absolutely no privacy.

Though the second bedroom was the size of a closet, the rest of that apartment was big and lonely. I was happy when Ethan moved to the city and needed a place to stay.

"Tell me about work," I said. I adored my little brother. I wanted to know everything about him, and everything everyone had said to him since I spoke to him last.

Ethan drank his coffee. "We had a birthday party in the VIP room, but Kevin got drunk and passed out in there and then vomited all over himself, and we tried to clean it up but we only had baking soda, so all night the party smelled like puke."

I thought Ethan should have been the president of the United States. "Were you working the VIP bar?"

"I worked downstairs, where we had two DEA cops sitting at the bar all night. Do they think I don't know what they are? Do they think anyone else dresses in rugby shirts in my bar?"

"How did they get in?"

"That's right. How did they get in."

"Maybe the door guy tipped them off."

"Kevin pays the door guy in coke."

I loved hearing Ethan's stories about the club, a very popular nightclub that year, so popular that no one I knew would have tried to get in without Ethan. I particularly loved hearing about Kevin, the misfit criminal junkie who owned the place, and how he managed to make a success of everything. "All the managers are stealing from him, and he knows it. But he can't bring in an accounting firm or the police or anything because he's stealing from the bar himself." Ethan shrugged. "I have got to get out of there."

I have got to get out of there is the most famous refrain of bar employees, but no one ever gets out of a well-paying bar, no matter how underworld the whole situation may be. For a year during graduate school I worked in a bar where the manager snorted lines right off the tables. He harassed the hostess and constantly accused us all of stealing, but it was a popular Sunday-night spot and I made far too much in tips to consider leaving. When I finished graduate school, I thought I ought to give the real working world a try, so I quit the bar and took a job in a film production office, assisting an ill-tempered and illiterate director of music videos and television commercials, writing treatments for her and buying her groceries. She had been through six assistants in as many months, but she brought in a lot of money for the company, and they had hired me because I seemed overly keen to please and probably ready for the abuse. I was twenty-six and had never had a daytime job. For nearly a year, I sat next to this director's best friend, a very fat fifty-year-old man called Hubby who, when the Thursday bagels were delivered late, would pound the desk and shout for a good hour, "Where are those fucking bagels?!" Hubby had matted hair and wore the same button-down yellow shirt every day, dark at the armpits and grease-stained above the breast. Just before I came to work at the production company, the owners had had to have a serious chat with Hubby because he had been smearing his feces on the walls

of the men's room. I would hear him on the phone noisily telling
people he was "sort-of on the producer track" or that he had been
"giving the music video business a try," but no one was ever sure
at all what Hubby did. He was a big, yellow, thirty-thousand-
dollar-a-year favor to the production company's unstable but lucrative star director. After eight months of writing treatments,
ordering cars, and playing friends with Hubby, I was suddenly
fired by the director over the phone with an onslaught of profan-
ities and insults. I never clearly understood why. "These fucking
shithead tomatoes have crappy black fucking seeds in the middle," she said, for starters. "Where the fuck are you buying my
groceries?" I put my tin of tea and my notebooks into my bag
and left the office without a word. Thanks to the municipal gift
of rent control, I would never go back to anything resembling a
full-time job.

Between coffee in the morning and work at the club, Ethan
went on auditions for soap operas, musicals, television commercials, the occasional independent film. He had picked up exactly
where I'd left off a long time ago being an actor, but he was
much better at it than I was: he acted better, he sang better, he
worked at bars better. Kevin called Ethan "the Stepford bartender" for Ethan's unshakable, pleasant demeanor. Customers
adored Ethan, and he was a minor celebrity south of Fourteenth
Street. Recently he had been cast in a popular off-Broadway en-
semble show in the Village, a plotless performance-art piece in
which good-looking young people banged on garbage cans and
tap-danced with brooms, but was forced to turn it down when he
discovered it paid in a week what he made in one night at the
bar. The longer he worked for Kevin, the less Ethan could see any
escape. Even in our sunny, expansive apartment, with its skyline
view and fancy zip code, Ethan was always itching to get out of
New York.

"Is Jonas stealing from them, too?" I asked. Jonas was Ethan's best friend from Claver, and the two of them followed each other from bar job to bar job.

"No!" Ethan opened his eyes clearly for the first time that morning. Then he thought. "I don't think so. Jonas is the only sincerely self-righteous person I know."

"Except your mother," I said.

"Except your mother," he said.

"Jonas loves that bar too much to steal from it," I said.

"Yes," Ethan agreed. "He feels a loyalty to Kevin a lot like love. Like many people, Kevin doesn't deserve it." Jonas was startlingly good-looking, imposingly tall, with olive skin and bright green eyes. When he and Ethan were in school, Jonas had been a roly-poly fat kid with the sort of overconfidence and ebullience that makes up for bad looks. During college, he had grown out of his teenage fat, but had kept his insistently jovial personality and the sense of superiority he had developed as a form of self-defense.

"Poor Jonas."

"Not poor Jonas."

"Let's play tennis today," I said. Ethan nodded. He often played lazy tennis with me on little to no sleep, which was the only way I could return his serve.

"You know what we should do later?" he said.

"Laundry?"

"We should get a board for the kitchen, a big board where we can write down all the funny things our friends say."

"And then we can do all the laundry."

"Or maybe after tennis we can cook a big lunch before I go to work."

Ethan and I had the same taste in food and friends, but it was nice to think that one or both of us might fall in love or get mar-

ried and leave the comfortable family home we had made together.

The phone rang. No one we knew phoned us before noon.

"It's Mom," I said.

We let it ring.

For the ten years I lived in that building, my next-door neighbor
threatened to kill me. He would hammer on my door—literally,
with a hammer—standing in the hallway in nothing but small
underpants, shouting, "You're finished, Tinkerbell!" or "I'm done
with you, wench, you're outta here!" After ten years, my door
looked concave and diseased, the hammer chipping away to re-
veal forty years' worth and at least eight layers of various colors of
paint. Three times a year I replaced expensively damaged locks
and knobs. He didn't threaten to kill me every day—only the
days he got drunk. But as the years wore on, he got drunk and
threatened to kill me more and more often. When he was not
drunk he was sociable and almost charming. He would invite me
over to dinner or ask my opinion on art shows or theater. "You
and I are the building's resident aesthetes," he said once, blinking
at me repeatedly and smiling, "but I have a few years' more practice." Kyle was an unpleasant-looking sixty-year-old with pock-
marked skin and splotchy eyebrows. He was just five feet tall,
and when he worked as a box-office manager at the Nederlander
Theatre, they had a special stool for him to stand on behind the
window.

For two blissful years, he moved to Napa to join a monastery
and sublet his apartment to a woman who pounded forty
thousand nails into the wall. I was much happier living next door
to a woman who pounded nails into our common wall all day
than I had been living next door to Kyle, who wanted me dead.

In the end, something went wrong with his plan to be a monk. He didn't get on well with the other monks, he told me one day in the elevator after he returned. He said, "You know, that crazy woman covered my entire living room wall in nails?"

"Who was she?" I asked.

He shook his head. "My aunt," he said.

While in Napa, Kyle had joined the Champagne-of-the-Month Club. Unfortunately, he had no friends to help him drink the champagne, so at least once a month he set to banging on my door, shouting about the different ways I would die.

I would see him in the building later and he would smile, wave, pretend that nothing had happened.

There are many recorded calls of me phoning 911 in a panic. The police would come—they were always surprisingly soft-spoken and kind, not at all what I read in the papers about New York City policemen. "I thought champagne made people happy drunks," I told them, teary-eyed and frightened.

They knocked on his door but Kyle never answered and as the police left they would tell me, "Just call us if he does it again." A few times they advised me to find someplace new to live, but in New York, giving up a rent-controlled apartment to save your life is as ridiculous as living in Queens.

The attacks slowed down once Ethan moved in, but did not stop completely. Kyle got to know Ethan's nights off, and managed to keep to himself those nights. Kyle didn't like tall men. If Ethan happened to appear in the hallway while Kyle waited for the elevator, Kyle would forget something in his apartment, or casually look for something in the recycling closet, or would pretend he was in a hurry and flee down twelve flights of stairs.

Naturally, the landlord was of no help. Owners of rent-controlled buildings don't mind when one tenant threatens to kill another; this sort of behavior generally clears out apartments quicker, allowing for new tenants and a hike in the rent. I wrote to the landlords telling them that my next-door neighbor had threatened to kill me and they wrote back, "He says you make too much noise. If your behavior continues, we will evict you."

Albert wanted to help. "I could talk to him."

"This is not a person you talk to," I said. "I talk to him all the time."

"It's better if a man talks to him."

I knew it would be no good for Albert to talk to Kyle. Albert was tall and muscular and had the chiseled face of a runway model; he had dark hair and pale skin and the broody sort of eyes you either feared or wanted. Kyle would be terrified and belligerent, or else run away or refuse to answer the door. "I think it's okay if you don't," I told Albert. "I have done all the talking there is to be done."

"Sometimes you can't handle absolutely everything by yourself," Albert said.

At his small press, Albert was having some trouble handling everything by himself. He had a great gift for knowing good poetry, but he had no gift for finances. He forgot which people to pay when, and he had no mind for things like royalties and percentages. His personal finances were indistinguishable from the finances at the press: Albert had only ever had one bank account. When it became clear that he needed some help with pecuniary matters, Albert enlisted a good friend of his from the tenement, a failed theater director called Bucky who lived on money his parents provided. Bucky was very good with numbers and a shrewd businessman—so shrewd that he had gradually begun to eliminate Albert from anything having to do with the small publishing company in the basement.

"Why don't you tell him to get lost?" I said.

"It's the deal he's cut with the distributor and the printers. He has some new investors, people who are taking care of all the money problems. He said we would just tell them I'm on hiatus, while I would go on like I usually do running the editorial. But it seems like he's sort-of taken over the editorial, too."

The poets were very happy to get their three-hundred-dollar royalty checks, and poor Albert had been strong-armed out of the only thing he had learned to love. He chose the wrong partner at a time when he needed someone on his side. Albert needed a brother like Ethan, is what I thought. I never said this. I didn't want to flaunt my good luck to everyone else. I took Albert to Ethan's bar. A cocktail was a good way to cheer someone up after I'd run out of cheerful things to say.

For his part, Ethan wondered why I wasn't in love with Albert. "He's smart and funny and much more gorgeous than most of your boyfriends," Ethan said one morning, almost pleading with me.

"We're just friends."

"That's no reason. Why can't you fall in love with one of your friends?"

"I don't know," I said. "Maybe it's because he's not already in love with me."

This frightened Ethan. I could see in the way his mouth became a perfectly straight, terrified line that he was imagining what it would be like if the two of us were to live together for the rest of our lives.

ELEVEN

An Evening at the Carlyle

The year I was fired from the film company and worked one night a week at an empty tourist bar in Times Square, I was very happy so long as I kept from making plans with people. I had wonderful friends, but any sort of commitment unnerved me. A mild dread of what's in store is not unreasonable for a young woman in New York who's just lost her job, I thought. Sometimes I managed to get places by blurring my focus and pretending I was dead, but oftentimes I would cancel plans at the last minute, walking to the Hampton Jitney and then sprinting back home, or else getting as far as the Seventy-seventh Street subway station and panicking on the stairs. Making plans with people in advance gave me enough time to imagine what a horrible time I could have.

One summer weekend, I had promised Albert I would accompany him to drinks with a record producer in from London. Since losing the publishing company, Albert had devoted all his time to writing punk-rock ballads and performing in small venues around town. Albert's music wasn't particularly interesting to me, but a lot of people thought it was very good and he had begun to get some attention in the alternative and underground press. There was a privately owned, important dance-music label out of the U.K. that thought Albert's songs, with a little electronic beat, could make some money. The director of the company had arranged a meeting with him just up the street from my building, on Madison, at the Carlyle Hotel. I was no more than the evening's accoutrement, but I began to panic ten hours in advance.

"You stand behind the bar like a big shot," Ethan scolded, "and you can't even keep a drinks date with friends?" He was perched on the window ledge, twelve stories high, smoking a cigarette. He was a coordinated person with good balance who didn't like to get smoke in the apartment.

"Why do you have to sit up there?" I asked him.

"You're more afraid of the subway than I am of this ledge."

"Get down!" I shouted. "Smoke inside!"

"You walk farther than the Carlyle to get groceries."

"I like this apartment. I want to stay home."

"Pretend it's work."

"But it's not work."

"Put all that theater-school training to use."

"I got fired from work, Ethan!"

"I know." Ethan nodded. He closed his eyes and nodded solemnly. "You're having a hard time." He stuck his whole body out the window and exhaled.

Albert phoned that afternoon. "I know you're considering not coming," he said, "so I am phoning to tell you that you absolutely cannot cancel."

"I wasn't considering not coming," I said.

"Yes you were. Of course you were. But you have to come. I don't want to have to make conversation with this chap on my own."

"This chap."

"You have to be there."

"I'll be there," I said. "I was never considering not being there."

"He's already interested in my music, so I just need to shut up long enough not to say anything to change his mind. Can you remind me just to shut up?"

"I will try to make amusing conversation," I said.

Albert was an outspoken communist who sometimes called himself an anarchist, and in any sort of social situation, he managed to offend most everyone. Albert was the sort of person who always had lots of new friends, because he was very good at alienating the old ones.

The Carlyle was one of my favorite places in the whole of New York. I liked J.G. Melon for the cramped, cozy space and the pecan pie, and the Central Park boathouse for afternoon cocktails in the summer, and I still liked the Plaza for tea or drinks at the Oak Bar, just like I had when I was a teenager. But the Carlyle was someplace I had discovered when I moved to New York in my twenties, a place I had found on my own without the instruction of Mrs. Burns or Page or any of the other New York friends I had as a teenager, not many of whom I heard from anymore. The New York of my teenage years seemed like a completely different city from my adult New York, populated by an entirely new set of people. These days, I got emails and phone calls from Clarissa all the time, but she was still in Oxford, getting her graduate degree in French literature. Sometimes I wondered if the reason Clarissa and I had remained so close was that she lived so far away.

I arrived at the hotel early, eager to have at least one drink before Albert and his record producer showed up, and I found my friend Tom at the very end of the bar drinking with a man I didn't know. Tom and I had gone to graduate school together, studying, he told people, The History of Misfits and What They Wrote. Now he wrote for magazines. He lived alone on Seventy-second Street in his parents' four-bedroom apartment, while his parents spent most of their time on Long Island. I often ran into Tom around the neighborhood, and was always glad when I did. He had a welcoming, easy way about him. He put his arm around your shoulder when he said hello and always looked you in the eye, but gently. It was this easiness that no doubt let people open up to him, and Tom wrote some of the most intimate celebrity profiles published anywhere. During school, Tom had written stories with characters he clearly knew well and adored. He wrote funny stories about women shelling peas at the sink and sisters so angry with each other that their bodies began to disintegrate. I thought Tom would be a great and serious writer as soon as he gave up this magazine business.

"We started talking about bourbons," he said to me, "and then we had to come in here and try some. We were having dinner in the restaurant. Have you had dinner in the restaurant?"

"No," I said, "I'm not bored of the bar yet."

"This is Henry," Tom said. "Katherine's a peach."

Henry shook my hand. He had soft, girl-like hands that were quite fine and pointed. His squinty brown eyes watered, and he was twirpy and pale, with skin less like porcelain and more like white paint. There was a large cyst above his left temple. He was not very good-looking. "I'm meeting a friend," I said, "but I came early so I could get a little bit drunk first."

"Sounds like a swell sort of friend," Tom said.

"He has a business meeting. He wants me along so he doesn't make an ass of himself."

"Who's that?" Tom patted the empty stool next to him, and I sat down.

"Albert Savage," I said. I looked at Henry. "That's his real name."

"God—Albert!" said Tom. "What an ass."

"Albert Savage?" Henry said.

"He used to publish poetry, and he had a very good name for that. Savage. Now he's a punk musician, and he's got a good name for that, too. But he tends to make people nervous."

"Nervous," Tom scoffed. "He's an asshole."

"Well," I said.

"He makes a living by stealing money from poets," Tom said.

"He didn't steal their money." I looked at Henry. "He didn't steal anyone's money."

"Call it incompetence, but I'll tell you what," Tom said. "Albert Savage is an ass. The whole of New York knows that. Stick around with us instead, Kate."

Henry said, "I have a meeting with Albert Savage in half an hour."

I looked at him. "Tom exaggerates."

"Katherine's a peach, though," Tom said. He flipped his shaggy hair out of his face.

It was a sticky summer evening, so I had a vodka gimlet on the rocks. I liked gimlets in hot weather. "Albert's not an ass," I said, feeling very bad that I'd undermined my friend before he'd even had a chance to undermine himself. Henry gave me a weak smile. He looked like a banker or a college professor, but not a record producer.

"Henry's got a couple magazines in the U.K." Tom said. "And he's one of England's greatest tennis champs."

"Doubles," Henry said.

"Doubles champ," Tom said.

"Former doubles champ," Henry said. "Shredded my shoulder."

"Albert thinks you're a record producer."

"I'm that, too," Henry said. He pushed his wire-rimmed glasses up the bridge of his nose. His delicate little hands grasped his drink. "I run a small media company. I'm not incredibly well liked, either."

"Henry's interested in starting a magazine over here," Tom said, lighting a cigarette and handing one to Henry. "You ought to write for him."

"What sort of magazine is it?"

"A music magazine," Henry said. "My life's great disappointment is I'm not very good as a musician." He blew smoke rings. "So write something about music for me."

"I'll give it some thought."

"Do that," Henry said. "Have an answer for me by the time I get back." He excused himself, still holding his cigarette. He walked with an assured purpose toward the hotel entrance, and one of the waiters had to take him by the arm and turn him toward the men's room.

"How's work?" Tom asked.

"What sort of work?"

"Work, you know. You were going to be a filmmaker."

"No," I said, "I was never going to be a filmmaker."

"Weren't you?"

"I was going to write stories, like you."

"Yes," Tom said. "We were both going to write stories."

"Remember that?"

"I remember. You once wrote a story while I was sitting next to you on the M4 bus. We were diligent."

"Have you been writing any stories?"

"I've been writing a hell of a lot of stories."

"Yes, I see your name all the time."

"You ought to talk to some of my editors. Why don't you let me set up some meetings for you?"

"I don't think so."

"You're being silly. Magazines are better than not writing at all."

"I wish you would write your own stories."

"Don't start. You and my brother."

"Why don't you come down to Sullivan's and tend bar with me? We'll tend bar and be happy and write our books."

"I'm happy right now."

"Well, you're a very happy sort of person."

"Have another gimlet."

I waved at the barman. "Can I put it on Henry's bill?"

"By all means. Where's Albert?"

"Probably still back at his house, reminding himself what not to say."

Henry came back from the men's room. "I hope you're putting those drinks on my bill."

"Thanks very much," I said.

"When was the last time you were in London?" Henry asked me.

"A long time ago. A year ago."

Henry seemed to agree that a year was a long time to have been away from London. "How did you find it?"

"I didn't even have to look for it," I said.

Henry looked at me. He was a little drunk. "So you liked it, then."

"Yes," I said. "I like London very much. I like the sidewalks."

"Ah, yes," Henry said, "we have beautiful sidewalks. I'm impressed you noticed."

It's not polite to insult anyone's hometown, but I hated London. The only nice thing I could think of to say was the thing about the sidewalks. I liked the sidewalks in London very much, but I hated the weather and I thought the people were sinister. I got the impression in England that when people asked seemingly innocuous questions like "Where are you from?" they were in fact searching for something meant to be used against you.

The bar began to fill up with tourists and older people from the neighborhood. Soon the jazz would start and conversation would be difficult.

"I have to get back and walk my parents' dog," Tom said. Tom had very casual lines for getting out of drunken evenings. He tossed them out as if they weren't really lines at all.

When Albert arrived, he was, as Henry would say, "on great form." He dressed in an untucked French-cuffed white linen shirt with worn-out jeans and brown loafers. His dark hair flopped down in front of his face in a preppy sort of way, not in the carefully styled Elvis Presley bouffant he usually wore. I thought Henry seemed charmed and comfortable. We drank two more rounds of gimlets. The jazz had started and we tried hard to speak above the music without shouting. We were just drunk enough not to think of going someplace else. I thought we were all having a nice time until Henry left again for the men's room and Albert's cheery demeanor immediately changed.

"I think you're being very rude, very inconsiderate," Albert said.

"What are you talking about?"

"It's incredibly rude of you to flirt with him like that when I've invited you here."

"You must be joking," I said.

"As if you are not here with me."

"Albert, the jig is up. He knows we're just friends."

"Well, he certainly thinks he's someone."

"Maybe."

"He does. He thinks he's someone."

"So what, Albert. You think you're someone."

"Yes," Albert said, "but I am someone."

"Are you."

"I mean, I really do things. This guy, he's like a pimp. All record producers are pimps."

"A poetry publisher is a pimp, too."

Albert nodded. After a while he said, "You're right. Fortunately I no longer publish poetry."

"Fortunately for whom?"

"Don't be a jerk."

"You were a very good poetry publisher, Albert."

"Yes. Well, now I am a punk musician."

When he came back from the men's room, Henry put his feet on my stool and his hand on my shoulder.

"I'd better go," Albert said, "before I get too drunk."

"We are all too drunk," Henry said. "Have a sidecar. Let's all have sidecars." Henry ordered sidecars all around. "Albert's going to make an album for me," Henry told the bartender.

Albert looked less pleased than he should have.

I said, "I'll write your liner notes, Albert."

"You can proofread my liner notes."

"All right," I said, sighing. "I'll proofread."

"I really am too drunk," Albert said. He had undone both his cuff links, and his long cuffs hung open past his wrists.

It was getting late, so Henry and I put Albert in a taxi and went up to a sushi restaurant on Second Avenue to see if they would serve us something to eat. We ate lovely pale toro and soft-shell crab. The chef held up the wiggling crab so we could see that it was alive before he dispatched it with a knife, quite dramatically and with great flair. Henry knew which nice cold sakes to order and how to pronounce their names. Afterwards I suggested Henry catch a taxi to wherever he was staying, but we walked for a while back toward the Carlyle and my apartment.

"I'm staying there at the Carlyle," Henry said.

"My favorite hotel."

"Would you like to come up with me?" Subtlety was not Henry's talent.

"No thanks, darling."

"I would like to see you every night for the next four nights if you're available."

I laughed. "What if we don't like each other after tomorrow night?"

He kissed me quite suddenly, without any warning, without leaning in toward me first. It was a hard, horrible kiss that softened into a very nice kiss. "I think we'll still like each other," he said.

"All right," I said. "That's fine." I would have liked to have gone up with him, but I kept thinking it was not the right thing to do. So often what I wanted to do was, I thought, not the right thing to do.

The following week, I ran into Tom at Citarella on Third Avenue.

"Don't buy any perishables," he whispered as he came up behind me. He was so handsome, Tom was. His hair was a mess and his clothes were always just disheveled enough. He had a diagonal scar from below his temple to the corner of his mouth. Tom was unusual and imperfect enough that all girls had a lingering crush on him.

"Why's that?"

"Because we're going for a drink, and I don't want the whole bar to smell like your fishy dinner."

"You want me to yourself all afternoon."

"Will you just hurry up and get your nonperishables and let's go?" His basket was full of olives and dry beans and crostini.

I was glad I had friends who were grocery shopping in the afternoon, when I was. I wondered what sort of people I would run into if I shopped in the evenings.

Tom and I took our groceries to Mediterraneo on Sixty-seventh Street, where I liked to practice my rudimentary Italian with the host. Gino always faked a heart attack when he saw me coming. "Cara mia, cara mia!" he shouted. "Non lo credo, che bella!" He seated us outside and brought us two glasses of crisp friuli.

"I want you to phone a couple of editors," Tom said.

"I can't."

"Why can't you?"

"I want to write a book, Tom."

"Yes, but when was the last time you wrote anything at all?"

"I don't want to be a journalist, Tom. I like bartending."

"I'm just saying it's not difficult work for someone like you, and you can get your name out there."

"I appreciate it. I think you're sweet."

"I'm doing it for me. Your success would make me look good."

"You look good on your own, darling. I see your name all the time." Though Tom was not writing the sorts of things I thought he should have been writing, he was the most successful of all of my graduate school friends.

"I'm talking about you, Kate."

"Talk talk talk, then." I was getting drunk and happy.

"Call my friend Dennis. You can write all about shoes and intellectuals. Write about whatever you want. I want to see you succeed."

No one was ever nicer to me than Tom. He was never in love with me. Tom was just a kind, kind friend. He knew to run into me at the market, and not to call ahead for plans.

———

Over the next several months, Henry phoned at least once a day. I was bored with the bar and I liked the attention. I told poor Henry countless times that there was no possible way I would ever move to London. "I'm an American," I said. "Are you trying to colonize me?"

"Colonize you."

"I know your type," I said. First appearances to the contrary, Henry was extremely charming; he did overtly romantic things, like sending flowers for no reason and ordering fancy dinners to be delivered to my apartment, but there was something about the grand gestures that I distrusted. Tom had told me Henry had a title, and Henry's title, though I liked the idea very much, made me a little bit cautious.

"You would keep your apartment," Henry said. "It wouldn't be a permanent move. But we cannot conduct a transatlantic relationship."

I agreed, but the logical thing seemed for us to not conduct a relationship at all.

Ethan had a callback for *Starlight Express* on London's West End.

"Didn't *Starlight Express* close about twenty years ago?" I said.

"Not in London," Ethan informed me. "Those English love their *Starlight Express,* and they're running out of nationals who can roller-skate."

Casting directors adored Ethan. He prepared thoroughly for every audition and always hit his notes. The casting directors doing *Starlight Express* had seen him many times before, and they kept looking to place him in something. Ethan's problem was he made so much money at the bar, only a leading man's salary would do. Now these casting directors got it in their heads that if they moved him out of New York, Ethan might be willing to take less.

"I'd like to get out of New York," he told me when he got the call.

"Why don't you date Henry? He'll put you up in London."

"I hear he's in love at the moment."

"Is he?"

"That's the word."

That afternoon, Ethan and Jonas and I went to the park to help Ethan practice his roller-skating, in case anyone tested him during callbacks. Jonas was no good at roller-skating, but he pretended to be an expert on everything. We practiced in the wide entrance at Seventy-second Street, which was closed to cars from ten a.m. until after three p.m. Older people with their nurses sat along the benches. Ethan was really lovely to watch. He was a good roller-skater, after all, and his thick blond hair bounced around as he twirled and skipped and made sudden, ostentatious stops. I sat on a bench for a while, and an older woman sitting in a wheelchair next to me giggled and giggled, watching graceful Ethan, and funny Jonas stumbling along next to him. Her young nurse giggled, too. It must have been close to a hundred humid degrees in the park that afternoon with no breeze, but that older lady had a heavy blanket across her lap.

"Go on then, Jonas, show me how it's done," Ethan was saying.

"You don't always have to stop with your toe down like that."

"You're the expert, clearly."

"You can shift your weight to the back."

"You just go ahead and show me your goods, Jonas."

"I'll show you my goods."

"That's what I'm asking."

"That's what I'm giving you." Jonas stopped with his weight on the outer edge of his wheels and fell over. The old lady laughed and laughed. Then, resting on her heavy blanket, I noticed the diamond. It covered half the ring finger on her right hand. It was a diamond worth recognizing. I looked up at Mrs.

Burns. I hadn't seen her since I was fourteen. She was frail. All the vibrancy was dead. It had been almost fifteen years since my last visit; there was no possible way she could remember me. Her nurse was not Ruth but someone closer to my age. Mrs. Burns shivered in the heat. Her hair was perfect, as it always had been, but her makeup was clumsy, as if no one who cared had been helping her apply it. I knew Page was living in New York: I had read in the gossip columns about her line of handbags and scarves. I had read that she was dating the vice president's nephew. Some grave family split must have occurred for Page to let her grandmother's makeup go bad.

Mrs. Burns would have told me not to be a fool, to take my opportunities when they came and to go to London.

I didn't say hello, because her falling mascara made me sorry, and because I had nothing interesting to tell her.

TWELVE

The Blizzard

Snow fell. The city became a vast receptacle of white. There were no cars, no fathers getting home, no clatter of plates and gossip from the opening doors of steaming restaurants. I fiddled with the top of my coat. Henry watched me, not offering to help. Snow landed on the backs of my hands.

"Let me," he said after some time.

"No, no. I've got it. Really, I've got it."

In time, that night is a gap, a wound, an accidental blip. That night extracts itself from every other snowy evening.

I steadied my thumb in the hollow of my throat. "There. I got it."

"Everything's gone white."

"Yes."

"What if we can't find your building."

"That would be a blessing."

"If we can't find your building, you'll come to London with me."

"No."

"Why not?"

I shook my head.

"Yes you will."

"No, Henry."

"Come to London."

"Stay in New York with me."

"I can't continue to invent business in New York. I have investors, you know."

"My job is here."

Between our voices, there was no sound but the snow. When I thought of that night later, I blamed the blizzard for my decisions.

"Your job. Your job is ridiculous, even you think it's ridiculous," he said.

"I can't live in London."

"You are more mobile than I am."

"More mobile. How is that? How am I more mobile?"

"I live in London," he said.

"I live here."

"I have to be in London."

I agreed. Of course I agreed, moving to New York would have been a silly idea for Henry, and there was not much for me to give up in a bar job.

"You are finished with your life here. The logical conclusion is to come to London and live with me, to love me."

I was quiet.

"We are an alliance," he said. "A team." He took my hand and slipped it into his coat pocket. "This is your opportunity to write the book you want to write. To be a huge success."

"I like to think I am already a success." I had won fellowships to graduate school. I was beginning to publish my stories in little magazines.

"You are. You are a success, of course."

"I can write here."

"But I will support you. Won't it be nice to write something meaningful?"

"Listen," I said. "I don't want to be dependent on you."

"Would you like me to anonymously deposit money into your bank account?"

The disappointing thing about Henry was that when he said things like that, he wasn't joking.

"No."

We walked against the blizzard, our close bodies making one figure on the sidewalk. Still we couldn't see each other clearly through the snow. "You listen," he said. "Do you want me to tell you there's someone else?"

"Is there someone else?"

"There is someone I've liked for a while. She's suddenly taken an interest in me."

"Congratulations to you."

"I want you, Katherine."

"Was that a threat right then?"

"It's not a threat. It's just telling you what's going on."

"So you waited to give me an ultimatum until you had a good one."

"There is no point in us going on like this. If you don't come to London, of course I will find someone else."

My toes were numb. I had ruined the pair of gray flannel heels I was wearing. "You don't have to give me ultimatums."

"Just come to London, just give us a chance."

New York is always very romantic in the snow.

"Can I keep my apartment?"

"No one in New York gives up their rent-controlled apartments."

I would go to London for reasons apart from love. I would go because I wanted to write a book, because Ethan was there in a West End show, and because I didn't want to regret a life of missed adventures.

THIRTEEN

Hiking in Heels

The climbing shop on Kensington High Street was my first sign of trouble.

"You're not scaling Le Dom in those," said the unshaven young man running the shop.

"They're Gore-Tex," I said.

The young man laughed and tried not to laugh.

"You'll get frostbitten," he said.

"But they're waterproof."

He smiled and laughed and set his hand on my back. "Look," he said, "please let me protect you."

I wondered why Henry was not protecting me. He had given the inadequate shoes to me on my birthday with a book about walking the Haute Route from Zermatt to Chamonix. I had been reluctant at first. The idea of dodging crevasses and carrying sixty pounds on my back for seven days in the middle of August appealed to me very little. I wanted to go to the beach in Croatia. But Henry cajoled and bullied. "You don't know the elation of a walk like that," he said, and "How can you not want to live, really live?" he said. As soon as I agreed to the beautiful challenge of the Haute Route, Henry changed his mind, deciding we would be better off climbing something simple like Le Dom: 15,500 feet high, but technically not very challenging.

"Look what I bought," I told Henry.

"What's that?"

"You see, these shoes have the tongue attached to the body."

"How human."

"You see," I said, "well. You see, never mind."

"No, never mind. Nothing I do for you is quite enough, so never mind."

I looked at him. "Well," I said. "Never mind."

The boys at the shop had asked me whether or not I was fit enough for the climb.

"Do I look fit enough?" I asked them.

They nodded and shrugged. "People tell you it's an easy mountain," said the boy with no facial hair. "But those are people who have maybe climbed a hill before." He was looking at my loafers. Even my loafers had two-inch heels.

"I have good genes," I assured him. I said, "I have running shoes. I do forty push-ups every day."

All the men in the shop nodded.

"She'll be fine, mate." I never trusted people who said "mate." "Mate" was a word people in England used to pretend they were a lot less rich and a lot more fashionable than they were. I bought the shoes anyway, because none of the other three men said "mate."

I bought the shoes and a pair of crampons and an ice ax. "An ice ax?" I said. "Are you sure?"

"Do you want me to show it to you in a book?"

"I don't need to see a book."

"It's a precaution," the man told me, the one who had said "mate." "Le Dom is not a casual stroll."

I nodded that nod that says *I am not stupid*, a nod I found myself using frequently this year in England, living with Henry.

"If something happens to you, I'll read about it and want to kill myself."

"Will you really want to kill yourself if something happens to me?"

"Just take the ax, please."

Later, Henry assured me the man in the shop had been right. "I forgot to tell you you'll need an ax," he said.

"Why would I possibly need an ice ax?"

"In case you slip. You use it to pull yourself up. Dig into a cliff. You know, that sort of thing."

"A cliff? On ice?"

"You never know what the conditions will be. It gets a little snowy."

On our way to Zermatt, we stopped in Vienna for the wedding of Henry's old roommate from school.

"Any git can climb Le Dom," the groom told me. "It's a practice hill."

The bride, a classically glamorous designer of women's clothing, said, "Darling, look at my heels," tilting her delicate stilettos toward me. "Even I have climbed Le Dom."

"Any git," the groom repeated.

"Of course, my toenails fell off," the bride told me, "but not until weeks later."

"Oh, not your toes again."

"I kept them for a long time," she said. "Entire toenails. I didn't want to throw them away, I wanted to use them for something."

"All she remembers is the thing about her toes."

"Plus I got to the top," she said.

"It's Le Dom. Any git can get to the top."

By the time we got to Zermatt, I had it in my head that Le Dom was too easy. As a girl who grew up in California and saw Disneyland's Matterhorn every summer vacation of her life, I could not come to Zermatt and feel happy climbing Le Dom. At the base of the small gingerbread town is that great iconic rock, the flat edge and sharp peak of the Matterhorn jutting into the sky as if everything were a backdrop, painted on. The imposing beauty of the Matterhorn in person is confirmation that not everything we were told as children was a lie. Comparatively, Le Dom is nothing but a round disappointment.

"Can't we please climb the Matterhorn instead?" I begged Henry.

"Too many tourists," he said.

"But then it must be perfect for me."

"Look," he said, "the danger of the Matterhorn isn't how tall or difficult it is, the danger is that some inexperienced Japanese tourist is going to fall down on top of you."

We were eating fondue, except that only I was eating fondue, because in Henry's many years of climbing in Switzerland, he had learned to hate fondue, which I took as a personal slight against how much I liked it. Henry disliked anything that smacked of tourism.

"You've climbed it," I said.

"Before the tourists got to it."

Henry actually ate the potatoes without dipping them into the cheese, and he did it with an unhappy look on his face, and I knew that later he would complain I made him eat plain potatoes for dinner.

The woman at the inn was skeptical that Henry and I would climb anything, much less anything as high as Le Dom. "Are you sure you're able to climb that hill?" she asked, eyeing Henry's sandals, orange cargo pants, and linen shirt printed with parrots.

"Why not?" he said.

"Are you going to climb the hill, too?" she asked me.

I stood very close to the desk so that she could not see my high-heeled loafers. "I think so," I said.

She shook her head and gave us a room key. As we climbed the stairs, my suitcase knocking into every step I ascended, she called after us, "There are a lot of challenging walks on the lower part of the mountains." She left a trail map outside our door.

Our guide was called Oliver. He would meet us halfway up Le Dom. The first ten thousand feet had come very easily, and Henry was pleased with my progress as a mountain climber. "You're like a little goat," he said. "You just hop hop hop up that hill."

"You're a goat."

"You're my little goat."

I thought of funny things while climbing, things like the names of the B-movies on résumés of washed-up actresses sent to me by my friend Brad when he was working at William Morris: *The Stud*, and its sequel, *The Bitch*. I thought of the time a friend at the Olympics sent me the Olympic Bomb Threat Checklist everyone had taped down next to their telephone. *Caller's Voice*, the checklist says, and lists options such as *crying* or *hoarse* or *familiar*.

"What are you laughing at?" Henry asked.

"The bomb threat checklist."

Henry never pressed for details.

The checklist says, *If voice sounds familiar, who does it sound like?* The checklist has several blank lines for *Exact Wording of Threat*.

I threw rocks into deep ravines and listened to them clatter their way down, the echo lasting long after the rock had presumably landed. I did this until I realized we had been climbing within an even larger ravine. We arrived at what seemed like the world's corner, with nowhere to go but back the way we came.

"How could there have been ravines within ravines?" I asked, bewildered, afraid of the large wall in front of me.

Henry tied a rope to my waist. "It would embarrass me to have to explain that to you," he said.

You have to trust the person you're roped to.

"I don't want to go up there," I said.

"There's no option," he said.

"I could go back down."

"We don't have enough daylight to go back down."

I suspected Henry was having an affair with his old assistant. She called too frequently, for no reason, and had pulled me aside at a party in Ibiza to tell me, "I know him better than you ever will." I had found a long strand of her blond curly hair in my brush after returning from a weekend away. People with curly hair don't brush it unless they've just taken a shower.

"Let's look at the map," I said.

"The trail goes up this rock, Katherine. Come on." He started up.

His mother had died mysteriously, which everyone knew and no one talked about. His father, at the time, had been seeing the prime minister's daughter, and when Henry's mother fell out a fourth-story window, there was no investigation.

"I can't go up."

"Then untie yourself and stay here." He continued up the rock. He clipped onto the stationary rope. As his carabiner hit each piton, every clank echoed into the valley.

"I can't go." I started to cry, and started climbing. *Questions to ask: When is the bomb going to explode?* I put one foot into a hold above the other. *Where is it? What does it look like?* I remembered, suddenly, reading in a mountain-climbing disaster epic to use your legs to push yourself up the rock, not your arms to pull. *What kind of bomb is it? What will cause it to explode?* "I can't go up," I said, crying into my mouth, and I clung to the wall as if it would hold me, looking only toward the top. *Did you place the bomb? Why? What is your address? What is your name?*

He unroped me at the top of the wall.

"You see," he said, "not difficult."

"You didn't even tell me how to climb."

"If I'd warned you, you would never have come this far," he said.

"Don't do that to me again!" I shouted. I thought of the inadequate shoes he had bought for me to wear, and how he had failed to remind me I would need an ice ax. I thought about the times he had lied to his staff about the financials of the magazine, and how he never remembered the birthdays of anyone in his family. I thought of Valentine's Day, when he and I both forgot our wallets at dinner and he called my brother to come pay for the meal. I tried to remember the reasons I loved him, but all I could come up with was those first few months of relentless courtship. I thought of the many, many tulips and the baskets of breakfast from Sarabeth's he'd had delivered to my apartment in New York, or the time a car came to fetch me unexpectedly from a horrible temp job and a borrowed jet flew me to the Lake District for the weekend. I thought of the dinners, the many trips from New York to London, the time he left an important meeting to rescue me from passport control when the grandmotherly immigration officer refused my entry into the country. The spectacular show had seduced me, and now I had followed him to Zermatt, where it turns out the Matterhorn is for real. I tried to think of the reasons I loved him right now, the reasons I had given up everything and moved to London, but I couldn't think of anything aside from the unpleasant alternative of a complicated return to New York and that I would be marrying a title. I thought of *The Sun Also Rises*, when Brett says, "Isn't it wonderful, we all have titles. Why haven't you a title, Jake?" Henry walked on ahead of me, following the map to the hut.

Our guide, Oliver, was sinewy and lithe and, it turned out, had gone to Eton with people Henry knew. I liked Oliver much better than I liked Henry that day. Henry had tricked me about the wall. Henry did not have the nicely veined hands and forearms that Oliver did. Oliver was sunning on the terrace of the hut when we arrived at our halfway point in the late afternoon, the two of us worn out and angry, barely speaking to each other.

"A storm up there today," Oliver told us. I thought he was looking at me with doubt. "We were up to our thighs in it," he said.

"Well, good, you've carved a path for us, then," Henry said.

Oliver shrugged. "It's an easy hill." He looked at me with squinty eyes. "How do you feel about snow?" He laughed.

"Look at these boots," I said.

Oliver nodded. "You're ready for snow."

I looked at Henry. "I'm ready for snow," I said.

The hut served canned beef Stroganoff for dinner, and afterwards Oliver revealed a bottle of grappa. "It's Croatian," he said. "Did you know the Croatians made grappa?"

Oliver and I drank out of coffee mugs.

"You get your little bit of Croatia after all," Henry said, throwing peel from his orange into the fire. Henry had not offered anyone a bit of the orange he had carried up in his pocket. Oliver and I watched him eat the entire thing.

"I wanted to go to Croatia," I told Oliver.

"You certainly like adventure."

"The beach is very nice."

"So is the grappa, apparently," Henry said.

We got drunk quickly at that altitude.

That night, in the sleeping room at the hut, all forty-five spaces on the long cramped floor of mattresses were full. I slept in a turtleneck and my furry deer stalking cap so that no part of me would have to touch the hut-provided linens. I slept between Henry and Oliver, accidentally facing Oliver. In the middle of the night, when neither of us was sleeping, and the light from the especially close moon lit everything up like daylight, Oliver mouthed, "Hello."

I looked at him. It was too late to pretend I was sleeping.

He adjusted himself so the shape of his body touched the shape of my body, so that his mouth breathed into mine. "Hello," he mouthed, and I could hear him, and smell the Stroganoff and grappa.

I resisted the impulse to put my hand on him.

The next morning, before the sun had come fully up, after a breakfast of porridge at the hut and no coffee, I was facing another wall. "If you can't do it, I'll pull you up," Oliver said.

"I can do it."

Henry climbed with a little help from Oliver, who pulled from below, sitting into the rope to help Henry reach the next step. Henry made the climb look very easy, and I paid special attention to where he found his holds.

"Come on, then," Henry shouted from the top, impatient. Other climbers were lining up behind me.

Oliver stood next to me, ready to belay. "I don't need you to pull me," I told him.

He mouthed, "Hello."

"I mean it."

"We'll see," he said.

He didn't tug on the belay, he let me do it all by myself, and I found every foothold.

"You're good at this," Oliver said, joining us at the top of the wall.

"She's my goat," Henry said.

I did not think Goat was the most endearing nickname in the world.

A light snow started at thirteen thousand feet.

"Maybe another storm," I said, alarmed, trying my best not to sound alarmed.

Oliver didn't respond.

"Can we still get to the top if there's a storm?" Henry asked.

"Yesterday we did," Oliver said. "Yesterday I had a group of Canadian college boys."

Henry slipped into a shallow crevasse. He yelped and was half gone. He swore and shouted, "Don't, Goat!" when I tried to help him out.

"Do we need to rope up?" Oliver said after Henry had pulled himself up.

"What do you think?" Henry said. "How many of those are there?"

"You just have to follow where I'm going." Oliver shook his head.

I followed Oliver very closely, carefully putting each of my feet where his had been.

A little farther up, Henry had trouble breathing. "Let's just stop for a minute," he said.

My feet were cold, I was afraid my new boots might be leaking, and the lack of caffeine had given me a headache. "Come on," I said.

Henry sat down and the snowfall made him all white. He didn't say anything. He caught his breath. He took off his glove and pulled a bag of gummy milk teeth from his pocket. Oliver stared. Henry said, "You're a crap guide, Oliver." Snow fell into the opening of Henry's glove.

I knelt next to him. "It's worse if you argue," I said.

"Your favorite," Henry said, smiling, handing me a row of gummy milk teeth.

I tied myself to him. "Come on," I said. "I'll pull you."

From where we were, we could see the peak. It was an easy fifteen hundred feet, straight uphill.

Oliver shook his head, took the end of the rope, and tied it to himself. "We're roping up for Le Dom," he said. He laughed.

"Of course we're roping up!" Henry shouted. "I fell into a crevasse!"

I pulled Henry up by his harness. "Stop it," I said.

"He's crap."

"Let's just quickly get to the top."

Henry wasn't moving much. I tugged him uphill. When I turned to look at him, his face was red, a vibrant red, and he looked as if he had no sense of direction.

One of my crampons came loose. I removed my gloves to fix it, but immediately my fingers went solid. I bent down to latch the crampon to my boot, and the pain in my head made me a little bit blind. I hesitated. Oliver stood where he was.

Henry came up beside me. "Don't take those gloves off," he said, handing them to me. "Put them on again." He took his own gloves off, bent down beside me, and fixed the crampon. "I'm the climber here," he said, and smiled, and kissed me. His face was glazed with mucus and saliva.

Other climbers, even the old ones, passed us on their way back down the mountain. We were by far the slowest group of the forty-five people who had slept in the hut the night before. They gave Oliver funny looks, and Oliver threw up his arms, and I looked at the ground and tried to concentrate on one foot in front of the other. I pulled harder at Henry, trying to get him to travel faster, trying to get to the top of the hill before the afternoon made everything more dangerous.

Two hundred feet from the top, I started vomiting large pieces of gummy milk teeth. I vomited pieces of last night's noodles, then I vomited the clear nothing I had in my stomach. "I'm having caffeine withdrawal," I said.

"It's your hangover," Henry said.

Oliver put his hand on my back. "How's your head feel?" he asked. Henry stayed away.

"Like I need a lot of espresso."

He didn't say a thing, he just started back down the hill.

"No!" Henry shouted. "No, no no!"

"I can stay here," I said. "It's just right there, I can see you all the way to the top."

We were tied to Oliver, and he had turned back.

"But the top is just right there!" Henry protested, tugging on the rope now with much more strength than he had a moment ago when I was pulling him uphill.

"She has altitude sickness," Oliver said simply. "We can't go any higher."

"She has a hangover!"

"Hurry up and go to the top," I said, "please."

Oliver looked at me. "Obviously, you are not a climber," he said.

"I'll go to the top," Henry said, untying the rope from his harness.

Oliver yanked the rope and Henry fell sideways. "I cannot leave anyone on the mountain."

"It's just Le Dom!" Henry cried. He sat in the snow.

"Your girlfriend needs to get to a lower altitude before her brain hemorrhages," Oliver said. He came very close to Henry and pulled him up by the rope, waist first.

"Le Dom is a peewee hill," Henry said to himself, to me.

I started down the hill after Oliver. "This happens to me, too," Oliver said quietly enough for only me to hear. "At the beginning of the season, if I don't give myself the time to get acclimated."

"Well," I said, "we had a wedding in Vienna, and we only have so much vacation."

"Is that so."

"I mean, we didn't actually have the time."

"Obviously not."

At the hut, the proprietors gave me a soda and Oliver left

without saying goodbye. Henry was meant to pay Oliver's fee at the guides' office in Zermatt, but he never went back to pay for anything at all.

As soon as we'd come down to a more civilized altitude, my illness had gone. I let my socks dry in the sun. My boots had leaked, and even after an hour in the afternoon heat just above the forest line, I couldn't feel my toes. The toenails were completely black.

"We're not staying here tonight," Henry informed me.

"We're not?"

"Wouldn't you rather get back down and sleep in a real bed?"

I looked at him. The walk down would take us eight hours at best.

"Wouldn't you rather have fondue and your loafers?" he asked.

"Look at my toes," I said.

He shrugged. "You're going to have to get down there at some point."

Threat Language: Well-spoken (educated). Foul. Incoherent. Message read by irrational threat maker.

I wanted to rappel down the first wall of rock we had encountered on the way up, but Henry said he didn't have the strength for it. "I'm not sure I can belay you," he said. "You can belay yourself."

I didn't want to learn how to belay myself on the wall of a ravine that looked as if its bottom was level with hell. Instead, I hooked onto the stationary rope and climbed down very carefully, crying the whole time but not saying anything. I had learned on the way up that exclamations were useless.

We walked into Zermatt well after dark, so that even the Matterhorn was invisible. "If we had climbed the Matterhorn," I told Henry at dinner, "I wouldn't have been sick." The Matterhorn is two hundred feet lower than Le Dom.

"If we had climbed the Matterhorn, my darling, a Japanese tourist would have dislodged a rock directly into your forehead."

"Oliver said he'd never failed to get a client up the Matterhorn."

"I am quite certain Oliver has never failed to get a client up Le Dom, until today."

I started to cry again. Not on purpose, but because I was so used to it.

"Oh don't," Henry said. I had let Henry pick the restaurant that night, and we were eating Italian food in Zermatt. "Don't," he said.

"My toes are black," I wailed.

"Not here."

"Which means I'll have to buy a new pair of shoes for the Highland Ball." I had been looking forward to the Highland Ball all year, with its dance cards to be filled and the brightly colored floor-length dresses and the gorgeous pair of beige heels I had purchased from Harvey Nichols with green leather vines sewn into the back. I had a lot of stored-up mucus from the quick trip to fifteen thousand feet, and it began to run and run. "I can't wear open-toed shoes for the rest of the summer," I cried. "And I didn't even get up the bunny hill."

"Le Dom is not a bunny hill."

"Don't patronize me."

"We should have never come to Zermatt, not for your first trip."

"I could have climbed the Matterhorn," I said. "I am technically very capable. It's the altitude."

"You're very capable."

"You didn't even tell me there would be a wall!"

"It wasn't entirely clear on the map. I didn't want to frighten you."

"You have a list of excuses."

"We should have just stayed in Vienna. You had all the right footwear for Vienna."

"I think it must have been the socks," I said. "I bought those nice boots from the shop on Kensington High Street. I don't know what went wrong."

"I don't know what went wrong, either." He stabbed his butter-sage ravioli.

Something washed-up actresses have in common is they all start doing films with the word *Fear* in the title.

Outside, on the short walk back to the hotel, feeling sad that I had eaten Italian food in Zermatt and that I had been more confident roped to Oliver than I had to Henry, I decided to ask him about what we both knew. "What if I told you I found someone else's hair chopstick in the sofa?"

He stopped. He put his hand on my face. "I would tell you that you should take that up with the housecleaner," he said.

As we walked back to the hotel, I remembered the way my brother looked when he showed up at the restaurant in Piccadilly on Valentine's Day to pay for our dinner. "I am only going to tell you this once," Ethan said while Henry went to the men's room. "And then I am never going to say it again." He looked pained and sorry and angry. "I am never going to like him." After that, I wished very hard for Ethan to say it again.

"It's as if the Matterhorn were never there," Henry said, glancing behind us where it should have been, but it was dark out and cloudy. We walked a little. "The thing is, I know when you tell the story about this trip, all you're going to tell people is that your toes turned black."

I nodded. He didn't not know me.

In college, I lived with a kind blond actor who kissed my face while I was sleeping and who spoke to me in tender tones of admiration. He said proudly to his friends, "She dyes her hair and doesn't pretend it's natural." He didn't get angry when I caught cold, or impatient when I asked him the details of his day or his family or his past. He knew exactly where the pain started in my arm when I'd been driving or skiing too long. He read me to sleep. He wore the clothes I bought him. It's not difficult for a person to love well.

At Henry's house in London, I put my crampons and ice ax in storage and quickly forgot they were there. I bought dark polish to cover the bruises on my toenails. The feeling never came back to the fourth toe on my left foot.

FOURTEEN

Rules for Saying Goodbye

One. Do not leave until he has mentioned two ex-girlfriends in casual conversation. If you are sure you want to leave and he has not mentioned two ex-girlfriends in conversation, mention two ex-boyfriends and see what happens.

Two. Leave if he starts writing songs about other people. These will be songs of loss and their details will have nothing to do with you. Shame on you for dating a musician. At your age.

Three. Once you have decided to go, say nice things about him to his friends. Say things they will repeat to him later. Also, and this should be obvious: do not fuck his friends. There is that one who will try to take advantage; the one with all the cashmere sweaters whom you have half a crush on who has already phoned you to ask if everything is all right. Do not do anything that will incriminate you once you are not there to defend yourself.

———

Four. Buy things to leave in his house, things he won't have the energy to throw out, like jars of the peanut butter you like. Do not leave things you might want later. Leave hair rubber bands and your toothbrush, but not your Sonicare toothbrush.

Five. Flirt with his mother. If his mother is not available, his sister or aunt will do. Flirt mercilessly until she adores you. If you do not smoke, take it up in order to share furtive cigarettes with her in the guest bathroom. Always carry very nice cigarettes, but not overly nice—Nat Sherman, for example, but not Cartier gold-tipped. If you have not already done it by the time you decide to leave, knit a scarf that matches her eyes. When she admires it, take it off your neck and give it to her. It will be easier for her to wear later if she doesn't think you knitted it specifically for her, and throughout winter and next fall, the scarf itself will remind him how gracious you were.

Six. Your handwriting should be ubiquitous: grocery lists left in his coat pockets, telephone messages used as bookmarks, notes on the refrigerator and in his bedside drawer, directions to friends' houses left in the passenger-side door of his car.

Seven. Cry politely. Do not cry like a horse.

Eight. If you must say mean things, say them in a delicate, lovely voice, the same voice you used to say "I love you," the same voice you used when you made promises you really did intend to keep. Do not shout or make ugly faces.

Nine. The last time he sees you should be the morning. He will come home from work and be surprised to find you gone. Be sure to smell good that morning, even if you have to get up before he does and pat a scent behind your ears. Touch his face softly, even if you have been arguing. Say "goodbye" tenderly. If you are very good, you will be able to give him that look that assures him everything will be fine, that he will come home and you will be nice again, that all your anger will have turned back to love. This will increase the impact of your departure.

Ten. Write a note on very nice paper. Make it simple. *Dear Henry, I have loved you completely.* Be too hurt to sign your name.

Eleven. Call a taxi. Have too much pride to phone your brother or your best friend. Leave in tears, broken, and make sure his next-door neighbor sees you. She is a stripper and she will comfort him. You will be safe knowing that he's in the arms of the stripper and not his assistant. Do not go back to retrieve things you have forgotten, like your climbing shoes or laundry you left in the dryer. Once you are gone, be gone for good.

FIFTEEN

A Friend in the Family

The summer after the spring I returned from London, my grandmother, who had lived in Krakow and Budapest and Cairo and Marseilles, died while living with my parents in Fresno. That day, Auntie Petra had shouted at her relentlessly for wearing good slippers outside to sweep some leaves. Sweeping leaves into tens of dozens of tiny piles was my grandmother's greatest pleasure. The day she had her final stroke, she had muddied a pair of sheepskin slip-ons, blissfully sweeping summertime leaves and grass cuttings into thirty piles along the edge of the driveway. Everyone was upset with fat, lonely Auntie Petra, which made her seem even fatter and lonelier. The last words my mother had exchanged with Grandma were, "Did Petra shout at you?"

"Shhh," my grandmother had said, "don' say any-ting, don' make 'em problem."

Then Grandma fell over, and in my mother's confusion and denial, she tried to prop her up with a chair. "Come on, Ma, sit up. Stop slouching."

Grandma had never gone to other people's funerals. She found them insulting, and full of hypocrites most of the time. "Who cares if you go to a funeral?" she would say. "What matters is how you treat people when they're alive."

At the very least, Grandma's funeral was an opportunity to dress well. There would be family members there I hadn't seen in some time, family members who didn't like me, family members who hadn't seen me since my college days, when I still looked like a boy. I wore a silk navy-blue wraparound apron dress, the one that accidentally opens too far in the back, the one my mother and I got on sale after the dot-com crash, a year no one spent any money in New York.

Ethan and I flew back together from New York, charging the last-minute tickets to our parents. He had returned from London in May after deciding not to renew his contract. Ethan disliked London equally as much as I had, unhappy with the weather and the people and the lack of heat in the dressing rooms at the theater. "No matter how often I changed my socks, they were always damp," he said. "And it's no fun without you there." We were very happy to be back to our old habits in New York, cooking for each other and getting on each other's nerves.

Ethan flirted with the flight attendant and had us moved up to first class, and by the time we arrived in Fresno, we were drunk on free first-class gin.

The red-brick church was the same church where my parents had been married, the same church where both of my brothers and I had been baptized. My cousins and brothers and I had gone to Sunday school in the basement, where a half-dozen of my childhood plays had been performed. That day, Ethan and I confessed to each other later, we didn't feel as sad in that church as we should have.

I looped my arm into my sister-in-law's. There had been rumors that she and I didn't get along, and naturally the rumors were true, but the last thing I wanted was anyone believing them. I linked my crooked arm to hers, and we strolled from the parking lot to the church with our heads bent toward each other in sorrow and friendship.

My cousins were already inside the church, my uncle's wife, Lou, already soaked in tears, this woman who had never invited Grandma to Christmas, who had only a year ago locked her in a 130-degree car on a humid day and then served Grandma cabbage soup to help her recover from the resulting stroke. Aunt Lou had made no secret of her loathing for Grandma. And yet, she was crying like a hurricane. She was praying out loud in Spanish. I couldn't stop looking. Aunt Lou was an even better actress than I was, with my arm in Peg's.

"Those are tears of joy," Ethan whispered to me.

My cousins looked bloated, which pleased me immensely. Doris, whom I had heard through mutual friends had a few years before sold all her real estate and cashed out for millions, had a horrible dye job for someone with so much interest-bearing capital. She had married a physically revolting mafia type, which practically had me squealing with glee, and her six-foot frame looked very well fed. Seeing my cousin look like an ugly stepsister was an enormous relief at my grandmother's funeral, and I silently thanked my mother over and over for paying for this beautiful dress that opened too far in the back.

I looked down the pew at my family: two handsome brothers, a voluptuous sister-in-law as much a knockout as she was a pest, my father youthful enough to still get carded by flirtatious bartenders, my lovely pink-cheeked roly-poly mother, more broken than anyone else in the church. Perfection, if beauty is what you're after.

Afterwards, at the lunch in the church reception hall, my father and two priests had to sit between my mother and her feuding siblings. These were feuds that had taken fifty years to develop, based on the sort of animosity that must begin in childhood. An agglomeration of unresolved arguments and slights: the time Uncle Dick slapped my mother back and forth across the face when she had refused to leave a wedding with him forty years ago, the time he bloodied her lip for dating a Japanese boy, the dozens of times Aunt Lou neglected to send invitations to Auntie Petra and Grandma for birthday or Christmas parties, the time Uncle Dick tried to discipline my brother Richard, his namesake, by pinning him against the garage with the car. Also, my mother was still angry with Auntie Petra for feeding her lard when she was eight.

I tried to forget the various ways I had tortured Richard and Ethan when we were little, tickling them until they vomited or popping their shoulders out of their joints or leaving them hidden when we played hide-and-seek.

My father gave a speech honoring Grandma and, in his kind but stupid way, did not forget to note the contention that had developed among her children.

My period started in the middle of lunch.

I leaned over to Peg. "You don't have a Tylenol, do you?"

She looked in her purse. "I'm sorry. Only Vicodin."

Peg's resourcefulness impressed me. "That will do," I said. I swallowed it with a shot of the Polish vodka on the table.

Richard kicked Peg underneath the table. "What are you doing?" he demanded.

"Your sister's sick."

Ethan leaned in, wanting to know what was going on.

"Richard's wife has drugs in her handbag."

"My wife does not have drugs."

"Your father gave them to me," Peg said.

Before the funeral, my orthopedist father had prescribed everything from sleeping pills to relaxants to antidepressants to my mother and Ethan and me, but we had no idea he had been so liberal as to prescribe opiates to Peg.

"He gave you Vicodin?!" I thought, for a moment, that Ethan might publicly interrupt my father's speech to complain about the inequity. "Exactly why?!" Ethan demanded, quietly.

"I have a pain in my back," Peg said in the certain whine that until five minutes previously I had deplored.

"A pain," Ethan whispered. "You have a pain."

Peg nodded.

"Give me one of those," Ethan insisted.

Peg complied.

"Give me one, too," Richard said, "and put them away."

My brothers swallowed their drugs with Polish vodka, Peg took one herself, and we found the remainder of the afternoon remarkably painless.

"Your children are beautiful," friends told my mother.

"Your children are one in their solidarity and in their grief," the head priest told my mother.

"Your children are drug abusers," I told her quite plainly. That afternoon, my brothers and Peg and I had not fought and we had not glared at each other because we were high, not out of respect for my grandmother, not out of the love we realized in sadness we felt for one another.

"Oh they are not," my mother said. "You are not."

"Yes we are. Daddy gave Peg Vicodin and it made me feel such a great love for not only her, but for everyone. For Doris and everyone."

"Peg did not have Vicodin."

"It's true, Peg did not have enough Vicodin for me to feel any love for Aunt Lou, but the whole thing was tolerable."

Mom was quite high herself, at that point, from all the Ativan Dad had prescribed to get her through the day. "I love you," she said. "But you are not on drugs."

I shrugged. "I am not on drugs," I said. I felt very content.

On the way out of the church, during that brief moment when the high wears off and melancholy sets in, I admired Peg for her bravery, her wanting to be loved, her generosity in sharing the drugs she knew she would probably never be prescribed again.

"Peg wants to be your friend," I whispered to Ethan as we were walking back to the car.

"She's after you," he said, as if I were an idiot. "Girls," he said, and rolled his eyes as dramatically as he could. He opened the car door for me. "You two, why can't you admit you'd like to be friends?"

After Grandma had died, my mother and Auntie Petra decided to blame their brother Dick for the death, adding to their collection of grievances against him. Uncle Dick was a general practitioner who had encouraged Grandma's doctors to give her a certain blood-pressure medicine my mother and aunt had long maintained was killing Grandma. "It's that drug that killed her," my Auntie Petra would argue that week and for years after my grandmother's funeral.

"We could sue for malpractice," my mother would agree.

Richard encouraged litigation.

"She was ninety," Ethan and I tried to remind them.

No one would sue for malpractice. Old age could kill. There were too many doctors in the family, and, my father would say, "I have to live in this town."

SIXTEEN

There Is Nothing They Can Do About the Scars

My mother never stops speaking before the answering machine cuts off. "It's hot," she says, "and I am so bored and I'm in the car, we're in the desert and Daddy is going potty and I'm hot and there's nothing to look at." We have asked her not to phone before eleven a.m., but she persists. My brother has told her, "People like us do not get up before eleven a.m."

"Unemployed people?"

"Bartenders, Mother."

We punish her by never picking up the phone. She punishes us by phoning again and again.

Sometimes she varies the punishment by not phoning for weeks, and though my brother and I are relieved when this happens, we panic sometimes and know, as she has told us, we'll be sorry when she's dead.

After Grandma died, Mother's threats of her own impending death took on a new tone of sadness. "You don't know," she would say. "I think of my mother every day."

When Mother visits New York, she visits longer than we ever anticipate. She visits for weeks at a time. "I hate Fresno," she says. "I hate that hellhole." She has lived in Fresno for forty-three years. For forty-three years she has said, "I hate this hellhole."

"Go on and do what you would do if I weren't here," she said that July after the second week of her visit. "I can read. I'll clean the closets."

"Don't clean my closet," Ethan said.

"It's a disaster," Mother told him.

"Don't clean my closet."

"Why?"

"Gay porn," I said. "He doesn't want you to find his gay porn."

Mother said, "That is not funny, Katherine."

I was not being funny. Ethan knew I was not being funny. He nodded and shrugged. "Clean out my closet," he said. "And clean underneath my bed, too."

Mother got a line down the center of her forehead. "I'll read instead."

"Your mother doesn't understand how hard I work," Daddy had said over Christmas as we sat together at the kitchen table for breakfast.

"She understands," I told him. "She understands she never gets to see you."

"That's right," my mother said. "Your father likes to have me here so he can leave me alone all the time and play golf."

"You encourage me to play golf."

"I don't encourage you to leave me alone all day."

"Well, I'm here all day now that you had it out with Pedro," he said, resigned.

"What happened with Pedro?" Pedro had been our family's gardener for eighteen years.

Mother looked up from the sink where she had been working. "He stole my persimmons," she said.

I waited for more. There was no more. "No one eats the persimmons anyway," I said.

"He was pruning the tree," my father said.

"It's the principle. I told him to leave them there. For eighteen years I had been telling him to leave my persimmons alone."

"You see," my father said, "so I don't play golf. I mow the lawn."

"Not in the winter," Mother said. "You prevaricator. The lawn has been fertilized for the winter. I have already hired a new gardener."

Daddy sighed. "We'll see how long this lasts," he said, his eyes on the morning's paper. "I bought one of those big mowers you just sit on and ride around."

My father could neither communicate very well with my mother, nor could he very well live without her. I understood Mother's frustration. My father always implied that he and I had nothing to say to one another. When I would phone and he'd answer, he would say immediately, "I'll let you speak to your mother."

"No, Daddy, I'll talk to you."

"I'll just get the gossip from your mother."

"Don't you have gossip?"

"Your mother fired the gardener again. I can't talk, darling, I'll get the gossip from your mother."

My mother took the phone. "I'm depressed," she said.

"Why?"

"Because I have wasted my whole life in this town and your father always leaves me alone."

The two of them had now decided to build a house on Lake Michigan, where each of them, separately, had spent their childhood summers. Mother had pinned all her hopes on this house and on the little town where everyone chipped in to buy a swimming pool for the local high school. My father thought the house would make him poor.

"I'm coming out to see the architect," Mother said that summer after Grandma died, "and I think I'll come see you kids for a while, too." I knew in the unusual flatness of her voice that I ought to prepare for something exceptional.

New York was alive. Ethan had come back from London, thrilled to be out of roller skates and working behind Kevin's bar again. When the feds couldn't get him on drugs, Kevin had gone to jail for tax fraud, and Jonas had been put in charge of things while he was away. Jonas had managed to land himself on the covers of *L'Uomo Vogue* and *Paper* magazine, and was constantly written up in Page Six or the Gotham column in *New York* magazine for the various men and women he managed to sleep with, which designer he had joined on vacation, the parties he did or did not attend. Jonas had parlayed his arrogant personality into a career, and everyone was falling for it. The most exciting new development in New York, though, was Clarissa's arrival. She had promised when we were eighteen that she would return to the States, and finally, ten years later, she had. For two generations, her Uncle Hugh had been the city's most sought-after tutor to undermotivated Manhattan private-school children. At sixty, he had decided to take his young third wife and move to Santiago, leaving a stable of well-paying students for Clarissa to look after. Clarissa rented an apartment in Williamsburg, a large empty loft she decorated with white furniture and the tiniest objects she could find. She had teeny-tiny dolls made from an inch of thread, and silver teaspoons so small you needed a magnifying glass to see the detail. She taped these things to her empty walls or left them alone on large, open bookshelves. In a sense, Clarissa's apartment reminded me of the conceptual fever dreams I'd had when I got the flu as a child: large heavy sounds and spaces colliding with delicate, pinpoint shapes and notes too high to hear. But also, Clarissa's apartment reminded me of the other dreams, the feeling I had when I knew I could fly.

I found a job at an unpopular new bar downtown. The building had, until recently, been Pageant, a legendary New York bookstore. It had been the bookstore featured in many famous films set in New York, in books and plays and a variety of critical articles. I remembered Pageant from our dangerous and exciting trips downtown when I was a teenager, when we would save our taxi money, disobey our parents, and take the vandalized subways to see how intelligent people lived. In Pageant, I had discovered Virginia Woolf, Ursula Le Guin, and Patrick Dennis's *Auntie Mame* books. I bought my first copy of *Lolita* at Pageant, without my parents looking out to monitor what I was reading. Later on, I bought *The Story of O*, recommended to me not only by Page but by Doris, too. Pageant had been, like the Plaza and Le Cirque, one of the few places I never felt homesick.

The new bar looked nothing like Pageant. I recognized the large, solid staircase and the wide plank floors, but the light and the excitement were gone. I made hardly any money in that bar, but I made some, and after having been away from a bar for so long, I was certain that no one else would hire me.

My parents had always worried that I would end up poor and alone, tending bar in any bar that would take me, becoming an alcoholic and telling people how talented I had been once. I dismissed them as alarmist and unrealistic. But now, Ethan had begun to worry the same thing.

"I don't understand why you don't just call Tom," Ethan would say. "Tom loves you."

"I have a job."

"I mean, you could really make money."

"Ethan," I explained as if he were still a ten-year-old, "I am not a journalist. I make things up, you see."

"You can refrain from making things up."

"No, *you* can refrain from making things up. You don't know what happens inside my head." The frightening truth was that Ethan did know exactly what happened inside my head. Though he was five years younger, I often felt that Ethan and I might, like a science-fiction novel, share the same brain. He voiced my thoughts, using my vocabulary, just as I was thinking them. His handwriting was so similar to mine, often I could not tell our phone messages apart. On days I had decided to make a roast chicken, Ethan would come home from the grocery store with an organic Amish hen and tell me, "I thought you might like to roast a chicken."

When Ethan started to worry that I was getting older and still living like a graduate student, I worried the same thing. In the three years since graduate school, while I had told myself and everyone else I was working on a novel, I had written nothing. Faced with the reality of being a failure in alumni newsletters and hometown papers and in the gossip that happened in my mother's bridge group, I decided it was time to call Tom.

"I knew you would call," he said on the patio of Mediterraneo, twirling his black linguine.

"I always call."

"No no no," he said, "I knew you would call me in regard to work. Everyone comes around." Tom had just taken an associate editorial position at a glossy men's magazine. Mine was, apparently, not the first phone call he had received from an old writing-school friend asking for work.

There was little I disliked more than appearing predictable. "You encouraged me for a long time," I said. "Anyway, I enjoy eating lunch with you."

"I'm glad." It was a warm day in June, and everyone was happy.

"I haven't written my book."

"No, I certainly haven't seen it on the shelves."

"What if I never write my book?"

"What if I never write mine?"

"Well, I think you should write it." Everything Tom wrote had you crying with laughter, and then, quite suddenly, just crying.

"It's always better to get paid for whatever it is you're writing," he said.

His linguine looked better than my insalata mista, and I picked at it, which he didn't mind. He pushed his plate a little toward me.

"I have some very good ideas," I told him.

"You can't imagine the ideas I hear all day. I stopped answering my phone, even at home."

"Listen."

He listened. I pitched him an article about Jonas's friend Jim Mullins, an enterprising young man who had invented what he called *the inflatable extra*: movie extras that inflated to look exactly like humans, for about a hundredth the price. They didn't need food, they didn't get cold, and they didn't harass the celebrities. Jim Mullins was all the rage inside Hollywood.

"Is he good-looking?"

"I don't know. He's friends with Jonas. Jonas's friends are almost exclusively very good-looking."

"Jonas is sleeping with my ex-girlfriend," Tom said, looking up from his linguine, as if this were a topic he had been waiting to discuss.

I shook my head. "He's gay, Tom. Queer as a three-dollar bill. Nancy boy, ansy-pay. Church member. Light in the loafers. Gladiola."

"I got it."

"Jailhouse turnout. Queen of Sheba. Camp as a row of tents." Ethan had taught me all of these useful phrases.

"I know Jonas," Tom said. "Let's have some more wine."

We caught Gino's eye and he sent over more of the friuli. We'd been through three glasses each. Working at the bar, I consistently made fun of people who ordered glass after glass of wine when it would have cost them almost half as much just to order the bottle. Idiots, I called them. Idiots.

I drank my glass of friuli. "Jonas is very good at getting himself publicity. Your girlfriends are very good at being lovely and photogenic."

"Anyway," he said, "be a writer."

"I am a writer, Tom."

"You are a writer. I know that. So am I."

"So are you. A few pictures in the tabloids doesn't mean anyone's sleeping together."

"I know that." He drank the whole glass in a couple of swigs. "Of course I know that."

I gave him a weak smile. "Anyway," I said, "be a writer."

Suddenly, in the lovely warm June afternoon, neither of us was quite as happy as we had been before lunch.

"When can you get out to Los Angeles?" Tom asked.

"Tomorrow," I said.

No one was happier than Jim Mullins.

Meanwhile, Mother was enthusiastically planning her trip to New York.

"Can you take time off from the bar and come out to Michigan with me to see the architect?"

"Sure."

"I'd like you to come with me, otherwise I'll get lonesome. Also, I'd like to know your thoughts on the new plans."

"Sure, Mother."

"And can you try to find a dentist for me in New York?"

My mother refused to go to the dentist in Fresno. She had not seen a dentist for twenty-two years because, she said, "I don't want the whole damn town gossiping about my teeth." About the only time my mother swore was when she used the phrase "the whole damn town."

"No one's gossiping about your teeth."

"You don't know, Katherine. What it's like in this town."

"Who cares. You hate everyone and you hardly leave the house anyway."

"I have to get work done and I don't want everyone talking about it."

"What kind of work?"

"Embarrassing work! Reconstructive dental work. I don't want you talking about it either. Please just make me an appointment with a dentist in New York."

I made her an appointment with the dentist of my friend Bruce. Bruce is the only person I know who has ever talked about his dentist when dentists were in no way part of the conversation. Also, Bruce has very nice teeth.

"I made an appointment for you," I phoned to tell her. "Bruce says this dentist is very good about having no pain."

"Is he gay?"

"Bruce is gay."

"The dentist, Katherine!"

"I don't know, Mother, I didn't ask the receptionist."

"I don't want a gay dentist."

I hung up the phone. Ethan had been listening. "Did she ask if the dentist was gay?" he said.

I told him, "This is a woman who gets out of bed once a week and is afraid that people are going to gossip about her teeth."

Ethan phoned her immediately.

"Mother, how long are you staying? Well, can you give me vague dates? Thank you, Mother."

"What did she say?" I asked.

"She says she's staying from July through December."

At Thanksgiving, Ethan and my mother had been having an argument about politics. My brother slammed the newspaper onto the table and stomped upstairs to his room as if he were a child. It's a big house with a long staircase. He continued shouting as he marched upstairs. "You!" he shouted. "You!"

"Why do you do that?" I said to her.

"What did I do?"

"You!" he shouted. "Are insane!"

"Why don't you just agree with him?"

"I don't agree with him."

"Why don't you just pretend?"

"Because I will not lie to my children." She brushed dirt from button mushrooms. She tossed one after the other into a large bowl. She did not look up, she gently rubbed each mushroom with a cloth. I could see the bald spot on the top of her head, the result of years of tugging at her hair.

"Then don't lie. Change your mind. It's none of your business, anyway." One moment we were three polite people sitting peacefully in my parents' kitchen, cleaning mushrooms and reading the paper. The next moment my brother and mother were violent, shouting, crazy-eyed people.

My mother's political views sometimes had little logic. Often her retorts included "because it offends me!" or "that's just the way it is." Unfortunately, usually the only argument to be made with my mother was "You're nuts," which she did not try to defend herself against.

"He brought it up," she said.

"He didn't bring it up, he was reading the paper."

She was visibly pained. There was that line she got down the center of her forehead, the same line you see in her wedding photos. In a moment she would open the refrigerator and eat every leftover she could find. She was not visibly pained to have disagreed with my brother, she was visibly pained at the thought of a son with ideas that offended her, a son who might someday want to marry another man.

"I don't care. I think what I think."

"You ought to think about changing your mind."

"He's wrong."

"I think you're wrong." I was relieved the argument had been so brief and that so far no one had put a fist through the sliding glass door.

"I know what you think," she said. She stopped a moment. She said, "I am his mother."

I picked up the newspaper where Ethan had left it.

There was a long silence. She opened the refrigerator and took the lemon sole I had brought home from dinner last night. "So," she said, opening the box, eating the sole, "what else?"

When they first bought the old farm in Harbor Springs, Michigan, Mother thought she could easily fly back and forth from California to supervise the planning and construction of their home. However, after one season of missed flights and jet lag and early-morning connections and overnight stays in Cincinnati, she decided the travel would be much easier from New York.

"You don't want me to come."

"I want you to come."

"No you don't, I can hear it in your voice."

"You're going to be uncomfortable all summer on the sofa."

"I'll sleep in your bed with you."

"Mother."

"You're going to make me sleep on the sofa?"

"Mommy."

She said, "You don't want me to come."

"You'll get bored."

"I have a plan," she said.

"What sort of plan?"

"A plan I'm not telling you."

"What good is a plan like that."

"You think you know everything," she said.

Clarissa and I met in Chinatown one afternoon to shop for dishes. For months since moving from England, she had been eating from paper plates with her grandmother's silver.

"Must find the right plates this afternoon," Clarissa informed me, "because tomorrow I'm having the Russian to dinner."

"I thought you were divorcing the Russian."

"Too handsome. Looks like Rudolf Nureyev. Can't bring myself to get rid of him."

I remembered what Nureyev looked like from the famous Karsh portrait. I didn't think those deep wrinkles and that wide mouth were so terribly handsome. "I thought you said he's in the mafia."

"He might be. There are a lot of middle-of-the-night phone calls and a lot of *da da, nyet nyet*. Anyway, it doesn't matter, because at the moment I can't resist him."

"He's dangerous. You're just desperate for danger after years of boring English people."

"Could be." She scanned a wall full of Chinese plates in reds and blues and pinks. "I want blue," she said. "Look for some nice blue, will you?"

"Please give me all his information in case something happens to you."

"If something happens to me, it was definitely him. Or his driver. He gets his driver to do everything."

Clarissa kept all the biographical and contact information for each of my ex-boyfriends, and she knew which of my exes I thought were most likely to stalk and kill me.

"Maybe I'll take the green," she said, holding a plate in each hand.

"White," I said. "Food looks best on white. Are you going to put vodka in the freezer?"

"Who told you that about white?"

"I read it in the Food section. Everything you read in the Food section is true."

"There is always vodka in my freezer, darling."

"I had to take the vodka out of my freezer. Coddling booze upsets my mother. 'Do you drink this every day?' she says. All I keep in my freezer is vodka and cocktail glasses."

"Well," Clarissa said, "that's what freezers are for. But get some peas or something to keep up appearances."

"All summer my freezer will be empty."

"How is Ethan feeling about this?"

"Ethan never gets upset about anything. He shakes his head occasionally. That's it."

"Ethan's very sensible."

"He's better at distancing himself from my parents."

"You can come to my house. I'll feed you vodka."

"Maybe your Russian can find us some really wonderful vodka."

"Yes, darling, and you can store it with no coddling underneath your kitchen sink."

I reached to a high shelf for oblong white plates. "Mother's not here yet and already I'm angry with her."

Clarissa nodded. She tugged the back of my hair. We bought white plates and took them back to Brooklyn on the subway.

During the six years I had been in New York, my mother had visited many times, dozens of times. I enjoyed our afternoons together lunching in the café at the top of Bergdorf's or getting dressed up and going to the theater. I enjoyed walking with her on Madison or across the park early in the morning for breakfast on the West Side. I certainly didn't mind when she rearranged my closets to make twice as much room as I thought I'd had. But by day ten, usually one or the other of us would start behaving badly and the visit would go sour. Either I would tell Mother the truth about how heavy she looked, or she'd tell me how I drank too much and had too many boyfriends.

This trip, the trouble started on her arrival at JFK. She arrived at our door frazzled, upset, a patch of hair at the back of her head upright because she had been pulling at it, her face blotched from hives.

"I had a fight," she said. She came in but wouldn't let go of her luggage.

"Let me take it," I said gently. "Sit down."

"Who won?" Ethan shouted from his room.

"I had a fight."

"Mommy, let go of your bag."

She released her luggage and sat down on the sofa. She looked at me apologetically.

"What happened?" I said.

She looked at me. She looked toward Ethan's door. "We were in the line for taxis. A lot of flights came in at the same time and the line was very long. A young woman cut in front of me. I told her not to, I said, 'I was here,' and she said . . . she said," Mother caught her breath. "She said, 'Shut up, you fat old bitch.' "

Mother pronounced each word with emphasis and then started to cry. She pulled a tissue from beneath the cuff of her sleeve.

"Who said this?" Ethan asked, coming out of his room.

"It was a long line and I had some time to think. I am fat and I am old. She really hurt my feelings. And I wanted to hurt her feelings, too."

"What did you do?" I stood in the doorway to my apartment, the door open. Mother's second suitcase was still in the hall. Ethan watched from the door to his room.

"I told her she had a very bad complexion. I said, 'I could lose weight, but there is nothing they can do about the scars on your face.' And the taxis didn't come, so I waited a while and said it again. I said, 'I guess they could try to blast them off with sand, but I hear that hurts a lot and doesn't really work.' "

Ethan began to laugh.

She looked at Ethan. "I said it like I meant it," she said.

"Mommy," I said, "well, that's very mean."

"I know," she said and really started to cry, so that the tears ran down and soaked the collar of her dress. "I wanted to hurt her feelings, and I feel so sad."

"You didn't mean to be mean," Ethan said.

"Yes I did," Mother said enthusiastically. "That is exactly what I wanted to do."

"Well, then you were successful!" Ethan said. "You see."

Mother had an endless supply of tissues underneath her sleeve.

I pulled her suitcase inside and shut the door.

My mother has worn to bed one of the same two oversized T-shirts for as long as I can remember. My father bought them for her on business trips. One is torn beneath the arms and worn out so that it is nearly see-through and says *Georgia Peach* in big orange cursive. The other is black and has naked cowgirls on it and says *Trainee. Mustang Ranch. Where Quality Keeps 'Em Coming.*

The first week of Mother's stay, I made a mistake I would not make again that summer. I had been seeing an Italian banker I quite liked. We loved the same books in different languages and he cooked beautifully. He was intense and charismatic and physically perfect. I would forget from time to time how stunning he was and seeing him would take my breath away. He had big, sad brown eyes that crinkled up at the corners when he laughed or when he saw me coming. He was beautifully rough-looking and tanned—surely the most gorgeous creature I had ever had the pleasure to take out in public. That first Friday of Mother's visit, he and I went to dinner for the third time. We ate six rounds of sushi and, after dinner, had walked over the Brooklyn Bridge. When I arrived home after three a.m., my mother was waiting, pacing the floor in her *Mustang Ranch Trainee* T-shirt, her short hair standing on end, her face blotched.

"Where have you been?" she demanded.

"I told you."

"But where have you been for so long?"

"Out."

She followed me into the kitchen while I fetched a glass of water.

"Did you kiss him?" My mother never asks questions like *Did you kiss him?* She launches them like accusations.

"I don't like the tone of that question," I said.

"Did you kiss him?" she demanded again.

"As a matter of fact, no, Mother, he had a cold and I didn't kiss him."

She was quiet and looked at me for a long time. "Ethan!" she shouted through the slatted doors of the kitchen into Ethan's room.

"Hmph."

"Can you have sex without kissing?"

Mother's first week in New York she spent on the phone to Michigan and cross-legged on the sofa with her house plans spread out before her. She was very sweet in the mornings, folding up the pullout sofa and straightening everything just so, making an extra effort to be quiet if Ethan or I had worked late the night before. In the afternoons, having spent several hours looking at her house plans, her mood would darken considerably.

"I don't like this architect."

"What's wrong?"

"He says I can't have a basement."

"You don't like him because he's gay," Ethan said.

"Mother, you're building beside a wetland," I said.

"I think he just doesn't want to bother building a basement for me."

"It will flood, Mother."

Ethan said, "If you build it, it will flood."

"He is not gay, he is married," Mother said then, to Ethan.

"He's gay. Katherine said he was gay."

I had met the architect and discerned that he was definitely gay. I had met his wife and discerned that she was definitely gay, too. Ethan had not even met the architect. Ethan preferred to have no emotional attachments to my mother's projects, which so often amounted to nothing.

"Katherine," my mother said in her most admonishing tone, "my architect is not gay."

The second week, Mother fired the architect and rehired him again.

I didn't tell Mother that Tom's magazine had just sent me out to Los Angeles, and did not tell her I had any professional aspirations outside of my own little stories and the unpopular bar. My mother tended to get her hopes up. If she had known I was writing for magazines, she would start to wonder why I wasn't the editor at the *New York Times*. She would start to get impatient for me to win a Pulitzer.

"I don't want to be in your way," Mother said when she arrived. "I want you to get your writing done."

"My writing, yes, I'll get it done."

"I won't be a nuisance."

"Believe it or not, Mother, I really don't consider you a nuisance." I meant it, then, when she first arrived.

One morning during the third week of her visit, while Ethan and I slept in after long nights at work, Mother got up early, made the effort of blow-drying her hair, and went out for the entire day. By the time she must have come home, Ethan and I were at work. The mornings that followed, she was up and out before Ethan or I got out of bed.

"Where do you think Mommy's going?" I asked him one day over coffee. I made coffee for the two of us in a press every afternoon when we woke up.

Ethan rolled his eyes. "I hope I get this pilot so I can escape this summer of madness." He went to his room and shut the door, which was merely a gesture at privacy.

The next time I saw Mother, I asked where she had been going every day for the past week.

"Columbia," she said.

"Where?" I heard her, but wasn't sure we were thinking about the same Columbia.

"I'm taking a class," she said. "I'm taking a course in American literature at Columbia."

I looked at her. "Why?"

"Because I am bored and have to do something with my life," she said.

"So what are you doing with your life?"

"I'm going to apply to graduate school."

I nodded. "What exactly do you expect to do with a graduate degree?"

"Teach," she said.

I didn't point out to her that with my graduate degree from Columbia, I had been bartending downtown for two years.

Mother and I went together to Michigan to see the architect. From New York to Traverse City there's a change of planes in Chicago and from Chicago to Traverse City there's a little twin-engine plane that invariably makes my mother sick. By the time we got to the architect's office, Mother was throwing up into a bin in the parking lot. Traveling with my mother is never a holiday.

"Commercial air travel is for assholes," I assured her.

She looked up from the bin. "I don't like that language."

My mother and dad had planned to travel from California to Michigan mostly by car, but I figured the occasional plane trip was inevitable, particularly if my mother planned on getting her graduate degree in New York. An idyllic and remote summer town in Michigan is too far away from anyone's bicoastal lifestyle to be convenient.

"How will you do this?" I asked her countless times that summer.

"You think you are a very clever girl."

"I think you're making a permanent travel mistake."

"You don't know what it's like to be from Michigan."

"I'm sure I don't."

"Do you know," she told me, "it is the only one of the forty-eight continental states you don't have to drive through to get somewhere else?"

"Yes, it's quite a challenge to get here."

"Do you have any idea what I mean?"

I had no idea what she meant, but I did not want to disagree too much. "Wherever you go, I'll come to visit you."

"I know you will," she said. "That's why I'm building here." She gestured to the turquoise lake beyond the architect's office, beyond the row of gabled houses on the sand. She said, "I'm going to fill up my new house with people."

I began to think my mother had encouraged me to be an artist because an artist could follow her wherever she wanted to go.

Mother and the architect had a personality clash. They argued over the definition of veneer. They argued over the sensibility of storm windows and wooden window frames and false mullions. They argued over which plants the architect had drawn on the elevations.

"They look like hydrangeas to me," my mother said.

"They're not, they're lilacs."

"They don't look like lilacs to me, they look like hydrangeas."

"There's not enough room here for hydrangea bushes. With the wetland they'll grow over the path."

"I'm just saying you drew hydrangeas, not lilacs."

"I drew lilacs."

They couldn't agree on a color of stone, or a palette for the outside of the house that would be best for the surroundings.

After the meeting with the architect, Mother and I ate grilled-cheese sandwiches and french fries at a fifties drive-in. "You see," she said, "he doesn't like to listen to me."

"Well."

I had to agree she was right, but sometimes I didn't like to listen to her, either.

My father phoned twice a day. "Hi, darling, can I talk to Mommy?"

"Don't you want to talk to me, Dad?"

"Sure I do. How are you, darling?"

"Fine, how are you?"

"Good. Can I talk to Mommy?"

He was homesick for her, and she was equally homesick for him.

"Poor Daddy is lonely," she told me one night after he phoned.

"Why don't you go back?"

She looked at me. She shook her head. "I have to do something with my life," she said.

Everyone at Tom's magazine had liked my Jim Mullins story very much. After the story appeared, it seemed that "inflatable extras" immediately became part of the American consciousness. At Ethan's bar, the doorman had said to Jonas, "Awfully empty in here. We ought to get some inflatable extras."

"Where did you hear about that?" Jonas asked.

"Read it in a magazine."

Jonas was a good friend, and he was thrilled to discover that I had an audience. "I'm going to get you a famous boyfriend," he said one night I dropped in at the bar.

"Not yet. Wait until I'm done with the Italian."

"Timing is essential here, darling. Now, I want you to do what I tell you."

"I don't want a mention in Page Six. I just want to make some money."

"You will do what I tell you, and you will like it." Jonas shook his head. "Dilettante."

"I don't want to be talked about. I want you to arrange more work for me, Jonas. Know anyone at *Vanity Fair*?"

"Why, darling? Things not so perky over at Pageant?" Jonas relished that the bar which had once been his favorite childhood bookstore was failing quite spectacularly, with great hype. "You can always come work here."

"No thank you." I had no interest in the high-pressure, high-volume atmosphere in that place. I had no interest in Jonas setting me up with D-list boyfriends, either, but for the next several weeks, whenever Jonas would ask me to visit him at work, there was a soap-opera actor or race-car driver or nightclub promoter waiting for me at the bar.

Jim Mullins was booked on all the morning shows. He started popping up on lists of most-eligible bachelors. Jonas set him up with one of Tom's ex-girlfriends.

"My teacher doesn't like me," my mother said one day after school.

"How do you know?"

"I can tell. I put my hand up and he doesn't call on me. Maybe I say stupid things in class."

"I'm sure you don't."

"Maybe I do."

I shrugged. "Well, he has to call on you once in a while. You paid for the class."

"He calls everyone by their first names," she said. "Except me. He calls me Mrs. Taylor."

"You're right," I said. "He doesn't like you."

"I'm going to win him over, though," she said, smiling. "With my term paper."

That weekend Mother spent on the sofa, absentmindedly tugging at her hair, writing her term paper longhand on college-ruled loose-leaf notebook paper, dog-eared copies of *McTeague* and *Sister Carrie* and *The Good Soldier* in front of her, highlighting the passages most useful for proving her thesis. Later, she paid me twenty dollars to type it—"Blaming Booze: When Good Characters Go Bad."

As far as I could see, not much needed to be straightened out in my life or in Ethan's, but my mother didn't see it that way. What my mother could see was that my brother and I were wasting our expensive educations by getting up at noon and spending too much time in front of the computer. "I am writing," I would lie. "I'm checking my email," Ethan would confess. What my mother could see was that I had no boyfriend and Ethan no girl-friend. Actually, I had several unimportant boyfriends, and so did Ethan.

She bought us matching coffee cups and scrubbed the cup-board underneath the kitchen sink. She bought me a new winter coat, a long sweepy one that flowed like water around me when I walked. She stopped short of having the oriental rug that had been my grandmother's cleaned. "When you move back to Los Angeles, we'll get it cleaned then," she said.

I had no intention of moving back to Los Angeles. I didn't know Ethan had it always not far in the back of his head.

One Saturday morning while Ethan slept in or pretended to sleep in, Mother and I went for breakfast at the Hotel Wales high up on Madison and strolled down afterwards, stopping into shops and looking for a dainty linen shirt my mother had in mind to wear during the summer evenings in New York. It's difficult finding sizes to fit my mother in any styles she'd wear. My mother likes the type of clothes skinny people wear.

"I'd like a black linen shirt with sleeves that fall just above the elbow, something that buttons up but not too high," she told one particularly aloof, bored salesboy in a shop that sold mostly handbags.

"I think they've got something like that at Bloomingdale's," he said.

"Bloomingdale's," my mother said flatly, glaring at him.

Outside, she turned to me, a little angry, very hurt. "Bloomingdale's? Do I look like I want to shop at Bloomingdale's?"

"You don't look like that to me," I assured her.

"He thinks I want to shop at Bloomingdale's because I'm fat."

"Maybe."

"Really?"

"I don't know."

"Bloomingdale's." She mentioned the incident several more times throughout the day, and into the next week, and occasionally for the rest of the summer.

Soon it became clearer and clearer that my mother's American literature teacher at Columbia really didn't like her.

"He rolls his eyes when I ask a question."

"I think you're imagining that," I would say.

She would pause and consider it. "I don't think so. He rolls his eyes. The other students won't talk to me during the breaks."

"They're eighteen years old."

"But what am I going to do if I don't go to graduate school?"

"Build your house."

"I am building my house," she said. "My architect is an idiot."

I didn't understand why she thought she was cut out for graduate school and I didn't want to hurt her feelings by asking her directly. During college at Fresno State University, Mother was so interested in furniture and boys and the school newspaper that she nearly flunked out altogether. She was put on academic suspension for an entire semester, and in the end only just passed after she met Daddy, who fell in love with her and wrote all her term papers.

Later in the summer, we went to Michigan again, to meet with contractors. I enjoyed accompanying my mother on these trips. I enjoyed the small town and the series of farms and barns along the two-lane highway and the buildings on Main Street that hadn't changed since 1881. There were flower boxes on every porch of every house and wide lawns that led down to the water, a lake so clear and calm you could see every color and shape of the pebbles on the bottom. Girls my age sat on Adirondack chairs near the beach, knitting and drinking wine. Teenagers on street corners had ice-cream cones where their cigarettes should have been. The summer days were eighteen hours long, and people played tennis at the town courts on the water until eleven p.m., when dark fell. Errant tennis balls floated in the harbor, and kayakers tossed them, wet, back up to the courts. My parents had bought a small cabin on the golf course, a temporary home while they tried to get their house built, and so far they had been there a lot longer than they had intended.

Mother and the architect fought about whether to use a local contractor or one from the larger town nearby. They fought about when to start building and whether or not it was time to start quarter-inch drawings. They fought about which trees to remove on the property and at which angle the house would face the lake. I could see my mother was quarrelsome, but I began to really dislike this architect. He raised his big, deep voice much too loud and pounded on the table with enormously muscular, furry arms. He had stopped even being considerate of her. He cut her off midsentence and spoke to her in the condescending tone that only family used with my mother.

"You see," she said, "the windows are not symmetrical."

"It would look ugly your way," the architect told her.

"But last time I told you what I like."

"You are not the architect."

The architect hadn't done much this trip but cause trouble, and afterwards he presented Mother with an enormous bill for his time.

"He charges me too much and he doesn't listen to me." Mother began to consider Dad's fear that the house would make them poor.

When Dad phoned, he was tender and kind. He encouraged her to keep the architect, or else to find a new one, and assured her that no one would be made poor.

That trip, Mother took me to a meeting of the Kiwanis Club, which she had joined in an effort to make friends in town. Mother had never been the club-joining type. When I was seven, she quit the Junior League after three meetings. I remember her telling her sister, in language completely out of character for my mother, that the Junior League president was "an anti-Semitic bitch married to the richest Jew in town." Throughout my childhood, she quit the PTA after a fight with my sixth-grade teacher, resigned from the board of the Fresno Art Museum after a heated disagreement over displaying found objects, decided the Literacy Council Board was full of "condescending old bags," and either gave up on or was shoved out of several informal quilting groups.

Here in Harbor Springs, in the backwoods of Michigan, members of the Kiwanis seemed, so far, to appreciate her forthright unpredictability, and she seemed to like them just as much. She was the youngest Kiwanis member by about thirty years, and the only woman. After breakfast, an old man I'd seen riding his bicycle around town approached me. "You sure are sweet-looking," he said to me. "Are you married?"

"No."

"Are you in love with anyone?"

"We'll see," I said.

He and Mother chatted about contractors for a few minutes and he said goodbye and as we walked to the car, Mother said, "Do you think he has someone in mind for you?" Mother was always very excited at the idea of me having a boyfriend, but always very unhappy with the reality.

I rarely saw Ethan, who pretended to sleep later and later and left for work earlier and earlier. The smoke from his clothes would drift out of his room, and Mother demanded, "Is Ethan smoking again?"

"I don't like that tone, Mother."

"I don't like Ethan smoking."

"He's an adult," I said.

"He's my son."

"It's the bar," I said. "Your clothes get just drenched in smoke." That was true, but I was sure that when Ethan left for work early, he walked half the way downtown before getting on the subway, so that he might have a little bit of peace on Lexington Avenue to smoke seven or eight cigarettes. Mother's visit had been trying for everyone, poor Dad included. I wished I had the nerve to take up smoking. Instead, I drank copiously when I went out in the evenings with Clarissa or the Italian. The Italian thought this was a lot of fun, the drinking and running around. He didn't have much of a tolerance, and I doubt he'd ever drunk so much so consistently in his entire life. I didn't try to make excuses after my third or fourth Manhattan. I feared becoming the sort of person who made excuses. Of course Clarissa understood everything completely.

"In London, the Halcyon was a very good place for recovering from the effects of affectionate mothers, remember?" she said.

"Of course I remember."

"And there was that lovely barman Dewey and his delicious sidecars."

"And then he left."

"Yes, he left and the other barmen wouldn't tell us where he'd gone." We sat on the stoop in front of Clarissa's apartment, waiting for the appearance of an aloof carpenter she had fallen in love with. He lived on the next block, and Clarissa was stalking him from her doorstep. She had given up the Russian recently, after finding a small silver gun in his overnight bag. "There are nice places in New York, too. We know a lot of nice places."

"Your mother's house," I said, "I think was the nicest place."

"And that breakfast place on the All Saints Road."

"And the path through Holland Park."

"When it wasn't raining."

"It rained every day."

"It was very good having you around last year, and putting up with me." Clarissa's mother had gone through a particularly bad time while I was in London. She had divorced her third husband and needed a lot of attention from Clarissa, who was still then finishing up her thesis at Oxford. I liked Clarissa's mother very much. She was languid and funny and she had a lot of harsh things to say about her countrymen, which I always enjoyed. She lived in Henry's neighborhood, between Holland Park and Shepherd's Bush; on days I felt lonesome myself, I would drop in with a bottle of wine or ingredients for soup, and the two of us would spend the afternoon together. She chain-smoked cigarettes, but never smoked in the house, so oftentimes we would sit in her garden, under an umbrella in the rain, while she smoked and we talked and our shoes got soaked.

"It was good having you around, too, darling. What would I have done?" After I left Henry, I had stayed at Clarissa's mother's house until I could find a decent ticket home.

"I ought to learn how to make a nice sidecar," Clarissa said.

She made entire pitchers of gin and tonics for us at her Brooklyn apartment. She had a talent for gin and tonics, rolling the limes with the butt of her palm and muddling them with the gin for a good while before slowly tipping the tonic into the pitcher over ice. "Did you read the article in this morning's paper that said scientists think loneliness could be genetic?"

"Loneliness?"

She nodded. "In which case, you and I are doomed."

When my mother's grade arrived from Columbia, she gripped the envelope for more than an hour before opening it. I paced from room to room, I sat down and got up, I made more than one cup of tea. For a very long time she sat on the sofa with that worried, vulnerable grimace of hers you see in photographs from when she was a child, that awful strain on her face that tries to be a smile.

"What if he failed me?"

"Mother, he didn't fail you. You went to class, you participated, you wrote 'Blaming Booze.' "

"What if he gave me a D?" she whispered.

"Well. Then."

"I can't go to graduate school with D's."

"You don't deserve a D." In fact, I had never worked so hard in graduate school as Mother worked in that basic undergraduate English class at Columbia.

"What am I going to do with my whole life?"

"Just open the envelope."

She opened the envelope. She looked at it. She started laughing. She laughed and laughed. "He gave me a C-plus," she said.

I laughed, too, disappointed. I said, "A C."

"C-plus," she said. Then we couldn't stop laughing. I hated that teacher.

Ethan was cast in a Diet Coke commercial, which was not a pilot but was something. Ethan said, "Dat's some-ting," like my Polish grandmother used to say. We still liked to mimic the way she spoke, her catchphrases like "dat's some-ting," or "you wan' 'em penis-butter and jelly?" or "don' make fun grandmama." The commercial gave him a reason to get out to Los Angeles for a little bit. In the fall, they offered him the entire campaign, the face of Diet Coke, which Ethan figured was even better than a pilot.

Mother and I helped him pack and Mother bought him a travel iron and Ethan felt happy and confident and looked very handsome, which was good enough for our mother. Seeing Ethan like that made her happy and confident, too.

My father phoned repeatedly to make sure Ethan didn't need a ride from the Los Angeles airport, and Ethan assured him every time as if it were the first time that he did not need a ride from the airport.

I was proud of Ethan but sad that I didn't make our mother feel happy and confident. She worried that no one would love me and that I would bartend until I was too ugly to bartend and that no one would ever like my stories as much as she liked them. She worried the same things about Ethan until he was rescued by Diet Coke.

"Maybe you should come to Harbor Springs and find a teaching job," she said.

I nodded.

"There are a lot of rich boys in Harbor Springs," she said.

"I don't like rich boys anymore," I told her. I told her this because it was true but also because I liked to wind her up.

"It's just as easy to love money."

My mother promised that if I married one of the impoverished, poetry-publishing-type boys I liked, I would be unhappy later. I told her not to worry, that I would not marry any of these impoverished boys or anyone else. This frightened her, as she did not want to continue paying my health insurance for the rest of her life.

She left New York in late August, shortly after Ethan went to Los Angeles, shortly before everything in New York changed for good. I was mostly relieved to see her go, but then the apartment seemed empty without her suitcases and blueprints and various classic paperbacks. In the end, she said herself she wasn't cut out for graduate school. "But I wanted to make sure," she said. She looked at me sideways. "You know Daddy helped me cheat in geography."

"I know," I said. "He wrote your English term papers, too."

"He did?!" she said. "I don't remember that. I don't think so."

"All right," I said. The following week, she would remind me that she wasn't cut out for graduate school because Daddy had helped her write all those English term papers anyway.

That fall, she and my father took a weekend trip to Michigan and found a new architect who seemed to share my mother's ideas of symmetry. Mother backed the car into a tree and Daddy didn't scream at her. When they returned to Fresno, my father gave up golf for the autumn and spent his weekends mowing the lawn, which my mother considered a romantic gesture toward spending more time together.

Just before her flight home to California at the end of the summer, Mother was dining alone at her favorite overpriced Greek restaurant on Seventy-first Street. She had started with the octopus, moved on to the swordfish baked in herbs, and finished with a hot chocolate and the yogurt smothered in honey and cherries. She sat, quite content, while Costa, the waiter, indicated repeatedly he would bring her check. A fine-boned woman and her young, serious daughter sat at the table across the way, and as Mother admired how attractive they looked in their short-sleeved linen shirts and matching summer sweaters, how elegantly they held their wineglasses, how their eyes lit up identically when they laughed, she overheard the woman tell her daughter, "Don't, darling. If you eat it all, you'll end up looking like her."

Mother looked at her hands and thought, *Even my hands are fat.*

On her way out, Mother couldn't keep from responding. "You should consider other people's feelings," she said with restraint as she passed the woman's table. Costa offered to wrap a baklava for the plane, courtesy of the chef. Mother refused, kissed Costa on both cheeks, and felt very happy for not having an impulse to hurt anyone the way she felt hurt. Walking back to the apartment in time to meet her car for the airport, she would tell me much later, she had a certain feeling of elation and freedom she hadn't felt in a long time.

Part Three

SEVENTEEN

Crying and Smoking

That January, everyone in New York was faking cheerfulness.

One afternoon, Clarissa showed up at my apartment. She was tutoring dull children on the Upper East Side at a rate of $150 an hour, a rate that made us both laugh, and she would often come by when she had an hour between students.

This afternoon the snow was everywhere, hiding everything but shapes in a plain white sheet, and Clarissa had lost one of her gloves getting out of the taxi.

"Plus my wallet has been stolen," she cried on my sofa, the tears starting at first all by themselves and then growing into good loud sobs. "Which had my green card in it and I can't get the green card replaced because they're all backed up after 9/11 and I have no passport because I lost it in Paris last month so I have no identification and can't get cash or any credit from the bank until they replace my green card so I am completely without means." She tried not to cry but at a certain point began to enjoy it. She hiccupped and sniffled delicate sniffles. "Plus I have no boyfriends, there are absolutely no prospects, and I have been rejected even by a forty-year-old ex-Mormon alcoholic carpenter in Williamsburg." From her bag she pulled a package of tissues printed with small blue moths. "What's wrong with me? I am the daughter of a specialist."

"I have no boyfriends, either."

"Don't make me laugh."

"I haven't heard from Stefano Naldi in over a week." I found the sound of "Stefano Naldi" so lovely that I always used his first and last names together even though there had never been two Stefanos.

"A week."

"He says he's depressed."

"Everyone is depressed."

"Let's have one of Ethan's cigarettes." When Ethan had moved to Los Angeles to get away from the sadness in New York but also to star in the new Diet Coke campaign, he left behind his discarded cashmere sweaters and various unfinished packs of gold-filtered party cigarettes.

"Let's." Clarissa is always very elegant and composed and even in her agitated state she lit the cigarette and inhaled slowly, gracefully, with cinematic perfection.

We were quiet for a little while and watched the snow.

"I have to go tutor Daniel on the Reformation."

I nodded. No matter how much time Clarissa spent with Daniel, he was always failing exams. No matter how many papers she outlined for him in descriptive detail, no matter the number of book summaries she wrote or paperbacks she notated or memorization games she invented, he couldn't manage to get anything done. His parents had told Clarissa they were hoping to get him into a decent university by playing up Daniel's quite questionable dyslexia. "Can you imagine," Clarissa would say, "lazy old Daniel whining his way through Dartmouth."

Of course, I loved to hear stories about Daniel and Clementine and the other boorish children who brought Clarissa to me and took her away in the afternoons.

"You wouldn't happen to have an old wallet I could borrow," she said.

"What will you put in it?"

"May I also borrow some cash?"

I had a wallet underneath my sofa. Every time I vacuumed I wondered what to do with that wallet, which was a perfectly good wallet but a cheap one bought off the street by a houseguest who had left it behind. Giving the wallet to Clarissa that day felt like a small victory, a satisfying solution to a problem I'd been considering for a while. I don't know why I let the wallet sit there so long underneath the sofa, anyway. For the better part of two years I had been too lazy to move it. Inside the wallet I stuck five twenty-dollar bills. "I would give you more," I said, "except they fired me from the bar."

"Fired you."

"They said I take too much time off."

"Really." She sipped her cigarette. She shook her head. "Fired from the bar." For a moment she stopped crying and considered the view. She opened the window and put her hand out. "This snow won't stick," she said.

That winter, it was always a relief just to talk about the weather.

We were quiet and listened to the traffic in the snow, and after a while Clarissa's tears started again all by themselves.

"Let's phone your father," I suggested, "he'll have someone expedite your green card." Clarissa's father is a famous cardiologist in Washington. He fixes the plugged-up hearts of all the senators on Capitol Hill.

"No," she gasped, "he can't know how irresponsible I am." She checked her makeup and watched herself cry in the mirror of a sconce. "I am nearly thirty, after all."

"My life is a shambles, too," I assured her. "The interest on my capital isn't covering my rent, my superstar little brother is going to have to give me an allowance, and I can't even seem to stay employed as a bartender."

"Still," she said, "you have citizenship."

I never learned how to smoke properly. I like the way a cigarette wilts and crackles, but cannot teach myself how to properly inhale.

"I am legally no one," Clarissa sobbed. "And I have a graduate degree from a very fine university."

A few days later I gave a dinner party. I had planned it for three weeks, inviting old school friends and newer friends and one friend I invited so that his sometimes jealous wife could meet my very gorgeous Italian boyfriend and perhaps stop maligning my friendship with her husband. I invited Clarissa but she said she was unavailable. In the end, she phoned from my street corner and came up anyway.

"I know I declined," she said, "so I won't stay for dinner. I wanted to come and thank you for always being so good."

"Stay for dinner," I said.

"The Curtis children canceled on me, anyway," she said. "Which means I am being paid four hundred and fifty dollars to stay for dinner. If you'll have me. I am opening this bottle of wine. Where is Stefano Naldi?"

"Coming," I said, though truly my very gorgeous Italian boyfriend was then half an hour late for dinner. "There's pink wine in the refrigerator."

"So we can pretend it's summer."

"Let's please pretend it's summer."

My guests talked about books a little, the new mayor a little, and four of my guests talked for eighty minutes straight about how to get the most gifts from an engagement and marriage. I expected every time the bell rang that I would open the door to

Stefano Naldi, but every time the bell rang, I opened the door to someone I'd forgotten I invited.

"Is Stefano coming?"

"Yes, he'll be here any moment."

"I hope you don't mind, we brought champagne instead of wine."

"That's lovely."

"Booze is booze. Let me open it for you."

"Did Clari find her green card?"

"It's stolen."

"Has anyone tried to use it?"

"It's a green card, darling, it's not like it has credit."

"No, but someone could try to hijack a plane."

"Clarissa, has anyone tried to hijack a plane with your green card?"

"If they have, the bank has not phoned me about it."

"You see?"

"Someone did try to buy gas with my Visa."

We waited two hours for Stefano Naldi. We waited and drank and we drank all the dinner wine.

"Why don't you just call your father? He'll have someone sort out your green card."

"Don't be ridiculous, I can't possibly tell my father."

"Why not?"

"He'll want to know what happened to my passport."

I asked my friend Ben to come to the kitchen to help me carve the chickens. "I need your advice," I said, "as a good male friend."

"We're out of wine, aren't we."

"Yes."

"My advice is not to mention it to the guests, just move on to scotch."

"I have bourbon, I can make Manhattans."

"We're even out of that pink wine?"

"But also, Ben. Stefano hasn't come. Shall I phone him or shall I just leave it and speak to him tomorrow?"

Ben said, "You're asking the wrong Jew."

I leaned into the living room. "Clari, could you step into the kitchen for a moment, please?"

Clarissa had her hands midair, grasping at nothing, pantomiming the elaborate story about losing her passport on a secret trip to France and taking up again with an ex-boyfriend who in the past few years had developed schizophrenia.

"I am a bad friend," she said, rushing into the kitchen. "I have crashed your dinner party and done nothing to help. Are we out of wine?"

"Stefano's not here," I said. "What do I do."

"You bloody well phone him immediately!" she hissed, irate. "Right now!" She marched me into the bedroom. "I want to hear this."

I didn't expect him to be home. I expected that there had been some sort of explosion on the subway.

"I don't feel like eating roast chicken and seeing those people," he said.

"Which people?"

"Your friends. Their chitchat makes me crazy."

"I'll speak to you tomorrow," I told him. I looked at Clarissa. My nose began to run. "He's not coming."

I managed not to cry during dinner. I served fourteen people three roast chickens, roast potatoes, escalloped potatoes, glazed carrots, braised peas, a cheese course, after-dinner drinks, and espresso with lemon twists. Everything that night was gorgeous and perfect, except that we ran out of wine and so drank bourbon with dinner.

The moment the last guest left, I latched the door and commenced crying. My crying is the opposite of Clarissa's. The facial contortions start before the tears come, and the tears are horrible and clumsy and not in the least charming like hers.

"He has behaved like an inconsiderate ass," Clarissa said, "and we will have nothing more to do with him. Anyway, what was he. One of those post-disaster romances. You don't want to live a cliché, my darling."

I let the tears run down my face to my mouth, where I like to let them run in so I can taste them; otherwise I like to wipe them off with my thumbnail and eat them.

"Let's smoke the rest of Ethan's cigarettes," she said. "Soon we'll be thirty."

We smoked and washed all the dishes and smoked again and didn't answer the phone when it rang. We let Stefano Naldi phone and phone. Every time he phoned I felt worse. Every time he phoned I cried some more. Clarissa was never shocked by my caterwauling and howling. She sidled up next to me on the sofa and smoothed my hair behind my ear. I wiped my nose with my sleeve. Ethan's sleeve, actually.

"I have a pain," I said.

"I have a pain, too," Clarissa said, "A funny pain in my face."

I looked at her. "I have a pain in my tummy."

"Don't worry." Lots of people can say *don't worry*, but I have never met anyone who says it quite with the assurance that Clarissa does. When Clarissa says *don't worry*, she says it with such intelligence and authority, with such classic movie-star beauty, somehow you feel worrying is entirely beside the point.

Clarissa came by the following afternoon much earlier than usual. "Shall we go out for lunch today?"

"I don't want to go out. I don't like it out there."

"I'm just feeling so dreary, being inside all those stuffy apartments. It's giving me a tingly head."

"Anyway my mother is arriving this afternoon and I don't know what time." I had been crying all day, trying to get all the crying finished before my mother arrived. With uncanny instinct, she always came to visit the day I broke up with a boyfriend, and the faking of cheerfulness would tax my resources for two weeks. I still had quite a bit of crying left to do, in fact, and felt it rising up behind my nose, pressing into my cheekbones, choked upward by the laughing muscles at the top of my throat.

"You look all pink, *cara*."

"Don't call me *cara* anymore." I hiccupped repeatedly, which brought on a fit of sneezing.

"He doesn't own Italian," Clarissa chided. "Just because one man is a twat doesn't ruin an entire language." She unbuttoned her overcoat. "And thank goodness, otherwise my degree in French literature would be completely useless."

"It's useless anyway," I said.

She stopped for a moment. "Daniel is failing French." She pulled a new package of Ethan's brand of cigarettes from her coat pocket. "I brought these to replace the ones we smoked. Do you have a watch I can borrow?"

"A match?"

"A watch. A wristwatch."

I checked old handbags. I never wear a watch but remembered Jonas giving me one with an image of a violent-looking buckled-up platform stiletto on the face. "How's this?"

She looked at it. "That will do. I am always late for everything and I seem to have lost the watch my father gave me for Christmas."

"Let's just have one of these," I said, unwrapping the package of Ethan's cigarettes.

"I have something wrong with my face," Clarissa said.

I looked at her. Clarissa's face is mathematically perfect. No one can look at Clarissa without looking twice. "What's wrong with your face?"

"I have a pain."

That afternoon, the ashtray was too small for the butts of all our cigarettes. We began to extinguish one cigarette on top of the other. Soon we had finished them all and I was checking Ethan's coat pockets and desk drawers for another pack.

Clarissa searched her bag for cough drops. "Have you spoken to Stefano Naldi?"

"He will make this all my fault. He'll say I'm a classist."

"Classist. Typical Bolognese."

"He'll say I'm unsympathetic, he'll say *You don't know what this winter has been like for me.* As if he is the only one who has lived through this winter."

"Thank God you didn't marry him."

"I never thought of marrying him."

"Didn't you?"

"I would never have married him."

Clarissa shrugged. She waved her cigarette. "Girls like us do not need to get married."

My mother had gained so much weight in the past year that she could no longer button her mink. "Am I going to get spray-painted wearing this in New York?"

"No one does that anymore."

"Why not? Is everyone too self-involved these days to care about the animals?"

I shrugged. "Fur is back," I said.

She tugged at the cuffs, trying in vain to get them to cover her wrists. "I don't think they stored this thing correctly."

We ate a late lunch in the overpriced Greek restaurant. I didn't tell Mother that for a few months now, going outside made me anxious. I tried not to flinch when busses drove past, or to jump when bicycles came too close. I focused on not stepping on the cracks. At lunch I was distracted and couldn't eat. My beet salad came and the beets had already made the feta all pink and runny. I started crying. I started crying and couldn't stop, and when Mother reacted I had no choice but to tell her about the dinner party and how I had broken up with Stefano Naldi just hours ago in a flurry of insults.

"This wouldn't have happened if you hadn't had sex with him," she said.

"All right, Mother."

"I know you don't want to hear that from me, darling. But I promise you it's true. Daddy thinks so, too."

"Does he."

"Does this mean you're going to quit your Italian classes?"

I shook my head. "They're nonrefundable."

"Good. Perhaps this whole episode hasn't been a complete waste."

"I'm just disappointed."

"Of course you are. If you keep having sex with all of these boyfriends, no one is ever going to love you."

That night Clarissa came by to return the one hundred dollars. "My father is going to have the green card speeded up," she said. "Thank God. I called him after six, when I know he's having a cocktail. He didn't ask too many questions. I told him it was an emergency and that you and I had plans to go to Rome this summer. Do you want to go to Rome this summer?"

"I have to get a job."

"But after that."

"I don't want to speak Italian."

She pulled me into the vestibule for a private word. With my mother present, neither of us wept and neither of us intended to smoke any cigarettes. "What did Stefano Naldi have to say for himself?"

"It wasn't very nice," I told her.

My mother interjected from Ethan's room, where she was having a rest, "I do not like that he used the F-word with my daughter!"

"Did he really?" Clarissa asked.

I nodded. "He didn't understand why I was upset. He said, 'You are going to throw me away over a piece of fucking chicken?'"

"That's a very good line. I like that line."

I had to agree. It was a very good line.

"Listen," she said, "come downstairs with me."

We went out and turned down Seventy-fifth Street toward the park. She pulled a new pack of cigarettes out of her bag. "I bought these to replace Ethan's that we smoked."

The weather was mild. We let our overcoats flap open. On Madison we ducked into the Carlyle and ordered two Manhattans. The Carlyle is good for drinks only on a Sunday or Monday. Other nights the Carlyle is good for jazz but not so good for conversation. The bartender there was called Mac and he knew us. He was the father of a very famous television sitcom actor, and one night later on in the spring we would go in to find that Mac had gone, forever, to California for retirement, and we hadn't had a chance to say goodbye.

That night there was no jazz trio and Mac set new cold cocktail glasses in front of us before we had finished the first round, and again before we had finished the second.

"Something's going wrong with me," Clarissa said.

"What do you mean wrong?"

"There's a spot on my brain," she said.

I looked at her. "Not really," I said.

"I think so."

"How do you know?"

"The doctor saw it. I have to go in again tomorrow. I may go down to Washington, just have everything done there."

"What sort of spot?"

"I don't know," she said. "A spot. Some sort of dark spot."

We smoked cigarettes and drank Manhattans and got very drunk and Mac called us "you girls, you girls," and neither of us felt like crying at all.

I didn't tell my mother about Clarissa's spot, and after that first day of Mother's long visit, we didn't discuss Stefano Naldi. Mother had come to town for three weeks of shopping and theater and to get away from Fresno for a little bit. I looked half-heartedly for a new job, but Mother, for all her nice intentions, undermined every effort. She bought matinee theater tickets or made late lunch reservations during the few hours I should have been seeing bar managers. She tried her best to keep me unemployed for the duration of her stay.

For Clarissa's thirtieth birthday at the end of January, Mother took us to the Carlyle for tea. I avoided Mac, not wanting my mother to think, necessarily, that Clarissa and I had developed first-name-basis relationships with most of the bartenders on the Upper East Side.

"You are not going to believe this," Clarissa said breathlessly as she swept in and sat down with us at a table in the restaurant. She looked an awful lot like her mother had in the London winter: her slender frame bundled up in bright colors, her skin vibrantly pink in the cold. She smiled and kissed us and reclasped the twist in her hair all in one motion. "Listen. I think Daniel was wanking today during our lesson." Clarissa knew how to make an entrance.

"Wanking?" my mother said.

"Poor thing," said Clarissa, "he just put a pillow right there and wank wank wank."

I liked this news very much. I thought this was the best Daniel story so far.

"Dyslexia didn't get him early admission to Dartmouth. He's going to have to shoot for something like Colgate, Bowdoin, Swarthmore."

"Dyslexia doesn't always work," I said.

"So he's just given up entirely, now he wanks during our lessons. At one-fifty an hour."

"Wanks," said my mother. "Really."

"Anyway, these are the last few lessons, I'm going away to Washington for a little while."

Hearing Clarissa say she was going away gave me a pain in the face, too. That January, many people started leaving, and the leaving didn't stop for a long time. Ethan and then Clarissa and, by spring, half the people who had been at the dinner party that night and most of the bartenders in my neighborhood had moved away from New York.

"I'll come back," Clarissa said in the pause that followed. "I'm just going for a little while, a little respite from the city."

She would come back, but never for good. Clarissa was never as well as she was then, that last January in the city.

Later Mother asked me, "Would you like to get out of the city, too?"

"I don't think so." It never occurred to me that New York could have been the reason I didn't want to go outside.

"You could go to Los Angeles."

"I could go anywhere, Mother. I want to stay here."

"But you're not doing anything, darling."

"For the moment. I'll do something. I'll find something to do."

"You used to do things."

I had written nothing since the Jim Mullins piece. I wanted to write stories, for myself or for magazines, but I hadn't found new ideas and hadn't found, really, the impetus to write. I had enjoyed bartending until I left for Christmas.

"Are you sure you're happy?" she asked.

"I am very happy, Mother, except I had a breakup."

"Maybe you should consider tutoring high school children," she said.

I didn't respond.

"Otherwise, you could be Ethan's manager."

The rest of that winter, no one seemed to phone, there were never any parties, there was very rarely an invitation to dinner or the ballet or a squash game. All the restaurants and bars were empty. There was a lot of snow. Everyone was tired, everyone was depleted. I sat indoors a lot smoking out the window by myself or talking on the telephone to Ethan or Clarissa or my mother. Some days I went down to the Carlyle for a cocktail after lunch and stayed, drinking cocktails, until the jazz started at night. Ethan sent me a box of oranges from his tree in Santa Monica, but the box never arrived. I read a column in *Vanity Fair* that claimed New York was darker and slower than it had been in a long long time.

In the spring, I took the train to Washington to see Clarissa. She felt a little weak and she was bald and had a vibrant red scar from just above her ear straight across the back of her head. She couldn't drink and shouldn't have smoked cigarettes but we did both anyway.

"Why stay?" Clarissa said. "You could give dinner parties but there's no one left to invite."

"I'm addicted to New York."

Clarissa had met a handsome mathematician on the Metro in Washington one night. Her hair had not started to fall out yet. He was taken with her shoes. Clarissa had a pair of turquoise ballet slippers she liked to wear around town. When the two of them got off at the same stop, she turned and said, "Are you following me?" He said, "No, but I might have if this weren't my stop." Now they had been seeing each other for close to a month. For this, and other reasons, she didn't see herself returning to New York anytime quite soon.

"What does Ethan have to say?"

"Ethan sold his TV show about our family. Ethan's making a killing trading on my mother's psychosis."

"He'll be rich," she said.

I shrugged. "It seems to me there's a glut in the market of mother psychosis."

"It's funny," Clarissa said, "the things we used to worry about in New York."

"What things?"

"You know, everything."

I knew. We worried about holding on to our rent-controlled apartments even though the hot water worked only occasionally and the doormen stole our packages and the landlords constantly came up with imaginative new reasons to try to evict us. We worried about how all the crying would give us wrinkles and we worried about the price of the cigarettes we would have sent up from the grocer downstairs. We worried about explosions on the subway and whether or not our insignificant boyfriends were alive when they failed to phone. We worried about taxi accidents and making enough tips to cover the weekend's activities and we worried that we drank too much or smoked too much or that our careers would never speed up, at least never as fast as everyone else's careers seemed to go. We worried that we had the wrong friends, or not enough friends, friends with not enough money or too much obvious money; we worried about who we knew and who they knew. For Clarissa, now, these were silly worries from the past, a normal life. Now she said frequently, "Now I have a cancer life." In some ways, Clarissa seemed much more content in her cancer life than she had in her New York life.

"You know," Clarissa said that night on the cold steps of her father's townhouse, "you should give Daniel a call. He needs a tutor."

"Maybe. I should."

I didn't make the phone call, mostly because I was afraid it might be a phone call that would keep me in New York longer than I wanted to stay.

Clarissa laughed at nothing, into the air on those cold steps. She started laughing, and laughed for a long time before she stopped. I looked at her. She laughed again. "You are going to throw me away over a piece of fucking chicken," she said.

I laughed too. It was a very good line.

EIGHTEEN

The Gallery Has Been Completely Vandalized

I was making a list of the celebrities who don't tip. David Byrne was number one. He never tipped in any of the three bars where I worked in New York. Rupert Everett, Parker Posey, Madonna, no tip. Tobey Maguire, Gwyneth Paltrow, Barbra Streisand. John Travolta's wife. Almost no tips at all.

Paul McCartney was once too drunk to tip.

There was no hope for David Byrne. I had spoken to other bartenders in the city, and he was known for taking back his quarters. David Byrne was universally disliked by New York's service industry. It's difficult to grow up and realize your teenage rock idol is a no-tipper, but that's growing up for you.

Recently I had discovered that if I wore the right sort of bra and a flimsy shirt, I got tipped much better and more often. The previous week, one of the regulars, a young Korean banker who lived in the neighborhood, left $200 for one beer after last call. Most of the young bankers in the neighborhood stayed longer and drank more and tipped heavily now that I had started dressing more like a slut.

"It's very sad," said Miguel, the Colombian busboy who was studying for his master's degree in architecture at NYU. "I like to think of myself as an enlightened man, more intelligent than most people, but when I see a waitress with nice breasts, I want to throw money at her. I can't help it."

He smoked his cigarette and let the other busboy get the tables. The other busboy was Mexican and younger and was not studying for a master's degree at NYU.

"You are not an enlightened man," Lily said to Miguel.

"What am I?"

"You are just a man. All men think they are enlightened," she said.

"But this is true," said Monica, Miguel's girlfriend, whom he had imported to the United States while he studied and bussed tables. "You are enlightened in your way, but you are just a man. You are just a simple man who likes a woman with nice breasts."

I didn't feel so bad about the conversation, because Monica and Lily had nice breasts, too.

"Still," said Miguel, "you girls are the ones showing them off, these nice breasts."

I looked around. I was the only girl showing off her nice breasts. Lily and Monica were wearing ample, dowdy-chic sweaters. I bent over the small prep counter to cut limes.

One of the owners of 74 Carmine was a young and famous director, and I got the embarrassing feeling that all these celebrities came hoping to run into him. The other owner was Lily, a balletic twenty-nine-year-old blonde who opened her first restaurant when she was a teenager and in the next ten years opened two more. Lily knew Jonas and Tom and most all of my friends from various places, which is how she came to hire me at the bar. I had not worked since the previous spring, after Clarissa and Ethan had left the city, and until Lily hired me, things had been looking, socially and financially, quite desperate. Lily had a handsome Dutch boyfriend to whom she was never faithful. She had small teeth and a nose like Myrna Loy and when she smiled she looked disarmingly young.

We all always drank too much. Lily started the evenings off with shots all around and everything was downhill from there. When a customer berated one of the waiters, we had another round. When the manager berated one of the waiters, we had another round. Anyone on staff could ask for a round, and it was bad manners not to participate. The secret to not having a hangover was not mixing alcohol and not mixing anything into the alcohol we drank. For example, if we did ten shots of plain vodka in one night, everyone was ready to start again the next day. If we did six shots of vodka mixed with lemonade or ginger syrup and one shot of tequila to keep us going, none of us drank for a week.

My friends who had real jobs liked to come in and see someone else working. They sat at the bar from six-thirty until they couldn't stay awake anymore, drinking sugary cocktails and telling me what happened inside a cubicle inside an office on the fifteenth floor of a thirty-five-story building in Midtown. They took the F train from work to the West Village to see me and to drink two or three ginger kamikazes, which they would regret the next day but which they would come back to drink again and again once they had forgotten the hangover. In New York it was easy to forget hangovers, and it was easy to forgive them. Sometimes a morning without a hangover made the struggle of the city even more obvious.

The smartest, best educated, most interesting people I knew were either unemployed or worked in restaurants. The blowhards I knew were bankers. The clever, earnest, boring people were doctors. The cutthroats worked in network news. The good-time girls worked in advertising and the frat boys had all become lawyers. The kind but stupid were social workers.

At six p.m. Geoffrey came in. He was our drunk regular.

Geoffrey was a segment producer for a cable network and I don't know how he got up every morning. He mixed alcohol and he liked drinks with sugar in them. He also liked expensive scotch.

"Hello, Geoffrey."

"My favorite bartender," he said. Geoffrey was trying to get on my good side because I was never nice to him. I was never nice to him because no matter how charming he seemed at six p.m., by midnight he was falling off his stool. Nothing else was as predictable as Geoffrey falling off his stool by midnight. Once every several days he sent Lily flowers and an apology. Lily liked him because he had a strong jaw and he sent her flowers, and until he fell off his stool, Geoffrey was not an unpleasant drunk.

"What do you want, Geoffrey?"

"Why are you so curt?"

"What do you want?"

"I want you to be nice and I want a margarita."

Miguel ignored Geoffrey. Miguel had said in the past, "Men like that are not men."

Monica had said, "Miguel doesn't like men with pretty faces." Miguel's face was rough and scarred and aggressively masculine. Women came from as far away as Los Angeles to have Miguel clear their plates.

People who hang out at bars gossip about their friends until their friends show up, and then they gossip about other friends. People who work in bars do the same thing. We gossiped about the regulars and we gossiped about waiters who had the night off and we gossiped about yesterday's gossip. Working in a bar confirmed all my fears that everyone I know, including my brothers and best friends and parents, was saying mean things about me behind my back.

Occasionally Lily's Dutch boyfriend would come by to drink one small gin and tonic. He was remarkably handsome but also remarkably dull. Everyone including the regulars and the prep cooks knew that Lily had had sex with the Saturday-night DJ in the bathroom the week before. We had all heard one way or another. The place was crowded, people talk.

Lily's Dutch boyfriend came in and sat at the end of the bar. He smiled hesitantly at me. I liked him, but I was never too friendly. I knew too many hurtful things to pretend I was his friend. "What about a big gin and tonic tonight?" I said. I said this every time.

"Just a little one."

I tried to believe he knew everything, that he and Lily had an arrangement. "A little one, then."

"She's extra caustic tonight," Geoffrey said.

"Caustic," I said. I shook my head at him. I would make a point of taking a very long time to refill his margarita.

The best thing about tending bar was I didn't have to pretend to like people I didn't like. The colder I was, the more the customers seemed eager to please me. I had the bar itself to protect me from all the sinister friendliness out there. If I didn't like someone, I didn't smile at them, or I smirked at them, or I condescended, or I just didn't give them a drink at all. All the seats at my bar were full by eight p.m.

"I like a woman who has had many men," Miguel was saying. "I like to know that she has had many men and that she has chosen me."

Lily was quiet. Monica had left without saying goodbye. I was cutting limes. "I get very jealous," I said.

"Jealous! Jealousy is useless. Jealousy is what a child feels for its mother."

"I'm not jealous of my mother," I said.

"You are not a child," he said. "What I am saying is this. I want to know a woman has enough experience."

I didn't say anything. I didn't want to be the kind of woman who doesn't have enough experience.

"You don't know what you're talking about," Lily said. "You talk just to hear yourself speak English."

"I do speak magnificent English," he said. He extinguished the very end of his cigarette.

The Tuesday-night DJ came in and began to set up his records in the booth at the end of the bar. He nodded to me. In a moment he would come over to pick up on the conversation we had been having for the past two weeks, since I accidentally mentioned a man I knew who had a perfect penis. The Tuesday-night DJ was now chronically preoccupied with what I had meant by "a perfect penis." No anecdote or explanation had been enough to sate him. Any time I mentioned a man's name, he said, "Is that the one with the perfect penis?" and we were off again, talking not about shape and dimension, but more loosely in terms of the beauty of men.

Lily had had enough of the conversation and said, "Robbie, you are beginning to make me think you're an asshole." Robbie and Lily had been friends since she opened her first restaurant. He was an antiques dealer who really sold used furniture, and Lily let him DJ on Tuesday nights in exchange for dinner and free drinks, which I saw as a noble philanthropic gesture at preserving cheap late-seventies design.

"I have got to know," he said.

I said, "I don't know what else to tell you."

"I want to hear and I don't want to hear," he said.

"I should have never mentioned it."

"Listen," he said, "you draw it for me and I'll tell you about the affair I had with my mother's best friend."

Gwyneth Paltrow came in. She lived up the street. I wanted to tell her that I had been making a list and she was on it, but Gwyneth was not stingy, only stupid. I thought she probably couldn't calculate 15 percent. She had wet hair. For the time being, it was still legal to smoke cigarettes in bars, which she did. She talked to Lily. Geoffrey pretended not to notice her. Miguel got up to clear some tables. I continued to cut more limes than I needed.

Adeline came in for the seven p.m. shift. She had one leg of her jeans tucked into her sock. "You have one side of your jeans tucked into your sock," I said.

"It's for riding my bicycle," she said, and bent down to fix her clothes.

Adeline was the only person I knew brave enough to ride a bicycle in New York City.

The man who sold fine tea to all the nice restaurants in New York had a crush on me. He had a crush on me when I worked at the bar in the East Village, and he had a crush on me now that I was working at a bar in the West Village. He came in frequently and was tall and polite but I was not interested. At least, for the time being I thought I was not interested. My mother was interested. "Did Pierre come in last night?" she asked every time we spoke on the phone.

"Yes."

"What did he say?"

"He said, 'Bonjour, Katrine.' "

"Why don't you just marry him and put us all out of our misery?"

I was surprised to hear her use the phrase "put us all out of our misery." Who was us all, I wondered.

I told Adeline what my mother had said. Adeline was twenty-two but seemed much wiser than I was. "Why'd she say that?"

"It hurt my feelings," I said. I followed her downstairs to the prep kitchen, where she began popping yesterday's candles out of their holders and I stood by the ice machine with the scoop in my hand, talking and not scooping.

"But your mother's nuts. Don't let the nuts things your mother says hurt your feelings."

"I know."

"Just try to assure her she's not always going to have to buy your winter coat for you."

"Well."

"She just wants to know that when she dies, you're going to have someone else to love you." Adeline had tattoos covering both of her arms and one of her legs. Her conservative parents had decided, after much debate, to love her anyway.

We came back upstairs and Adeline ate cucumbers from the bar. Pierre arrived. "Your husband," she whispered.

Pierre sat next to Gwyneth Paltrow. They knew each other already; Pierre collected celebrity friends. Pierre was gentle and funny and had a large French nose and once you met him, you wanted to keep knowing him. He repeatedly glanced my way, trying hard not to glance my way. I placed his usual drink in front of him, and Gwyneth drank from it. These were the days before she got married and started a family. She told Pierre how shabbily she was being treated by her inattentive boyfriends. She spoke too loudly, I thought, for a badly tipping celebrity who would have probably preferred her gossip not be spread all over the headlines of the *Post*. I caught Pierre glancing at me and I winked at him. He looked away quickly and placed his hand over Gwyneth Paltrow's.

"I smashed my thumb," Adeline said. She held it up so I could see. "Hanging my show." Adeline had taken portraits of some of the staff and some of the regulars as her senior thesis for art school.

"How do I look?" I asked.

"Glamorous, shy, and happy."

I am none of those things, I thought. "Good. I am glamorous, shy, and happy."

"Maybe not shy," she said.

"Definitely not shy," Geoffrey said. He needed a refill on his margarita, and I was ignoring him, and now I would continue to ignore him.

"But you're glamorous and happy." Adeline smiled. She smiled a smart smile and I knew she was thinking that I was none of those things. "Your husband is flirting with Gwyneth Paltrow," she said.

The bad weather had gone on and on that November, but the bad weather goes on and on every November, and every autumn we complained about it as if it were the first. That year, though, an autumn the rain made New York especially sad and the mayor raised the prices on cigarettes anyway, that year the weather did in a lot of us. I stopped speaking to at least one friend whose sadness demanded too much, and I surrounded myself with people who liked to drink and stay out until the sun came up and people who didn't like to talk about anything personal. I preferred good-looking people, rich and motivated people, people who knew other good-looking, rich, and motivated people. In New York, these sorts of friends were very easy to find.

Clarissa never let her sadness be too much. Her hair had begun to grow back in patches, and she was entirely unself-conscious about it. She had moved back into her Williamsburg loft and behaved as if nothing had ever gone wrong. She sat on my sofa or next to the window facing Seventy-fifth Street smoking cigarettes and told breathlessly funny stories of her own sourceless depression. "Whatever you do," she warned me, "don't kiss Pierre. You can't go around acting out of loneliness. Just because he has a mouth doesn't mean you have to kiss it."

"I know."

"Think of how your actions affect other people."

"It won't kill him."

"I am talking about me. I am the one who'll have to help you get rid of him." She was lying on the floor, her leg pointed in the air, practicing the reclining big toe pose from yoga. "You should try Zoloft. It's more expensive, but it's less likely to call you in the morning."

That afternoon, I was off from the bar and Clarissa was done with her students so we took the subway downtown to watch Adeline hanging the rest of her show. People had always looked at Clarissa in the subway. People would stare at her unabashedly, actively, as if they were imagining scenarios of where a girl as beautiful as she was could be going from Sixty-eighth Street to Spring. Girls that lovely, whether they were downtown models or Upper East Side second wives, hardly ever left their neighborhoods. If they did, they generally did not take the subway. After Clarissa got cancer and left the city to live at her father's house in D.C., she found Martin the mathematician, who had been staring at her on the Metro. After Clarissa didn't look as beautiful and always refused to wear a scarf or a hat over the scar across the back of her head, people would stare at her on the subway for other reasons, reasons she felt she had earned.

Downtown it was raining a very cold rain and people with frowns on their faces pushed plastic-covered baby carriages in and out of the expensive, useless stores and markets in SoHo. Tourists huddled under umbrellas, holding sodden maps and shouting at each other. Clarissa and I wanted a drink before meeting Adeline, but it was too early to drink cocktails without feeling ashamed of ourselves. Clarissa knew a gallery on Broadway that had a nice coffee shop in the back and we went up there and through the many rooms of bad art to drink tea out of paper cups. The rain and the grumpy people shoving bundled-up strollers along the sidewalks we used to like had depressed us a little bit, and we both really wanted bourbon, not tea, so we left our paper cups half full and wandered back to the street.

"I think it was your idea to have tea," she said.

"It's too early to start drinking."

"In the future, let's please remember that I am more sensible about these things."

We walked to the bar at the SoHo Grand, where we shared one Manhattan, and then shared four more. Cliff, the bartender, was our friend who by coincidence had played Young Dad in a Ford Motor Company commercial which I had written during my very short stint in film production three years before. Clarissa and I knew an alarming number of bartenders in neighborhoods all over Manhattan and Brooklyn, which curiously never led us to believe we were alcoholics.

"You won't be going anywhere if you drink another one," Cliff said.

"We won't be going anywhere," said Clarissa.

"We'll walk it off," I said.

Later, we took one of the pretty white umbrellas from the lobby of the hotel and walked along West Broadway, looking in the windows of the overpriced dress shops and makeup stores and the lighted windows of other people's lofts. The windows in SoHo were an important reminder to us always that we must work very hard and not be lazy. We were very lazy then.

At the gallery, Adeline was standing on a stool with one side of her jeans tucked into her sock, hanging pictures. The pictures were very exciting. I thought of the word "exciting," rather than "good." The pictures were more than good. They surprised and impressed me. They required energy and made you hungry for something you couldn't place.

The studio was dry and warm but not overly warm. Rain knocked into the windows and Clarissa and I sat quite happily in two folding chairs, watching Adeline measure and remeasure, hammer and hang. She had drawn a quarter-inch blueprint of the gallery and detailed which photos would hang where and at which height, and she worked more seriously than I had ever seen her. She worked so seriously, I felt a little bit intimidated by her, and a little bit sorry that I had never worked quite as hard. If the pictures had not been so compelling, Clarissa and I would have been bored sitting there, if we had decided to sit there at all. Instead, looking at Adeline's portraits that evening was like having good conversations with several complex and good-looking people.

"How do you look?" Adeline asked.

"Glamorous and shy and happy," I said. In fact, I didn't think my portrait looked glamorous and shy and happy at all. I thought Adeline had captured every part of me I didn't want people to see.

"I don't know." She looked at the picture of me for a little while. "You look like somebody I would be friends with." She smiled and nodded at me. With her tattoos and swagger and one side of her jeans tucked into her sock, Adeline did not look remotely like someone I would be friends with. This drew me to her, the way we're drawn to anything that looks like it might be an adventure.

Work could cure almost anything, even the November blues. Behind the bar, I felt confident as I did nowhere else. I concentrated on nothing more than standing up straight and I high-poured the liquor from above my head, so the liquid made a lovely arc into the shaker I held very low. For this I sometimes got applause. I had a very good memory and never forgot a customer or what he drank and whether or not he tipped well. I remembered the names of customers and the names of people the customer talked about, which everyone thought was remarkable. This was, of course, completely unremarkable. I have always had a good memory for names. But the fact that the customers thought I was remarkable and that they applauded when I backwards-poured a cosmopolitan made me happier than I would be anywhere else for a long time.

Thursday night, while Geoffrey got expensively drunk at one end of the bar and Robbie got drunk for free at the other, while Pierre flirted with a preppy, fine-featured magazine editor who drank twice as much as he did and while my friends Clarissa and Tom gossiped about our other friends while devouring kimchee and gamja buchim, Lily and Miguel and I were very happy to hear of the success of Adeline's thesis. Her professors had passed her with the highest grade, and one of them had phoned a famous dealer to see her project.

"Remember that smashing your thumb is good luck," Lily said.

"Remember that me coming by drunk is good luck," I said.

"You see what happens," Miguel said, "when I am in pictures."

Adeline was pink-cheeked and breathless with the prospect of her future. She carried large trays of ban chan and bulgogi out to the boisterous, preweekend Thursday-night crowd, unfazed by their complaints or reprimands or unreasonable requests, and she must have been floating above herself, the way I felt when I got my first fellowship to graduate school, or the way I looked forward to elaborate tree houses after my mother won the California lottery.

"Mr. Derderian is coming next week," Adeline said. "The dealer."

We had a round of shots to celebrate.

Lily said, "Pierre knows Derderian the dealer."

We looked over at Pierre. We waved. He smiled and waved back, bashful and eager. Pierre knew everyone.

None of us who worked at 74 Carmine ever had money for taxis or new clothes or health insurance, but we always had the money to drink as much as we liked after hours. That Thursday night after the restaurant closed, we went out to celebrate Adeline's great success. Pierre drove us to the East Village in his big red Range Rover, because under no circumstances was Pierre ever drunk, and he liked going out with us on binge nights.

"Are they any good?" he asked me about the pictures.

"They're exciting," I said.

"Exciting."

"They make you wish that Adeline were your best friend, they are that good."

"How's yours?"

"I'm unphotogenic."

"How does Miguel look?"

"Arrogant, provincial, uncertain."

"They must be very good," he said.

Behind the bar there was a big tank with a mermaid swimming in it, and the mermaid was one of the ex-managers at 74. None of us got too drunk that night, which meant it was a good and happy night, and we had a whole section of strangers at the bar toasting Adeline. It rained on us later as we waited outside the club for Pierre to bring the car around, and the lightning came so close to the tops of the six-story buildings across the street that we thought the old wooden water tanks might catch on fire. We huddled together for safety and because it was fun to huddle together early in the morning, outside in the sideways rain.

We never thought of ourselves as poor. If things got bad, as they did the following spring after the smoking ban, we would find roommates or rich boyfriends or debase ourselves by asking our parents for money. We girls could always make a little bit extra by swimming as a mermaid after hours. Jason, the gay waiter who was also a dancer and whose coke habit was usually just barely under control, had a $300-a-month apartment above a crack den in the Bronx. He let us all know that if things were really bad, we could move in and split the rent for $150.

We never thought of ourselves as poor until one of us had an emergency.

"Someone broke into the gallery last night." Miguel was sitting at the bar when I arrived at work the next day, smoking and tapping his ashes into a collins glass. "They have destroyed everything," he said.

I looked at him. I had stepped in a puddle on my way to work and both of my loafers made squashing noises. "What do you mean, destroyed?"

"I mean," he said, "the gallery has been completely vandalized."

"How?"

He motioned toward the kitchen. "Adeline is downstairs with those candles she does."

Adeline did not look ravaged by despair. She looked ordinary, the way an ordinary person looks when everything is a disappointment. "Who did it?" I said.

"I can't quite believe it."

"How did this happen?"

"No matter how hard I work," she said, "it just doesn't matter."

"Why did they destroy everything?"

She popped candles out of their holders with a butter knife. "Something like this will just make me a better photographer."

"But why did this happen?"

She looked at me. "Stop asking those questions." She shook her head. "I could go on for the rest of my life trying to answer those questions." She worked hard on the candles.

"Are you angry?" I asked.

She looked up. "I feel very lonesome," she said.

"I feel lonesome, too."

"I know." She nodded. She went back to the candles.

"What about Derderian, the art dealer?" Jason asked when he heard.

"There won't be any art dealers," Adeline said simply. She had spent everything she had earned at the restaurant printing those photos and framing them in handmade museum reproductions, now in pieces on the gallery floor. "There won't be anything until next time."

"What about insurance?" Lily asked.

Adeline shook her head.

"Next time there won't be a Chelsea gallery the university arranges for you," Miguel shouted to us from where he was sitting. "It will be years from now and your professor will have found other students to support." We were eating the staff meal in the dining room, but Miguel was having his dinner and a cigarette at the bar.

"These things just make you work harder," Adeline said. She spoke as if she were making us feel better. She did make me feel better. I had that searing pain in the chest you get when your heart has been broken.

"That is feel-good American pop psychology," Miguel said, wandering over to the edge of the dining room with a cigarette in one hand and his collins-glass ashtray in the other. "These things do not make you work harder. These are the things that crush your spirit."

"I feel fine," Adeline said.

"I am correct," he said, shrugging. "You feel shocked right now. Later, you will be too angry to work. We all know Adeline is the most gifted, but she does not have the money to produce the photographs again. She has had her chance and she has been very unlucky. When you are poor, you must be as lucky as you are talented."

"Miguel," Lily said.

"You're a communist," Jason said.

"This is America!" I said. I was heartbroken and I felt very patriotic.

Adeline looked at Miguel. "I will never be too angry to work," she said.

"You will see that I am correct," he said and went back to the bar.

Adeline looked at us, and we all looked at our dinners. "You guys," she said, in her twenty-two-year-old midwestern twang. "These are the struggles that make you successful."

Jason looked at her. Jason had been struggling out of college for the past eleven years. "You're very sweet and cute," he said.

Those tattoos are not cute, I thought. They were expensive and they hurt. I was beginning to think, more and more, that Adeline and I would become friends because of the tattoos, rather than in spite of.

"I will give you the money," Lily said.

We looked at her.

Adeline said, "No, Lily. It's thousands of dollars."

"I'll give you the money."

"It would take me years to pay you back, Lily. Years and years."

"You won't pay me back," Lily said. "I'll pay you to reproduce the show for me."

Adeline said, "The gallery is out of commission."

"You can hang the show in here." Lily was getting excited. "I would like those photographs in here, of Jason's handsome bottom and Miguel looking grumpy. People can buy the photos from me."

"And we can have an opening one night," I said. "A Sunday when no one's here, we can have Derderian come then, Pierre can bring the press and investors and we'll pack the place with Lily's celebrities and your art school friends."

Jason said, "You can be Judy Garland and I'll be Mickey Rooney!"

Lily said, "We'll have Pierre get Derderian drunk so he signs you immediately."

"He won't need to be drunk," Miguel shouted from the bar.

We didn't talk about it much longer. The plan was so brilliant, we didn't want talk to ruin it.

In the three weeks leading up to Adeline's show, Pierre stopped flirting with me, which infuriated me and caused me to develop a crush on him. Jason's cocaine habit was temporarily out of control—he was storing lines of coke on top of the hand-towel dispenser and inhaled them standing on the toilet. Lily moved out of the apartment she shared with her handsome Dutch boyfriend and announced to us all in case we were wondering that she had told him she would be seeing other people. Miguel and Monica had been married at City Hall so that Monica could work under Miguel's student visa. In an effort to become more of a gentleman, Robbie gave up asking about the perfect penis. Clarissa's doctors in Washington had tried to remove another small tumor from her brain, but only got most of it.

"What does that mean?" I asked her.

"I don't know. Lots of bother for me is what it means."

"I don't understand."

"I should have just eaten apples, like the holistic people say."

"What happens next?"

"We shrink it. We shrink it down so it's just a dried-up old scab of a cancer, and I lose all my hair again and probably get very fat."

"You didn't get fat last time."

"I know. The second time is supposed to be worse."

Adeline sent out a postcard of Miguel looking grumpy, which guaranteed at least a certain number of girls showing up. She printed the photos and framed them just as beautifully as they had been the first time, but this second time round she lost her enthusiasm. There was no blueprint of the restaurant. There were no quarter-inch drawings. She measured haphazardly, marking her space with a pencil and getting everything almost right, right enough, but there was none of that serious perfectionism I had seen at the gallery a month before. I thought that Miguel had been right about disappointment.

Before she went into the hospital, Clarissa warned me not to develop a crush on Pierre. "This is the oldest trick in the book," she said. "The old dismissal switcheroo."

"I am not developing a crush."

She rolled her eyes. She pointed her toes toward the ceiling. "I know you, darling. I know you better than you know yourself."

"All right."

"Believe me, he's not right for you. If you talk yourself into fancying him now, you're going to have at least six months of a vaguely pleasant, confusing, and sexually unfulfilling farce of a relationship. He will fall in love with you, things will end badly at best, you will have lost a perfectly good friend and source of fine tea, and I cannot promise that I'll be here in six months to help you."

"You'll be here," I said.

"I mean here in New York," she said.

"I knew what you meant."

It was a very long winter and spring without Clarissa.

The Sunday night of Adeline's opening, Robbie spun salsa. The prep cooks made 250 rice crêpe vegetable rolls and a hundred beef skewers. Lily's sister, the pastry chef, made teeny-tiny pecan wafers and bites of rice pudding set into spoons. Adeline wore her hair tied back loosely in a girlish twist and a naked-colored dress that showed off her tattoos. Pierre and Lily managed to bring in a good number of celebrities, including everyone's friend Gwyneth and the young film director who owned half of the restaurant. I lined up soju shots at the edge of the bar again and again until every guest was a little bit drunk. Pierre's friend the magazine editor drank more than anyone and offered Adeline a job as a photo assistant. Mr. Derderian stayed sober and wondered if Adeline wouldn't do a series of the artists he represented. Miguel lounged in the back of the dining room with several admiring women, including an actress called Emily Watson who had been in a few films no one at 74 had happened to have seen but who everyone knew was remarkably talented.

"I appreciate a woman who has a great talent," Miguel said as he came to the bar to do a shot with the staff.

"You have never seen her before," Monica said.

"But it is clear to me she has a great talent."

"How is it clear?" Monica asked.

"I have known a great many extraordinary women, and I can spot them when I meet them."

"You can."

"Of course I can."

"The problem with Miguel," Lily said, "is he learned to speak English."

"He is exactly the same in Spanish," Monica said. "He is Miguel in all languages."

For the rest of the evening, Miguel spoke exclusively in Spanish, and the only person other than Monica who understood him was Gwyneth Paltrow. Gwyneth Paltrow and Miguel spoke quite intimately for a long time, and Monica left early.

"Miguel is stealing your husband's girlfriend," Adeline said.

At the end of the night, Adeline had a new job and a proposal to do some pictures for Derderian the art dealer, if not a deal for him to represent her. What we didn't know then was that after losing everything, losing the momentum of that first big chance and seeing the mean destruction of her work, Adeline would not be able to take pictures quite as exciting for a long time. The pictures she took of Derderian's people turned out to be no good, she thought, though they were technically very fine; but she was right: you couldn't see all the human weaknesses you did in the photos she took of the people at 74.

Before midnight when he fell off his stool, Geoffrey managed to get Lily in the bathroom alone. We all knew what went on in the bathroom between Lily and our handsome drunk regulars.

"I can't pay attention to that," Adeline said to me toward the end of the evening.

"She's such a fantastic girl," I said, pouring shots for just the two of us and Jason. "What can she find remotely attractive in him?"

"Let's pretend it's not happening."

"He's been sending her flowers for months."

"Well," Adeline said, "let's pretend it's not happening tonight."

Everyone, including your brothers and best friends and parents, is gossiping about you.

We were all very drunk that night. Pierre left earlier than I would have liked, but not before arranging specific dates for a weekend I could visit him at his country house in Connecticut. He gave Emily Watson a ride home.

When everyone but the staff had gone, I lined up a last round of shots on the bar. I didn't toast Lily because she was still in the bathroom with Geoffrey. I thought of toasting Adeline, but we had been toasting Adeline all evening. It was at least the tenth shot of the night, and we had used up most good ideas. I thought for a moment. Jason was tapping his foot. "To hard work," I said.

"To work," they said, with no enthusiasm, and we drank.

NINETEEN

The Heiress from Lebanon

I have never, but for that first night with Delia, vomited in the back of a taxi.

Delia moved into what had been Ethan's room on Seventy-fifth Street. She had relocated to New York from Argentina, where she had lived on and off for twelve years after dumping her fiancé and moving away from Lebanon, Tennessee, when she was eighteen. We had a mutual friend, a foreign correspondent from Austin called Poppa, who introduced us during what became an unruly ten hours of drinking and salsa.

"Meet Deeley."

"Delia," she corrected.

"Deeley needs a place to stay, and I told her you take in strays."

"Occasionally," I said.

"I'm sure I'll find someplace." Delia had been staying with Poppa, in his dank one-bedroom on Avenue D, and both of them were tired or uncomfortable with the arrangement.

"Kate loves stray cats like you, Dee."

Our friend Poppa, who at first was our friend and then was one of Delia's boyfriends and then wasn't our friend anymore, called Delia "a person in miniature." Once she started talking, quick and funny and seductive, you forgot how little she was. Men loved Delia. There was something more than just her prettiness, something Poppa said "makes gay men think twice," something he also said "gives married men nightmares." It was more than the red hair and soft southern accent, or the tender gestures she made when she spoke, or how she put her hand on the inside of your wrist when she was telling you something important or funny or sad. I was impressed and fascinated with the way men responded to Delia. I had never seen anything like it.

"I'm sure you don't want a stranger in your house," she said.

"How long do you need to stay?"

"Until I find an apartment."

I shrugged. "You're Poppa's friend," I said, "you're not a stranger." With Ethan and Clarissa both gone, I was eager for some company.

Delia had a small inheritance from her father's side of the family: a famous, now diluted Louisiana coal-mining trust that gave her just enough money every month to cover cocktails and taxis and an occasional pair of shoes. The trust had put her through college with enough money to develop very expensive habits. "It was a dirty trick played by my great-grandaddy," she told me that first night, before I had thrown up my Manhattans in the back of the taxi. "You get your money in such an unevenly structured way that in college you think you like cocaine and heels, but then you get out to the real world and realize your income affords you only flip-flops and crack." That first night, she drank a lot more slowly than I did. "I did my time with crack," she said. I nodded, like we'd all done our time with crack.

Everyone in New York had been fired from their jobs at the banks, from their jobs at the restaurants, at the magazines, the agencies, the nightclubs, the hotels, the Gotham Writers' Workshop, the production offices of all the better shows on Broadway. Even the drug dealers I knew were out of work. The new mayor refused to live in Gracie Mansion. Televisions had been installed in the backs of taxicabs. Cigarettes had been taxed to $10 a pack, but even then you couldn't smoke them in bars. An art student had left in the Astor Place subway station an ominous black box marked BE AFRAID, and everyone was.

The winter had made me homesick for California, and I started to write a story about a couple living in a house on the San Andreas Fault. I imagined the house looked exactly like Ethan's in Santa Monica: a doll-sized Craftsman bungalow with citrus trees in the back and bougainvillea spreading over the terrace. In the story, the house had begun to split right down the middle of the center staircase, one half falling east and the other sliding west, and the couple ignored the split completely. The couple in the story ignoring the split reminded me of myself and Henry, and I became very sad about a lot of things in the past several years that simply hadn't worked.

In pursuit of a job, Delia phoned cousins she had never met and people she remembered from soccer camp twenty years previous. She phoned friends of friends of people she had known from Nashville or Buenos Aires or her travel through Europe and South America. Delia had a talent for friendships. People who met her wanted to be liked by her, and there were remarkably many of Delia's acquaintances who considered her their best friend.

"I need a job where there is social interaction," she said. "Otherwise I'll drink too much."

We were on our second bottle of wine. Unless we started a third bottle of wine between the two of us, we never felt as if we were drinking too much. "I'm sick of social interaction."

"You work in a bar," she said, explaining everything.

"Too much social interaction, you'll have to drink to put up with it."

She nodded. "That's the way people are, deluge or drought." She had found a pair of binoculars in Ethan's dresser and sat at the window, spying on the neighbors.

Delia hated the thought of work, and had decided that if someone was going to pay her to do something she didn't feel so inclined to do, then she would do only the most frivolous thing possible, and so she became a public relations specialist. She was very good at it and a hard worker. "I am going to teach the world not to wear denim on denim," she said.

"Or you could teach them to read books," I suggested.

"Or eat unrefined sugar." She shrugged. "It doesn't matter what you're selling, if you're going to whore."

In truth, denim was not important to Delia, but being the best at what she did was very important, and she liked making money.

"How long can I continue this fakery?" she asked me once she had been employed for three months and given a small promotion. "I don't feel like a PR flack. Do I look like one?" she asked sincerely. She waited for an answer.

"I don't know," I said. "I don't know what PR looks like."

I was spying on the neighbor across the street, the man with one ear who watched baseball all night and masturbated with his underpants on.

At the bar, before he got drunk, Geoffrey asked Delia what she did for a living. Until then they had been pleasantly chatting, Delia giving him that wink she saved for no one, that wink that passed over her face so quickly you were never sure whether she had just winked at you. He said, "So. What do you do here in the city?" and she turned right from him as if he were suddenly not there, as if he had never been there and they had never been talking. "Darling," she said to me over the bar, "I believe I'll need another drink." Delia had a smart way of making people feel, with her sigh or her glance or her casual but pointed disregard, as if their questions were very boring.

Very qualified people I knew were sending out a hundred job applications before being given just one interview. Delia's first interview came from her first application, she and the company's president went out for five martinis, and Delia was hired on the spot.

"This means I have to go to work every day," she said, concerned. She was painting her toenails in our living room. Delia had no use for manicurists. She thought they were a ridiculous waste of money and time and she was always vaguely embarrassed for the girls she would see sitting in the windows of New York's ubiquitous manicure shops, staring blankly into nothing and waiting for their nails to dry.

"This is terrible news."

"I feel like I've disappointed both of us."

"I admire you," I said. "You're very brave." Delia's getting a job had left me with the childish, raw embarrassment that I couldn't imagine myself doing the same thing.

"I promised myself when I left Argentina that I would never work in an office again."

Delia was usually not the type to break a promise. "This is not just an office," I said. "This is New York PR. This is mythical."

Her toenail polish reminded me of the smell of the girls' dorm at school. Recently, smells and tastes and places I had forgotten made me very nostalgic. One afternoon at Bergdorf's, I saw Page's new line of handbags and a big knot grew in my throat. A lot about Delia reminded me of Page: her voice, her gestures, the subtle way she had of getting people to behave exactly how she wanted. I remembered the terrified and exciting feeling of sitting with Page at the river, smoking cigarettes in the spring. The autumn we were sixteen, Page and some other girls had signed their parents' names to release forms and pooled their money to rent a room at the Ritz Carlton in Boston, where they met Page's brother and his friends from a boys' school nearby. I had not been included, and so had cried permanent stains into my pillow. I remembered disinterestedly kissing my second and third boyfriends in different classrooms in the schoolhouse, and taking my top off for one of them, who thanked me by saying, "I love you." There was that horrible time for Clarissa in varsity doubles. At school, we had all thought we were uniquely tormented, that our remarkable insights and sensitivity would curse us till death. We wrote angry poems and identified with all the daughters in *King Lear*. If we had known then that the onset of cancer is age twenty-nine, we may have spent more time being happy.

I have never worn polish, but only because I can't paint it on straight. In fact, the irony of a girls' boarding-school dorm is that the people who live there are rarely concerned enough with beauty to actually paint their nails, but always the types to find this sort of enterprise alluring, mysterious, unattainable. I have always liked the smell of one girl in a room painting her nails.

"Now look what's happened to me," Delia said.

"No more morning coffee together," I said. Every time I opened my mouth, I wanted to shut myself up.

"I have to buy a work suit. I have to buy some black corduroy hip-huggers, patent-leather pumps. I have to buy pumps. I am the girl who walks to work in pumps." She looked up from her nails. "Please don't ever let me wear nylons."

"No more listening to news on the radio until the classical music starts in the afternoon," I said.

She was looking at me. "Don't let me ever," she said, "ever buy those nylons that come in a plastic egg."

"This is New York," I said again. "They don't sell those here." I hadn't seen nylons in plastic eggs since I was a child in suburban California.

"I can't wear my clothes from Argentina."

"You'll have to take the subway during terrorist hours."

"I have to wake up to an alarm clock."

"You'll have to get an alarm clock."

"I will have no time to see the blossoms in Central Park."

I had been telling Delia how I looked forward to the blossoms every year. I had made a special point of telling her how sorry I felt for the poor slobs who worked all day in an office and couldn't go out to see the blossoms in the spring in New York and sit under them and smell them. I was going to have a difficult time now convincing Delia—and myself—that she was not a poor slob. "And you can't meet me out at all hours to get drunk after I'm done at the bar."

"Oh yes," she said. "Oh yes I can."

I hadn't been bad very often in my life so far. I was twenty-nine and had never touched an illegal drug, never lied on my résumé, never had casual sex or even a fling. I was bartending downtown and I was a big flirt and wore revealing shirts unbuttoned practically to my navel, but I had the bar itself to protect me from the world on the other side. On the other side of the bar, when I was buttoned-up and bespectacled, people never recognized me arriving or leaving or drinking on my days off, sometimes not even the people I worked with. Delia brought home very delicious seven-dollar bottles of wine and we drank them thirstily and ordered pizza from downstairs or else made healthy casseroles from Delia's low-fat cookbook and she tried, as many had, to teach me how to really smoke cigarettes, though I would never get the hang of it. "I am definitely not wasting any pot on you," she said. "If you can't even inhale a cigarette." In the evenings we would go to the gym together and afterwards get drunk and laugh about the instructors. We had an Australian instructor called Gavin whose selection of songs every week made embarrassingly clear the specific events of his life. Through the music he chose for spinning class, we followed Gavin's separation from his wife, a brief reconciliation and inevitable divorce followed by a long period of sadness, then a longer period of anger, and then, suddenly, spirited happiness at finding someone new to love. I don't know what happened with Gavin's new love because by then Delia had moved downtown and I didn't go to spinning or even the gym anymore.

Delia had a budget of $100 a week to spend on cocktails alone, not including bottles of wine, which she budgeted into groceries, and not including drinks with dinner, which she budgeted into eating out. In New York, then, cocktails in any respectable bar cost upwards of $12. Twelve dollars paid for the drink itself and for the certain pleasure, unique to New York, of having paid that much. Cocktails were more reasonable in the less fashionable bars, but the less fashionable bars did not cater to the sorts of people Delia intended to meet. One hundred dollars lasted her usually from Sunday afternoon through Monday night, and for the rest of the week she made dates with various boyfriends or else flirted with men wearing nice watches who invariably paid for her drinks.

I met her one evening in a new restaurant downtown we

couldn't not explore. "For one drink," we promised. "Just one." There was never just one drink. In fact, there were never just two, because odd numbers was Delia's policy on everything from flower arranging to cocktails to boyfriends. Delia got to chatting with a man in cuff links, a banker called Andy from Memphis who took us through the kitchen to introduce us to the chef. "I own this place," Andy said, "but you won't read that on Page Six." In New York, it didn't matter for the moment whether what people said was the truth, and I tried not to make any judgments on what I thought was a lie. We went downstairs to the prep kitchen, where everything was as spotless as if it had never been used, and Delia taught me how to snort Andy's coke from the stainless-steel surface of a prep table.

"Try not to chew up the inside of your mouth," she said.

Cocaine wasn't anything I would have paid for myself, and it made my throat sore for three days afterwards, but I liked the feeling it gave that I was going to solve all the world's problems. Delia had to restrain me from phoning my mother and telling her to try it.

Later I said to Delia, "If Andy owned that place, he would have sent us home in a car, not a taxi."

She agreed, but she looked at me sideways, and I knew she was disappointed that I had said something so obvious out loud.

The two of us and her most important client—one of the only single men on the Fortune 400 list—snorted coke one night from the banister in the eleventh floor stairwell of the boutique hotel next door to Delia's office. "He's gay," she said. She lit a cigarette and smiled and whispered, "But anyone can give a blow job."

On more than one occasion, we ended up in some developer's whitewashed loft at an unspeakable hour of the morning while he cooked for us whatever he had in his refrigerator and wondered out loud whether Delia would stay the night and I would go home. Those nights that I was along, Delia never stayed the night. She came home with me and we laughed in bed about the pomposity and desperation of whoever we had met that evening and usually she made it to work the next morning in the same clothes she had been wearing the night before.

This sort of thing went on for some time: the drunkenness and drug use and the boys with money. I came along sometimes, or else one of Delia's dozens of other very close friends came along, but for Delia this sort of thing went on every night. Occasionally we worried that she might be doing herself in, but she got up every morning and went into work and did a good job and her clients adored her, so we thought she must be onto something.

Once Delia arrived, Kyle stopped threatening to kill me. She cheered him up considerably. He seemed enamored with Delia and happened to appear in the hallway whenever she did, happened to be at the market at the same time, happened to join the same gym, happened to walk the same way to the subway. "Your new roommate sure is pretty," he told me one day in the lobby. More than once he invited her over for champagne.

"Don't go," I warned her. "Who knows what he might put in your champagne."

"You think I can't handle him?" she said.

"Is it worth the free champagne?"

"Shouldn't I just go over there and use his stemware instead of having to wash ours in the tub?" She was washing out her teacup in the bathroom sink. Sometimes, in that apartment, the water in the kitchen would stop for weeks, one of the landlord's funny jokes.

"I'll wash the stemware," I said.

"I'm doing you a favor, darling. It's the gay ones who fall in love with you the most," she said. "They make very nice allies. Let me go over and charm him a little bit."

The super in my building must have been savagely and heterosexually in love with her, because Delia couldn't charm him. I imagine he didn't like her late hours, when she would let the door to the lobby slam on her way in after the doormen had gone, or else he resented the various good-looking suitors he must have seen coming and going at all times of the day and night. He never minded my late hours, when I let the door slam, and he never minded the occasional boys who came to see me, but something about Delia made him delirious with rage. If the super happened to catch Delia coming or going, he would hurry out of his apartment and besiege her. I rarely saw the super. He must have been keeping watch for Delia through the peephole in his front door. His attacks on her became more and more vicious, more and more profane. At first he launched semi-intelligible tirades about the time she came in, and later on started in about the number of boys who came in and out, and finally she could rarely leave the building without the super chasing her down Seventy-fifth Street, calling her a slut and a whore and spitting his venom all over the pavement. One morning as she left to get the paper, he came out of his apartment in his underwear, hair no one should have ever seen rising above the elastic of his pants, his turgid tummy and other pornographic shapes bare to the morning and sweating in the cold, pointed his finger at her, and said in a quiet, serious tone, "I am going to really fuck you." We knew it was time for Delia to find a new place to live.

By the end of the week, Delia had moved into a two-bedroom fourth-floor walk-up with high ceilings and original moldings at St. Mark's and Avenue A. It suited her that on the noisiest, liveliest corner in New York City, she found a silent apartment at the back of the building facing a garden, and woke every morning to sunlight and birds.

Poppa was the type of person who always knew new places to dance or to eat cheaply or he knew the doormen and bartenders in swanky nightclubs where we would drink all night long without paying.

"If you don't drink," Poppa would say, "you are actually losing money."

One of these nights when no one was losing money, at Jonas's bar in the VIP room, a night Poppa was so smitten with Delia he would not stop talking, he said, "Delia is one of these magic people who just exists without trying."

"*You* exist without trying," she said. "Where are your cigarettes?"

"One of these people who never has to put gas in the car, never has a stomachache, never gets bit by a mosquito while everyone else gets eaten alive." He caressed her hair.

"I must protest," she said softly, joking, but protesting.

"Your voice is like a scarf," he said.

"Don't talk to me," she said, "dance with me."

No one got up. An intoxicated exhaustion fell over the table. We had already noticed that Reggie Jackson was sitting in the booth next to us. We were surprised not so much to see a baseball legend in the booth next to us as we were that all three of us knew who he was. We were also not surprised that he kept looking over to where we were sitting, as if he were waiting for an invitation to join us. Delia looked at me. "Do you want to dance with me, darling?"

I nodded, but none of us moved. She took my hand. Poppa had annoyed her, we all could tell. Now she had taken my hand, which was somehow a gesture against him.

"You like me," Poppa said, trying to convince himself and all of us.

"Oh, but I do," she gushed. "I adore you."

He took her other hand.

"Why don't you get on the phone, darling," she told him, "call some company. Why don't you ring up some of your nice friends?"

We liked Poppa's friends. Poppa was kind and gentle and too sweet to be particularly sexy, but he had a collection of dangerous, creative, unshaven friends we found irresistible. Delia had sex with no fewer than four of Poppa's friends before Poppa became an interest himself, and even then Poppa was too tender and sincere and refined for Delia to have sex with, which must have been very confusing for him, and quite a blow to his ego.

"He used the phrase 'make love,'" she told me one morning over coffee, after she moved out but before we could relinquish the tradition of the morning together. She had come home with me because I was afraid what might happen if I put her into a taxi alone.

"Make love," I said. I have never known a girl who could stomach the phrase. It's a mystery to all of the women I know how it remains in the language, when simple natural selection should have removed it. It's so touchy and fraudulent, *make love.* It's so far from anything a girl in Delia's position was prepared to do. "Poor Poppa."

"Make love," she said again, with a shiver. We were in a cramped diner on Madison. Delia lowered her head and her voice. "He said, 'I want to make love to you,' and I said to him, 'Aren't you going to rape me?'"

I tried and tried to bring myself to have a one-night stand with one of Poppa's friends. One night when Delia told me I had better "slut it up" before my prudishness wore too thin, I managed to kiss Lucas, an English journalist passing through New York after a six-month stint reporting bad news from Pakistan. I didn't manage to kiss anyone else for the rest of the summer, and

Lucas and I wrote emails to each other afterwards every day for a year.

All you saw of the world on Avenue A was tattooed teenagers and traffic and garbage splayed along the curb, excrement from the neighborhood's pets, people hurrying or arguing or speaking to each other in tense voices. Up three flights, Delia's apartment was a little oasis of gauzy curtains and soft white walls and black-and-white photos in frames. The books on her shelf were good books. There was always something delicious in the refrigerator. Her house was warm in the winter and cool in the summertime. She would pour you a glass of wine, which you would drink from hand-blown glasses brought with her from Argentina. She never answered the phone when she had a guest. When she smoked in the apartment, there seemed to be a vacuum outside the nearest window. You would sit on her overstuffed sofa with your feet tucked under you and she would make you laugh and laugh, and no one could ever believe how fortunate they were to have a friend like Delia, one of those people unassumingly blessed by luck and charm and bone structure.

"Sometimes," she said one evening, sitting by the window in her apartment and smoking the beginning of a cigarette, "if I'm in some man's hotel room and I can't sleep, I walk up and down the corridors of the hotel, and I see all those little bags full of people's dry cleaning hung out on the doorknobs, and it makes me feel so lonely to see all those traveling people with no one to take the dry cleaning in for them." She paused to sip her cigarette. "Those sorts of things just make me want to go right back to Lebanon and marry some private-practice doctor and forget there even is a life beyond a day's drive from town."

"Then don't go walking down those corridors," I said. "That

sounds like dangerous business." I didn't want to know what Delia got up to in strangers' hotel rooms.

She looked at me. She nodded. "It gets very claustrophobic inside those rooms."

I hated hotels. I tried never to go anyplace where I didn't know someone who would put me up. "Yes," I said.

She said, "Do you know those little dry-cleaning bags I mean? Have you ever had to use one?"

"Just to pack muddy shoes."

"Sort of reminds me of Argentina," she said. "For twelve years I felt like a tourist."

"I feel like a tourist wherever I am."

"That's something I wish I had never seen, an empty night-time hotel hallway with all those dry-cleaning bags hanging around. Anyway, that's about the time I usually make my escape."

I nodded. I had never escaped from a hotel room, but it sounded like something I ought to try.

More than once, other friends of mine told me she was crazy.

"Someone who lives in Argentina for twelve years and moves to New York now? Of all times?" Clarissa was never terribly fond of my newer friends. "She must be insane."

"She's impulsive."

"She must be insane to have an impulse like that."

"Oh, Clari, you like her."

"Of course, we all like her. She's quite adorable. Quite adorably nuts."

I thought Delia would have a lot in common with Tom. Tom was handsome in that dangerous, crooked-faced way that Delia particularly liked. A few months after Delia had started her job, just after my story about the house on the San Andreas Fault appeared in a fancy journal out of Texas, when spring was arriving and everything seemed to be looking up, Tom phoned to tell me he had been appointed the editor of one of the country's oldest men's magazines. I was very proud of him. Tom was a loyal, generous friend and I wanted to see him get everything he wanted. He worked hard and had not had a girlfriend since his ex started running around with Jonas. Tom liked smart, pretty redheads and I thought he would certainly like Delia. But the night we all met for dinner, Tom excused himself to the men's room halfway through the main course and never returned.

"I was so drunk, I forgot why I got up from the table," he said later. "So I got in a taxi."

"We missed you," I said.

"Anyway," he told me, "I think your friend Delia is not right in the head."

"What do you mean?"

"She has a voracious appetite."

"We were hungry."

"I mean, it's obvious she's really after something."

"We're all after something."

"Not like that. It's like she's insatiable, she's going to devour everything she sees. People like that end up in hospitals, you know."

"I guess so."

"She reminds me of something depressing."

"What does she remind you of?"

"Something very depressing. I had to get in a taxi."

Editors of men's magazines have no truck with depressing. Not many people I knew would see the sadness in Delia that Tom did. Not long afterwards, Tom met a quiet blond neurosurgeon and moved in with her.

———

Delia had a string of boyfriends, many of them at the same time, but at any given time she had her usual. For a while, she had a TV producer called Willy and he was her usual. Willy was under the impression that Delia was a gentle southern creature and that I was a hardened New Yorker corrupting her with fast times and my callous attitude.

One night I looked tired, so Willy patted me on the head and said, "Don't be tired."

I don't like to be patted, and I told him, "Don't pat me. If you want to touch my hair, then pull it a little."

I was exasperated with him only because Delia was always exasperated with him.

He laced his fingers through my hair and gave me a nice gentle pull. "That's right," I said.

After that, he told his friends and Delia's friends and anyone else who would listen that I liked to have my hair pulled. He always made it sound like a very deviant sexual perversion.

One day in January, a year after Delia arrived in New York, she woke up with a broken arm and had no recollection at all of how it had happened.

I showed up at her apartment unannounced, dropping in before work at the bar, and found her lying on top of her bed, her arm in a cast. "I spent the day in the hospital," she said.

"Did you wake up at the hospital?"

"I took a taxi. I woke up in my bed." She showed me the trousers she had been wearing the night before. "The best I can make out from the color of the dust is that I fell down the stairs here, coming home."

I nodded.

She stared at the ceiling.

"Who was with you last night?" I said.

"Don't know."

"Who did you have plans with?"

"Don't remember."

I looked at her for a long time. She had no expression.

"I tried to reconstruct it from looking at my phone, but now I'm afraid to call any of those people to see what happened."

I knew what she meant.

"This is not such a nice thing to happen, you know?"

I knew.

She said, "I'm not a stupid girl, Katherine. I know when there's a problem."

I looked at her, her arm slung across her chest in the sort of large white cast I hadn't seen on anyone since I was a teenager playing girls' soccer. "Well," I said. I had nothing more to say. I may have been more reluctant than Delia to admit there was a problem.

I didn't think she would go. No one goes back willingly to the small town of their adolescence.

"I'm going to find myself a nice private-practice doctor," she said.

I was wrapping those hand-blown wineglasses she brought with her to New York, packaging them for the trip south. I didn't want her to leave. I had just learned to be bad, and I wasn't very good at it yet. "Is that going to make you happy? Marrying a doctor?" I couldn't have been happy, I thought then, with a private-practice doctor. The clever girls I knew thought we could be happy only with world-class financiers or Nobel Prize–winning, MRI-inventing, cancer-curing geniuses, men equally as remarkable as we knew we were. We could have never imagined that the comfortable lives our mothers or step-mothers had lived could be our own comfortable lives as well.

"I am not altogether sure you need to forget what's out here to be happy in a little southern town," she said. She was drinking a beer with her injured arm and smoking a cigarette with the other. "Try not to chew up your mouth."

"I'm not going to do any of that stuff without you."

She nodded. "Nashville isn't so far away," she said, which I knew already.

"Nashville is far away in my head," I told her. She scowled at me, the truth too obvious to say out loud.

"This all seems like a long nightmare," she said. I didn't know whether she meant the ordeal of her broken arm or the whole yearlong ordeal that was her time in New York.

"It will apparently be over soon," I said. I felt suddenly angry and outraged and quite superior, with my nine years' endurance of blizzards and homicidal neighbors and other disasters of the city. What did Delia know about a bad dream? She had made us believe, for a little while, that we had been missing something. In a way, I felt tricked. She couldn't have known all the things we were missing.

She put her good hand on my wrist. "Can you believe we all knew that was Reggie Jackson?" she said.

She left like she came in: surprisingly, abruptly. She left in a taxi we caught outside her apartment on St. Mark's Place. After the taxi drove off, I went into the hot dog place across the street and ordered two vegetarian hot dogs with mustard and onions. After that I walked to work at the bar, where everything was the same as usual. Robbie was there an hour before we opened, fiddling with the speakers. Jason was downstairs, cleaning the espresso machine. When I said hello, he shook his head slowly, and I knew that meant he didn't want to speak until his hangover had passed.

I expected to hear from Delia once in a very long while, maybe, on her way through town with her southern husband. I expected to get a wedding invitation. I expected occasional stilted phone calls and annual Christmas photos only people in small towns have the energy to send. I didn't hear from her too often, though. Delia never bothered sending Christmas cards, and she got married quietly at her parents' house one weekend in Lebanon.

She phoned me from the taxi on her way out of town. "That was some fun!" she said.

That spring was hot, the kind of dry spring that precedes an oppressive summer. I phoned moving companies to check prices on moving all my things to Los Angeles. I looked up language schools and thought halfheartedly about spending the summer in Italy. I wrote long, flirtatious emails to Lucas, who always wrote back. Every so often I would wear my skimpy undershirt and rack-enhancing bra on the public side of the bar. I tried my hardest to tongue-kiss strangers. "That was some fun!" she had said. I started, slowly, to put all my things in boxes, waiting for the final thing that would give me a reason to leave.

TWENTY

The Journey Out

Clarissa came back to the city in June. Her posture was rounded, her face bloated, her hands pudgy and dry. Her boyfriend Martin, the one she had met on the Metro, came, too. He had found work at an engineering firm in the city and moved into the loft Clarissa kept in Williamsburg.

The first week she was back, I invited her round for lunch, which I ordered in from the Greek place up the street. I ordered all my mother's favorites: the octopus salad and the grilled halibut, the tzatziki and the baklava and extra, extra, extra olives. Pierre had brought me tea fresh from his trip to the plantations in Bhutan. I wanted everything as lovely as possible for Clarissa. I bought an expensive pink wine. I arranged two chairs at the window and bought a pack of party cigarettes, in case Clarissa felt well enough to smoke.

By then I had packed nearly everything in my apartment, but I had no plans to leave. For months I had stalked the streets for sturdy boxes I could drag home with me. Looking for boxes had become my favorite hobby. I knew to look in front of the drugstore across the street just after midnight on Tuesdays and Thursdays, to catch good boxes before the employees broke them down and tied them together with string. I knew to check with the bars on Second Avenue early in the afternoon, before I left for work, to get the good strong liquor boxes. Even after I left the city, I would continue to scope out nice prospects in the gutter. "Look at that," I would say, longing to take every good piece of cardboard home with me. "Not even a weak spot."

I knew I would leave New York soon, but I didn't know when, and though I missed California, I wasn't certain I was ready to go back.

I had not anticipated Clarissa's horrified reaction to the way I was living. "What is this?"

"I'm just packing up a few things."

"A few things. Where are all your nice frying pans?"

"I mostly eat at the bar."

"Where is your lobster pot?"

"I put all my winter hats in it. It's in one of the larger boxes somewhere."

She stared at me, shocked.

"Well," I said, "do you want me to cook you some lobster? Nothing is taped up yet. Except the books."

"You taped up your books? You put your books into boxes and taped them shut?"

"I've been buying new ones. It's a good idea. You know, I had been reading the same books over and over since school. You should box up your books. It's liberating."

She marched around the apartment, clearly alarmed, almost panicked. "I had no idea things had come to this. Why didn't you tell me?"

"Tell you what? I want to move, and this way I'll be ready."

"Darling, they're going to box *you* up. Who knows about this?"

I thought for a moment. "I'm not sure. Lucas, maybe."

Clarissa knew about my emails to Lucas. She had pointed out

frequently that I talked about him more than was necessary. "Where are you moving?"

"I don't know yet."

"Are you moving out of this apartment or out of New York altogether?"

"I don't know."

"Well, you can't just move out of New York altogether. What will I do?"

"I'm not moving out of New York."

"Do you think you're going to find something in the city comparable to what you're paying here?"

"I'll move to Brooklyn."

"Brooklyn, ha! You couldn't get a parking spot in Brooklyn for what you pay here!"

"I don't really want to move to Brooklyn."

"I can see you don't plan on sticking around this place." She peeked inside an open box. She pulled out a box of matches from Raoul's. "I could use some matches. Can I have these matches?"

"The boxes are no inconvenience, really."

"Darling, something has got to be done. You're ready to move now. I mean, now." Clarissa could always be trusted to take action. "Where do you want to go?"

"California, I guess. Los Angeles."

"Los Angeles. Good." She took a pen from her bag and wrote the details on a take-out menu someone had slipped under my door. "Where to? Will you live with Ethan?"

"I don't think I can impose on Ethan. Maybe I don't want to move to Los Angeles."

"Will Ethan hold on to your things while you make up your mind?"

"I think so."

"He has a garage or something?"

"Ethan still doesn't have any furniture."

"Oh. Is he planning on moving, too?"

"Ethan doesn't like to have a lot of things in his way."

"Clearly that does not run in the family." She scribbled down Ethan's address on the take-out menu. "Estimating from the cost of Martin's recent move, I think this is going to run you in the neighborhood of three thousand dollars."

"That's what I was expecting." I had saved my money from the four articles I had written in a special account dedicated to the escape I was having trouble planning. Tom had sent me to Miami to cover a dance music conference, where I shamelessly used all of Henry's contacts, and to upstate New York to talk to a man who carved entire staircases from one piece of wood. Tom and I both wanted to write big, important books, books we hadn't thought of yet but were sure would be essential, ground-breaking works of fiction and nonfiction that would ask new questions and inspire change. Instead, Tom worked fourteen hours a day putting out a magazine about music and starlets, about men behaving in inappropriate ways and beating the system, and I called him up for work when I needed money or wanted to go someplace.

"Why didn't you tell me about this?" she repeated, collapsing onto a box of books and removing her jacket. Since she got sick, Clarissa was always cold, even on a humid June afternoon.

I didn't say anything. It hadn't occurred to me there was anything worth telling her.

"When did you start packing?"

"February, I guess. Sometime after Delia left."

"After Delia. Of course. The role model."

"You don't like Delia."

"I adore Delia." Clarissa rolled her eyes. "Not everything is just one way or the other, darling."

"Yes. This is why I have been in the middle of a move for a while."

"I can't eat in here."

"I got food from the Greek place."

"Can you put it in the refrigerator? Let's get out of here."

"We could go down to the Greek place and eat there."

"Let's. Martin will be mad at me. He loves that Greek place."

Clarissa phoned the movers for me, and they all came by on a Wednesday afternoon to give their estimates. By the end of the week, I was scheduled to be out of the apartment and on my way to Los Angeles within ten days.

"Don't go," Clarissa said. She was more upset than I had prepared for. "I made a mistake calling those movers."

"You didn't make a mistake."

She made rooibos for us in her teeny-tiny teacups. "I want you to be happy, but I want you to be happy in the same place I'm happy."

"I might not be moving to Los Angeles."

"That's quite a shame, as all your things will be there."

"Let's go to Rome," I said.

She looked at me. She shook her head. "I'd like to. I thought we would, you know."

Though Clarissa looked unwell and I knew all the details of her treatments and the uncertain outlook, I did not like to think of her as sick. She did not like to think of herself as sick. But when it comes to making plans for leaving the country, a cancer life kicks in. "You go," she said.

"Not without you."

"Yes without me. Go, Katie. You don't know what's going to happen to you. I don't know what's going to happen to me. Go."

"We won't go for long," I said.

She shook her head. "I want to stay here with Martin."

That afternoon, before I thought too much about it, I bought a ticket to Rome and booked myself in for two months of language classes at Parliamo Italiano, a school just off Piazza Navona.

I wrote to Lucas in Brussels about my plans for the summer, and hours later he had found a place for me to live, with a hapless journalist called Giancarlo in Giancarlo's mother's palatial apartment off Via Nomentana. I gathered the numbers of friends of friends to contact when I arrived in Rome, lists of places to eat and out-of-the-way places to buy vegetables or the best, the very best gelato. I bought a straw hat with a rim large enough to cast a shadow over the entire top half of my body. I dug my old Italian tapes out of a box full of stereo equipment.

The day the movers came, the morning of the afternoon I was leaving for Rome, I had washed my jeans in the building's machine in the basement. Just before my car came, as I was packing and repacking my two suitcases in order to fit in two more pairs of shoes than were reasonable, I went down to the basement to discover that someone had stolen my old, ratty blue jeans right out of the dryer. I started crying. I cried for well over an hour. The loss seemed very personal. How could a pair of old jeans mean to anyone else what they had meant to me? I cried into my open luggage, over the sundresses and flip-flops. I cried into the sink in my bathroom. I cried in the newly empty living room, not bothering to sit by the window while I fake-smoked a party cigarette, and I kept crying, enjoying the sound.

My usual driver came to pick me up. He ran a one-man underground car service and was half as expensive as the cheapest car service you might find in the phone book. He had been driv-

ing me to and from the airport for ten years. He loaded my suitcases into the trunk, and I could not stop sobbing.

"Don't cry," he said to me from the front seat. "You are a very
nice girl."

"Someone stole my jeans!" I wailed. "Why would anyone steal
my jeans?!" I couldn't catch my breath. I was really going at it.

"You're going to find better jeans," he said.

"That's just not very nice, is it?" I was savoring the feeling of
all those tears streaming down my face. They felt like a light sort
of caress. I stuck my tongue out to the side a little and tried to
eat them.

"No." My driver shook his head with conviction. "No, it's
horrible, horrible. Don't worry. You're going to find jeans that
are nicer." I cried all the way to the international terminal, and
expending all that energy felt wonderful.

When I stumbled out of customs at Fiumicino, Lucas was there,
at the front of the crowd waiting for passengers. I was not expecting him, and had not seen him in well over a year, but I recognized him immediately.

"What are you doing here?" I asked, stunned and thrilled to
see him, dressed nicely in a white button-down shirt and loose
linen pants.

"Someone's got to get you to Giancarlo's house."

"But what are you doing here?"

"I'm here to see you."

"But why?"

"You're my friend. And I kissed you, remember?"

"Yes."

"Do I look like a cad? I can't make arrangements for you in
Rome and then not see to it that you're all right."

"What about work?"

"I took off from work," he said. "And I've booked my own hotel, because I don't want you getting the wrong idea."

I was very happy to see him. I said, "I don't think I have the wrong idea."

Giancarlo was a classic *mammone*, an Italian momma's boy, except that his mother lived not in the same apartment, as was usually the case with *mammoni*, but in the even larger apartment next door. This sliver of independence gave Giancarlo the notion that he was quite an exceptional young man. Having a pretty American writer come to stay with him for the summer strengthened this notion. The evening Lucas dropped me off with my luggage and left me to get acquainted, Giancarlo was crestfallen to learn that I would be dining out.

"But look," he said, "I have cooked a pasta."

"I am so sorry, Giancarlo, but I didn't know Lucas would be meeting me." I was enormously relieved to be eating out—by the time I arrived, Giancarlo had boiled the pasta into a solid block, and then he let it boil twenty minutes further while I got settled in my room. Giancarlo was the only Italian I would come to know who boiled his pasta for a good thirty to forty-five minutes. He had obviously never cooked in his life.

"Lucas," Giancarlo waved his hand. "Is he one with the red hair?"

"No," I said. "No, not red hair, quite."

"I know a journalist in Brussels with red hair, I thought this was your Lucas who had made the arrangements."

"I can't imagine he could be described as having red hair." Lucas's hair was a dark blond, curly and wild, but I didn't know him well and it was possible that his beard could have been red.

"Look here," said Giancarlo, gesturing to the jar of brownish pesto on the counter, "why don't you just eat a little bit of pasta with me, we get to know each other?"

I was not so concerned about spoiling my dinner, but I was very concerned about eating Giancarlo's pasta. "Maybe just a very small plate," I said.

"Yes, yes," he said. "A very small *prima piatta*."

Giancarlo had laid out his sprawling apartment in a very unusual fashion. His bed and television and working quarters were in the dining room, while the rest of the house was completely vacant. For the two months I stayed there, I would occasionally open a door I thought was a closet to find another bedroom or wing of the house. These bedrooms and separate wings were, however, completely abandoned. Giancarlo's bed was where the dining table should have been. The dining table was on the terrace, which was itself nearly the size of any regular apartment. That first night, I sat at the table outside, not without trepidation, waiting for Giancarlo to serve my *prima piatta*.

He carried out two of the largest bowls of pasta I had ever seen, and followed that with two very small, Clarissa-sized teacups into which he poured a minuscule amount of wine. "I like to have a little wine with my dinner," he said. "Do you drink?"

"Oh yes," I assured him, "I drink." I hoped that would give him the cue to change the glasses and pour forth the wine, but he corked the bottle and put it back in the refrigerator. I did not know how to begin with my enormous slice of pasta block. Giancarlo had not set the table with knives. I cut into the thick mound with the edge of my fork, and tried to eat by using my old trick of pretending I was dead. It occurred to me, after two or three bites, that the pasta seemed quite savory, particularly for having been boiled into a log.

"This is peculiar pasta," I said.

"Ah yes," Giancarlo was proud to tell me. "It's tortellini. There is no tortellini where you are from, is that right?"

"Tortellini," I said, chewing and chewing. "What's inside of the tortellini?"

"Prosciutto. You know prosciutto is our specialty here, yes?"

I had not eaten meat since before I'd left for school. Even when I had roasted chickens for many dinner parties, I never ate a bite. I liked the idea of cooking meat for people, but I had not eaten it in almost twenty years. Usually the texture of meat made me sick, but this tortellini had been boiled beyond texture.

"Prosciutto, really," I said. I continued to eat. I did not want to be impolite.

"The wine is good, no?"

"Yes," I said. "The wine, the wine is delicious."

Lucas came to fetch me later in the evening.

"Oh," Giancarlo said when greeting him at the door. "You are not the same Lucas I expected."

"No? Whom exactly did you expect?"

"My friend Lucas."

"Oh." Lucas was puzzled. "The entire time we were making the arrangements, you thought I was someone else, a friend?"

"Yes. I thought you were a friend."

"I hope these arrangements are okay," Lucas said to him.

"Oh yes," Giancarlo said, waving off his comment. "Katherine, she is a lovely girl. I did not feed her too much."

In the elevator, Lucas asked me, "You ate dinner?"

"He forced me. I ate a block of pasta and ham that had been boiled for an hour at least, and I haven't eaten ham since I was ten."

"I'll take you someplace to wash that taste out of your mouth."

Lucas had studied in Rome during university, and he still

knew all the best places in small corners of the city. He took me to a seafood restaurant on the second floor of a narrow, three-story residential building just off Piazza della Minerva. There were stone walls and wood floors and windows that opened onto two quiet streets, so that between the sounds of restaurant conversation and laughter, you could hear the occasional buzz of a single *motorino* or the click click click of a woman walking alone. We ate bowls of tender snails steamed in wine and langoustines so fresh I wondered if the restaurant didn't breed them in the back. We drank the house white from a liter carafe and washed everything down with shots of frozen limoncello. Afterwards, we walked to one of the tourist spots right in front of the Pantheon and drank espressos. No other city is quite like Rome at night. Whoever did the lighting for Rome at night did a beautiful job. It is quite theatrically lit.

"So you've moved all your things to Los Angeles?"

"My brother doesn't have any furniture."

"That's going to make it very difficult for me to convince you to move to Brussels."

I laughed.

He smiled. "I'm not joking," he said. "Brussels is the ideal place for someone like you. It's vibrant and young and full of the smartest people from all over the world."

"So is New York," I said.

He shook his head. "Brussels is different. It's a very small town. Also, I would like to have you there. I would take very good care of you."

I nodded. I was surprised to find myself, for the first time, attracted to the idea of being taken good care of.

I pitched Tom several ideas that would take me for a few days to Brussels. I pitched a story on the making and acquiring of the rarest and most delicious beers in the world, which he liked. The week after I arrived in Rome, I missed my language classes and flew to Brussels for a few days to do some reporting.

Lucas borrowed a car and we drove up to northwest Belgium and down to the Ardennes, tasting beers and eating gorgeous Belgian food along the way: thick waterzooie, mussels in light broth, frites and waffles we would stop for in tourist traps along the side of the road. The food in the tourist traps was delicious. A cold summertime fog rolled in at night, and we stopped in towns along the Semois to watch the clouds move just above the water. Near Orval, we walked and walked to a café in the hills that could be reached only on foot. The first night of our trip, arriving in Bouillon very late, Lucas confessed he had reserved only one hotel room.

"Good," I said. "I'm glad you didn't get the wrong idea."

We had been trading jokes and ideas and secrets by email for close to a year and a half. Seeing him again in Europe, I remembered why I had kissed him that night in New York, how tranquil and unthreatening he was in person.

After I had been in his home little more than a week, Giancarlo dropped any pretense of being a genteel host and regularly wandered from his dining room/bedroom to the kitchen and back through the hall to the dining room in his tight black underpants and a purple T-shirt that stretched snugly over his pudgy tummy. He padded across the terazzo floors, absentmindedly scratching whichever experimental facial hair he happened to be growing, absentmindedly scratching other places, too. I tried not to look, or to visibly react. I spent most of my time in my room or at the dining table on the terrace, studying irregular verbs.

Giancarlo rarely ate at home. Mostly he went next door to his mother's apartment, where I was never invited. Lucas told me that for Giancarlo to take me next door to his mother's for dinner would give the wrong impression of the nature of my relationship with her son. On the rare and sorry occasion Giancarlo cooked for himself, he boiled eggplants into a watery soup, or else tossed a block of overboiled pasta with a few olives he never bothered to pit. One sweltering Roman afternoon, Giancarlo came home with a full watermelon, cut it into slices, and put the slices in the freezer. Before eating them, he let the slices thaw in the sun, so they took on the floppy texture of warm, wet towels. I felt quite sad for him. I made a couple mild suggestions regarding how long he might boil the pasta or that it might be tastier to grill the eggplants; I offered to show him how to pit an olive, but Giancarlo did not take kindly to cooking tips from an unmarried American woman.

One afternoon I asked him, "Is there a place in the neighborhood I can take my laundry?"

"You know," he said, "I think we have laundry here." He took me to a bathroom in the rear of the house, through a hallway I had thought was a closet, and beneath a stack of newspapers and gossip magazines dating as far back as twelve years Giancarlo unearthed what looked like a brand-new washing machine. "I believe it works," he said, "but I don't know how to use it."

"Is it hooked up?"

" 'Hooked up'?"

"To water and a drain and things?"

He looked bewildered. "Maybe we just plug it in," he said.

I said, "I think we need more than just a plug. There has to be someplace for the old water to go." I looked around, but the machine didn't seem to be attached to a drain. Giancarlo cleared some old paperbacks from the crack between the machine and the wall, but after peering down there and feeling around, he declared, "I am quite sure you just plug it in."

I nodded, and later on I took a walk through the neighborhood to find a laundromat.

Lucas loved hearing everything about Giancarlo, especially pleased with himself to have placed me in the home of such a catastrophic buffoon.

"His sister is an even worse cook than he is," I told Lucas one weekend he had flown down to Rome to see me.

"Is it possible?"

"She had a party at the house, and I offered to help with the preparations. She shouted at me for putting too much olivada on the crostini, and then she boiled the pasta even longer than Giancarlo does. She opened a can of tuna, tried unsuccessfully to toss it into two pounds of disintegrated farfalle, and served the whole mess to her guests."

"Did you join them?"

"I told them I had a dinner date."

"With whom?"

"I took a taxi to Corso d'Italia and ate a pizza by myself."

Lucas joined me in Rome on the weekends, or else I flew up to Brussels on assignment for a story. I didn't tell my family I was seeing anyone. There was no reason to raise alarm by telling Ethan or my parents I had been seeing another English person. Lucas lived too far away to be anything serious. I had learned my lesson on international romances during the Henry disaster.

At the end of August, I returned to New York and bought an inflatable mattress for my abandoned apartment. I loved the empty, uncluttered feel of the place, and suddenly understood exactly why Ethan had avoided buying furniture. I set my computer on a coffee table I found discarded on Seventy-seventh Street and wrote articles for Tom's magazine while sitting on the floor.

In Los Angeles, Ethan had unpacked my dishes and put my

books on his built-in shelves and was, after three years, finally cooking food in his own kitchen. I planned on joining him there, but I was in no rush. "You've already missed the orange blossoms," he said. "There's nothing to hurry out for now."

I tried to convince Lucas that things between us were over. Through the hot, romantic Italian summer and into November, I tried to remind him how different we were—how, as they say, an ocean divided us. No one either of us knew thought Lucas and I could sustain a romance. Continuing through the fall and winter to fly back and forth between Europe and the United States would only prolong the inevitable, which I preferred to get over with as soon as possible.

"I am moving to Los Angeles," I told him one cold morning in New York.

He smiled. He had charmingly crooked English teeth. "I don't see you buying a ticket."

"I promise you I am. I promise you this is never going to work out between us."

He smiled and counted out twenty-four kisses. "Next time I will give you twenty-five," he said, "and after that, twenty-six, and by the time we are eighty, I will have to give you a hundred thousand kisses in the morning."

"I am not sure about that math."

He sighed. "All right, Kate. You check on the math, and I'll make the tea."

His calm, his easiness, made trying to end things with him very difficult.

Part Four

TWENTY-ONE

Engagement; or, A Hostage Situation

There were no Americans anywhere. I had not had enough to drink. It was after midnight at Murphy's Pub in Strasbourg, and the rotund Irish president of the European Parliament was expounding to me his ideas for securing Europe's economy. "Douche bags," he told me conspiratorially, "sponsored douche bags. On all of Europe's airlines."

"Vomit bags?"

"Vomit bags," he corrected. He was drunk. "Puke bags. They're good for your health, good for the environment, and good for liberalism." He laughed and laughed. He put his arm around me and laughed.

I had spent the day with the younger Members of European Parliament, scribbling down notes on the various ways they insulted each other. The president had not chosen the most discreet candidate for his attention that evening. He thought I was the innocuous girlfriend of a *Tribune* political correspondent, which I was, but I happened to be in Strasbourg writing about the ungentlemanly antics of the Members of European Parliament for Tom's magazine. "Here comes Fubini," the president said and gestured toward a slender, beautifully dressed young man just entering the pub. "Now, Fubini's a douche bag. But an admirable douche bag. He's been through every woman in the Labour Party. And most of the women at the BBC." The president's advisors had herded him away from a swarm of eager Irish journalists to the relative sanctity of Lucas, a well-trusted wire reporter, and had inadvertently landed him with me. "I hope none of these lads has got any condoms," he continued. "The freedom of Europe means 'Lads, take off your condoms!' I hate condoms, don't you?" I nodded in agreement, and, ignoring the disapproving looks from Lucas, I excused myself to the ladies' room to take notes.

By then I was no longer trying to convince Lucas that things between us were over. I had tried all the obvious reasoning: "New York to Brussels will not work."

"It's worked so far," he said.

I had tried: "Too many compromises will have to be made, and someone will end up very unhappy."

"Then let's just do this until we're unhappy," he said.

I had tried: "But English and Americans don't get along in the long run."

He said, "You know the wrong English people."

Lucas was handsome in an awkward way and he lacked the reckless glamour of my previous boyfriends. I found ways to get to Brussels. I had never focused so hard on my career: I wrote articles on the women of Parliament, on the assistants in Parliament, the English in Europe, the Italians in Europe. I had stretched the limits of my professional imagination for ideas of what had not been said yet pertaining to Brussels in the context of a glossy lifestyle magazine. I won a small travel fellowship from an arts foundation. I used funds I had saved in my money-market account.

Lucas came to New York on his holidays and stayed with me in my empty apartment.

"Never fall in love with a journalist," Clarissa warned me. "No one is ever happy with a journalist."

"How do you know that?"

"Haven't you read any books, darling? Anyone who's read a book with a journalist in it knows they'll make you unhappy." She folded her torso completely over the length of her legs. I sat on the ledge of my living room window and smoked a cigarette. "Anyway, they're poor," she said.

"I'm not falling in love."

"I know that, but I don't want you to trick yourself into believing you're in love when you're not."

Ethan asked, "Are you in love with him?"

"No, no," I assured him, or assured myself. "I could never fall in love with him."

"Careful about never," Ethan said.

As the real cold of winter set in, Lucas rented a large, drafty, three-hundred-year-old stone house in the Belgian countryside and I went to join him for what was meant to be a proper weekend of eating and shooting and drinking champagne with his friends. Just before the weekend began, an unexpected snowstorm knocked out the electricity and closed the roads all over northern Belgium, leaving the two of us stranded in the freezing wilderness, miles and miles from anything resembling civilization. For three days and three nights, we sustained ourselves on champagne and a large wheel of raclette. The fireplaces in the living room and kitchen and bedroom failed to keep us warm. Sleeping with two pairs of socks on my feet and a sheepskin cap failed to keep me warm. There is nothing to make you realize your tender feelings for electricity like going without it in a three-hundred-year-old stone house in the middle of the forest in the dead of winter. I love electricity. I mean I really, really love it.

The third night of the blackout, grumpy and cold and feeling the flu coming on, I asked Lucas to please find some chicken soup without the chicken, because there is nothing I hate much more than the way chicken squeaks between your teeth like old gum, but I wanted the noodles and broth. Lucas was such a good sport that after a long search in the unlit pantry, he found a can of hearty chicken noodle soup, removed all the pieces of hearty chicken by the light of a candle, and heated the soup over the fire.

I told this story to Ethan, who said, "Oh God, Katherine."

"Why? Oh God what?"

"Oh God." Ethan took a long sigh, and got that familiar look of alarm on his face. "If you were at my house in the middle of a three-day blackout and asked for chicken soup without the chicken, I would give you a slap. I would give you slap soup without the soup."

It never occurred to me I was falling in love with Lucas.

I liked Brussels. I liked the social life—I liked the smart young international polyglots gathered in one very small town, in very small smoky bars with very nice, cheap beer, and I liked that no one went to the market without running into someone they knew. Lately, New York seemed to have become a very small town as well, but in New York, the beer was not cheap, and I never liked the people I ran into at the market anymore.

"You can't use that line about Fubini," Lucas warned me later that night, after the scene with the EU president at the bar in Strasbourg.

"Why not?"

"You can't use it. It's not right. Everything else is fair, but not that."

"It's fair."

"I depend on these people for my career."

"You're not the one writing the article."

"They'll all find out who you are."

"I'm using everything," I said.

"We'll see about that."

"You're not the boss of me," I told him.

No one was more surprised than I was when Lucas asked me to marry him. In fact, I was one of the only people surprised. Lucas had said, "I think you should move to Brussels and be with me." I had said, "We don't even know where this is going, Lucas." And he had said, "Will you marry me?"

"What did you say?" Clarissa asked.

"I said yes, of course."

"So what you meant to tell me was, 'I'm engaged,' not, 'Lucas asked me to marry him.' "

"Yes. I'm engaged."

"Well, congratulations. I like him."

"You don't think I'm foolish to marry a journalist?"

"It's too late for that conversation now. Anyway, you're a journalist, too, darling. Now let's just talk about how nice he is to you and how he doesn't try to squash you."

"No, he lets me talk all I want."

"It's difficult for girls who like to talk to find someone who doesn't always try to shut them up."

I told Lucas that although I was fond of visiting Brussels, I had no interest in starting our life together there. "It rains," I said, "and the whole town is full of your ex-girlfriends."

He was going off for a few months to cover the war in Iraq. "Well, you don't want to come to Baghdad."

"I think I'd like to go back to Rome."

"Good God, Katherine, the way they drive there it's equally as dangerous as Baghdad."

"I'd like to live there, to get settled and really learn to speak."

"We'll go to Rome, then."

"And on the longest day of the year, can we go north? We can go to Brussels on the longest day of the year."

"Of course."

"To visit your friends and drink beer."

"I've always wanted to go to Copenhagen for the longest day of the year," he said.

"We'll go to Copenhagen, then."

"We can do anything we want to do."

The article about the caddish MEPs was published while Lucas was embedded with troops in the Iraqi desert. I was disappointed at first that Lucas wouldn't be able to see the magazine until his return. After the piece came out, though, and after the trouble it caused, I was happy to have Lucas as far away as possible.

"Well, I don't want to work in Brussels anymore anyway," I told him when he heard through friends exactly the degree of outrage prevailing in Parliament, before the president and Mr. Fubini had threatened to sue the magazine but after the English and Italian tabloids got hold of the story. Lucas phoned me from his satellite phone on the terrace of Saddam Hussein's old palace in Tikrit, after receiving an email from his Liberal Party friend in Brussels. Every time we spoke from Tikrit, Lucas reminded me how expensive it was to speak on the satellite phone.

"It doesn't look good for me, either," he said. "And it's not going to be the easiest thing in the world for you to overcome when you want to write from Rome."

"I'm not worried about writing from Rome. I'm worried about being with you in Rome."

"You don't understand," he said.

"What don't I understand?"

"That you won't even be able to write about fashion. No one is going to let you near them."

"You haven't even read the thing."

"No, I've been a little busy here, you can imagine."

There was no response to the piece in the States. I was disappointed. I liked the attention I was getting overseas. "Americans don't even know there is such a thing as a European Parliament," Tom explained. "Of course no one's noticing. No one knows who these people are."

"Well, they didn't really know who they were in Europe, either, until all the news about this article. Lucas says no one will go near me again."

"Maybe we can get you something writing for travel magazines."

"I don't want to write travel pieces."

He nodded. By then, Tom was past encouraging me to do something he wouldn't enjoy doing himself.

Lucas and I arrived in Rome, and no one from Cardiff to Moscow had forgotten the scandalous things that American girl had written about Parliament in that tawdry American magazine. I tried writing a piece about the new antismoking laws in Italy, but even the mayor's office would not return my calls. I was able to get an interview with a young unknown shoe designer who was also an heiress, but no American magazine was interested.

"Maybe it's time for you to work on your novel," Lucas said.

"I don't have a novel."

"Maybe it's time for you to start thinking about what it is you really want," he told me.

I kept trying to remind myself that I was very lucky to be engaged to a man who told me to think only of what I really want, but from the moment we arrived in Rome, in February in the freezing, driving rain, I could concentrate on little aside from the things that went wrong.

At first, I thought of anything that went wrong aside from Lucas.

I took language classes. The language classes were full of German college students and one grandmother from Arizona and a woman from Paris who thought she had enrolled in an Italian

Language for Business course. The classes were held in an airless room on the third floor of a narrow building facing a corridor off Piazza Navona, and the seven of us in class drank espresso after espresso, trying to stay awake without sunlight in the stale air from eight until noon. I tried to make friends, but no one was interested in group dinners or weekend cocktails in out-of-the-way places. No one wanted to come over to my house for a knitting circle. I learned later I had taken the wrong language classes; I had chosen, again, old reliable Parliamo Italiano, a school that catered exclusively to tourists. There were no expatriates anywhere.

I shopped by myself for a wedding dress. I went to all the best designers in Rome. I went three times to Alberta Ferretti, hoping each time that the dress I liked in the picture would fit me the way I wanted it to. Girls in the shop felt very bad for me, looking by myself for a wedding dress and determined to fit into a gown that didn't suit me. "Dov'è tua madre?" they would ask, and I would shrug and tell them California, and speak as little as possible before they started speaking to me in English, which they invariably did, and which made me feel very bad about my Italian. The third time I went to Alberta Ferretti, the girls there stopped taking me seriously, and I had to beg them to bring my dress out from the storeroom.

My mother refused to visit. "My passport expired ten years ago," she said. "I don't want to leave the country. I have my house in Michigan." My mother had once been quite a vigorous traveler. She had gone on trips for weeks at a time, leaving us with our grandmother and tracking down famous chefs for lessons or to volunteer in their kitchens. My mother learned to chop onions in Lisbon while I was in kindergarten. She learned to roast a chicken from Brian Turner in London, and had charmed James Beard during a trip to Vienna, during which he taught her how to appreciate sweet wines. My mother had once been lots of things she wasn't so much anymore, including depressed.

"But I live here now," I tried to tell her.

"Yes," she said, "and think of all the frequent flyer miles you'll rack up coming to visit me."

After Lucas had returned from the war, he was intermittently very sad or very happy, and rarely anything in between. During the twelve weeks he was gone, Lucas reminded me every night over the satellite phone both that the moon reflected a remarkable white light over the Tigris and that the other reporters in Camp Britney thought he called me too much.

"Have you told the soldiers you're marrying an American girl?"

"They haven't asked."

"Have you told anyone you're getting married?"

"They haven't asked, I said."

One of the reporters who had been in Tikrit at the beginning of the invasion had hung a magazine cover of the American pop star Britney Spears in the former ballroom that was now the journalists' quarters, and even the colonels referred to the dormitory-style barrack as Camp Britney.

Throughout the course of his work there, Lucas was surprised to see a lot of young men shot into pieces, and a lot of teenage boys with their bodies beaten to blue tissue and blood.

"Everyone sees that," I told him, "even those of us at home."

"But I saw blood splattered over the remainders of people's dinners," he said. "I saw blood splattered over people's takeout."

"I saw those photos," I said. Later he would nod, as if there were nothing more he could say to me. I didn't know they had takeout in Iraq.

"The satellite phone is eight dollars a minute," he would remind me.

"I don't care. I am just here waiting for you and I can't focus on anything, all I can do is read the wire all day and wait for your name."

"Wait for my name where?" he said.

"Your byline, Lucas. I'm looking for your byline."

"Don't wait for my name," he said.

In Rome, when Lucas sensed I was getting forlorn, he would call in sick to work and we would walk in the parks or, later, when the weather improved once spring rolled around, ride our bicycles. In the evening he would play to me on the guitar, and much later, when I met the gay American couple who lived downstairs from us, one said, "You're the one with the romantic husband who serenades you on the balcony."

"*Fidanzato*," I said.

"He seems a little standoffish," the other one said.

I said, "He's just shy." I didn't tell them that Lucas had heard from our next-door neighbor that those two American boys were *incubi*. Nightmares. They had been complaining and complaining about the stalled construction on the elevator in the lobby. In order to get to their apartment, they had to jump over the empty pit where the elevator shaft would go.

I went to the market next door to the train station and had a fight with the woman who sold tomatoes. I had been buying tomatoes from the same woman since we moved to Rome nearly three months previous, and she never let me choose them myself. Instead, she would give me a brown bag of all the bruised, split-open tomatoes, and leave the beautiful ones right in front for everyone to see. One cool spring morning I felt, finally, that my Italian had advanced enough to discuss the bad tomatoes.

"Non voglio i pomodori brutti," I said.

The old tomato woman started shouting at me. She shouted

at me rapidly and in idioms I didn't completely understand. I told her to please give me the pretty tomatoes at the front. She shouted and shouted and waved her hands about and insisted she had given me the nice, delicate tomatoes. She said just because a tomato is small doesn't mean it's *brutto*. I didn't know the words for bruised and split-open, so I gave the tomatoes back and went home.

My mother phoned. "What are you cooking tonight?" She liked to hear the details of all the Italian food.

"Artichoke soup. I bought teeny-tiny artichokes and bright green and white leeks."

"The markets must be wonderful this time of year."

"Yes," I said. "The markets are wonderful." I was lying in bed, sad from the argument with the tomato woman. "Tell me the gossip," I said.

"Well," she sighed. "The gossip." She sipped something. "Daddy is suicidal and doesn't want you to have a wedding because we'll have to invite Richard and Richard will become a problem."

I said, "You want me to cancel the wedding because no one gets along with Richard?" I laughed. She was serious. I said, "Is Dad suicidal?"

She said, "No. But he doesn't want you to have a wedding." During a family trip to San Francisco to see Richard's new house, Richard and Ethan had argued almost violently over where to have dinner, and Richard had hurled all sorts of creative gay epithets at Ethan. Ethan had hired a car and driven back to Los Angeles on the spot, promising never to speak to Richard again.

"Daddy doesn't want Richard to make a scene in front of everyone's friends," my mother said.

"Don't invite Richard."

"Daddy doesn't want to have a wedding and exclude your brother."

"So the only possible solution to this problem is not to have a wedding at all?"

"That's what Daddy says."

"You just tell Daddy to keep Richard on Ativan." Drugging Richard seemed to be the only way to put up with him.

After the conversation with my mother, I went to the post office to see about purchasing stamps. The clerk refused to sell any to me. There was much confusion, until finally the clerk succeeded in explaining, half in English and half in Italian, that the post office no longer sells stamps at all.

I phoned Clarissa. She enjoyed hearing the unexpected difficulties of living in Rome. "The post office doesn't sell stamps," I told her.

"It's all right," she said, "you just get them at the tobacconists."

"I need my letters weighed for correct postage," I said, "and the sink is broken and the plumber can't come for three weeks."

"You can wait three weeks."

I was upsetting myself now, for no reason. "I know what will happen," I said as calmly as I could. "The same thing that happened when the shower door broke. He will need a part. He'll need an essential part that he doesn't have but that he'll bring back in another three weeks, and nothing will ever get repaired."

"That's the drawback of the relaxed Roman lifestyle you looked forward to, my darling."

"Well," I said, trying suddenly not to hyperventilate and trying not to think of the conversation with my mother or the draining altercation at the market, "we have a cupboard filled with gorgeous wine and I eat the most delicious Parmesan in the world."

"You have lunch on the Circo Massimo."

"I walk through the orange light on the Forum every afternoon. It's silly to get upset about the sink."

"You rarely had water in your kitchen in New York, anyway."

"That's right. I forgot that."

"You washed your pots in the bathtub."

"The doormen stole my deliveries."

"The doormen would shout at you for wearing your Rollerblades in the lobby."

There was a pause.

"How's Lucas?" she asked.

"Perfect. I love Lucas."

"Yes. Well. Good thing. Are you still planning on marrying him?"

I paused, considering replaying the conversation with my mother but was too upset to repeat it. "How's Martin?"

"Martin. He's darling." There was another pause. "There's something I've got to tell you."

"What's that?"

"I don't want you to get angry with me."

"What is it?"

"Don't be upset."

"Don't be ridiculous."

"You're going to be disappointed. I don't want you to be too disappointed."

"Did you break up with Martin?"

"No no, not that. Not yet."

"Clari. Tell me."

"I'm pregnant."

"Miss Clarissa," I gasped. There was nothing she could have told me that would have made me happier, or more surprised. "Are you really? Are we really going to have a small Clarissa? How?"

"In fact, you know, I don't know how. I really can't imagine how, I've felt so ill from all that's gone wrong with me. Poor Martin. Immaculate conception, I guess."

"You're the holy mother."

"Probably," she said. "Will you send me gold and myrrh?"

"I can't," I said. "There are no stamps at the post office."

"Send diamonds. Those will do."

"Mrs. Burns would say you're too young for diamonds."

"Oh, I am," Clarissa said. "I am much too beautiful still for diamonds. Better just send me incense."

"How about a hologram key chain of the pope and Jesus?"

"I must admit, you don't make it sound like the most romantic city in the world."

At least once a week, someone threatened to throw themselves off the Colosseum. From the window at the back of our apartment, I could see them perched at the top. I would run outside to wait for hours on the opposite side of the Fiori Imperiali to see teenage girls or middle-aged men or very young mothers plunge head-first into the cobblestones below. To my enormous disappointment, no one ever jumped. The Italians are a bunch of babies.

Albert visited from the States, touring with his new album. Albert was quite well known in dance music these days, thanks to Henry's hard work and keen ear. I'd instructed Albert to stay at a hotel on Capo d'Africa, just around the corner from our apartment, and I looked forward to having a friend in the neighborhood temporarily.

Rome has the most beautiful terraces in the world. From the hotel bar at Capo d'Africa, it seemed you could see directly into the arches of the Colosseum, that if you got a running start you might be able to jump right in. The city had the kind of heavy pollution that makes sunsets orange, red, and violet, like a forest on fire. No painter could have dreamed up anything more beautiful. Albert and I drank gin and tonics and leaned against the railings, over the street.

"You're a lucky girl," he said. Albert's first afternoon in Rome, he had gone to Battistoni and bought himself a dandy white straw hat. In his summer linen suit and the dandy hat and his loafers with no socks, he looked nothing like the punk musician Henry represented and everything like the Great Gatsby.

"You're a superstar DJ."

He tugged my hair. Albert knew I liked to have my hair tugged. "That sky is an actual purple."

"You ought to move here. Why don't you get Henry to just move you right into Capo d'Africa."

"Wouldn't that be perfect."

"Yes," I said. "You would be the only person in Rome who speaks Italian worse than I do."

"You have a certain tone of desperation." He signaled the waiter for more drinks. "I would introduce you to my friends here," he said. "Except they're dying to leave. A *New Yorker* writer and his wife. They hate it here."

"That's transitional."

"They told me going to the grocery store is like going into battle."

"They don't lie."

"Nothing can be worse than the Gristede's near my house." He meant nothing can be worse than that grocery-store smell unique to New York: the stench of milk gone bad and fruit decomposing and old meat misplaced in the dry-goods aisles. He meant the reliably filthy floors and the angry customers and the cashiers who ignore you if they are not directly hostile.

"It's worse, Albert." I found the predictability of New York's sad and putrid grocery stores very comforting. "The Italians don't line up, and everyone's shoving everyone else." I tried to concentrate on the purple sky and the Colosseum. Living in Rome was something I had longed to do my whole life, and I wanted to be in love with the city. I wanted to be in love with Rome because I had forced Lucas to come here, and it was my responsibility to be happy. "Hating the grocery store, that's universal to Americans," I said. "Americans don't understand why everyone is shoving in front of everyone else." Once at a wine bar during lunchtime I sat next to a drunk American diplomat who was hysterical about the state of the grocery stores. "You can stand in line for weeks," she cried, really cried, with authentic tears she tried to hold back, "but everyone is going to beat you back with their *pane.* You will never get to the front of the line."

"I have sixteen cities on this tour," Albert said. "It gets really lonesome."

"Gets really lonesome in one city, Albert."

"Yes, yes. Cry me a river."

"Cry me the Tiber."

The sky darkened. I wanted to go someplace for dinner.

"Shall we have another drink?" Albert said.

"Shall we eat some dinner? We can have wine."

"Let's go to dinner."

We ate dinner at Luzzi, a hallway of a restaurant near my house. The place had waxy red-checkered tablecloths and wineglasses that were maroon on the bottom from years of improper washing. The waitresses were angry and the owner was a drunk, but the food was delicious and the wine was cheap.

"This place is small."

"It's the best food in Celio. After dinner, the waitress will offer you one of her cigarettes."

"What a life you have."

"What a life," I said.

"Is it lonelier than touring?"

"Touring stops."

It was dark now, and you couldn't see the Colosseum from Luzzi unless you stood up and walked to the corner. Albert and I ate big, steaming bowls of pasta e fagioli and drank the good,

cheap red wine. We sopped up the broth at the bottom of our
bowls with warm, crusty bread and ordered tiramisu to share. Lucas was working late, waiting on news about the Italians at war.
Lately, Lucas was always waiting on news about the war. While I
was still in New York, he would call me at all hours from Tikrit,
always on the verge of something, always waiting on a story from
the soldiers in the Fourth Infantry Division, or ready to go out
with them in their Humvees to cover a raid. The twelve weeks he
was covering the war, I became obsessed with murdered journalists, or journalists caught in misdirected fire, and I had worried a
permanent crease into my forehead. At the *Tribune* in Rome, the
office shifts were arranged so that if Lucas was not home by six or
eight p.m. he likely wouldn't be home until midnight. There was
nothing to worry about but how grumpy he would be when he
got in. I was quite happy having Albert around for two days, so
that I didn't have to eat dinner alone.

Lucas and I were attacked by a dog one night coming home from
the gym. We had been to a late spinning class and had eaten In-
dian food at a take-out place on our walk back to Celio. A mangy,
skinny, unkempt dog snarled and snapped and lunged at us,
while his aged owner walked on ahead of him, unconcerned that
his vicious pet was attacking passersby. As we tried to defend
ourselves with Lucas's bicycle seat and the chain lock, the owner
stood back and admonished halfheartedly, "No no, Pepe, no no."

"You're a shithead!" Lucas shouted.

"Don't call him a shithead," I whispered.

"His dog is trying to kill us."

"I know. Don't call him a shithead."

"You're a shithead!" Lucas shouted.

When Lucas and I had retreated behind a fence, the owner
shouted violently at Lucas for swatting the animal with a chain.

"You shouldn't have called him a shithead," I said.

"I am trying to protect you!"

"Just. You know. The Italians don't like to be called shit-heads."

"Don't go ahead and tell me about Italians," he hissed.

We walked home in an unhappy silence.

I could not get over my jet lag. After three months in Rome, I was still getting out of bed at one in the afternoon. If Lucas phoned from the office, I would quickly shake off the sleep. "I'm just running out to the market," I would say, or, if I had ignored the telephone all morning, "I've just been across town getting organic sugar," after which I would have to race across town to find organic sugar. I didn't want Lucas to know how much I'd been sleeping, and I didn't want him getting the impression I could be depressed.

"Are you depressed?" my mother asked.

"I don't understand how you get that impression."

"Maybe I just think everyone's depressed." My mother had been trying to conceal her disappointment that I planned to marry a journalist who had taken me out of the country and had neglected to buy me an engagement ring. My father, of course, had done nothing to conceal his disappointment.

"I'm very, very happy, Mother."

"How's Lucas?"

"He's perfect."

There were many worse places to be living, I reminded myself. I occasionally spoke to Ethan, who assured me that the whole world deposits its garbage in Los Angeles. He had come to the conclusion that only the lowest common denominator chooses to live in Los Angeles, and that those who haven't actually chosen to live there are offspring of the lowest common denominator.

Lucas and I lived in a small apartment. We had no oven. There were the beautiful high ceilings and terrazzo floors and art deco moldings that one associates with fancy apartments in Rome, but the place was just a rectangle and had no storage. Clearly it had been designed as a holiday home or a bachelor pad: for someone who didn't need to stock paper towels. The owner of the apartment had assured us that it had everything we might need, but instead of drinking glasses there were empty Nutella jars, and instead of cereal bowls, there was Tupperware. I was homesick for my wineglasses, for my flatware, for someone to complain to when I had to turn off the hot water heater in order to turn on the stove.

In the lobby, the hole for the elevator remained dangerously open, littered with mail to departed tenants and the wrappers from hundreds of cones of gelati. There was never a sign of workmen. When it rained, which it did a lot that year, the entire lobby would turn to mud.

Sometimes, particularly if Lucas worked at the office until midnight, I walked past the Vittoriano monument, up the Corso to Piazza del Popolo, and to the garden bar at the back of the Hotel Russie. It was the loveliest garden in Rome, I thought, and the staff kindly tricked me into thinking my Italian was better than their English. The drinks were expensive, but I was lonesome and had no work to do, and the Hotel Russie was the only place in Rome where I could always count on seeing beautifully dressed people. Rome was not like the rest of Italy: in Rome, the rich people tended to dress with the flamboyance of circus performers, and everyone else dressed like peasants.

One afternoon, sometime between lunch and dinner before the sun had gone down but just as the Italians were walking home from work or buzzing down the Corso with their briefcases latched to the backs of their *motorini*, after Lucas had phoned to tell me he'd be quite late at the office waiting to hear news on the fate of Italian hostages in Iraq, I went out for a stroll through the Forum. The sky was pink and orange, too beautiful for me to go home, so I kept walking, past Piazza Venezia, up the Corso and detouring past the university, through the quiet Piazza della Minerva and up behind the Pantheon. If I heard one more American tourist refer to the Pantheon as the Parthenon, I thought I would drink myself into a stupor from which I might never recover.

That evening, I overheard no tourists remarking on the beauty of the Parthenon but decided I might like to drink myself into a stupor anyway. All over Rome there was the ubiquitous image of those four young Italian hostages crouched against a wall, pleading for someone to hurry and rescue them. Lucas was working just a few blocks from the Corso, but I missed him unreasonably. I wanted to talk, and the waiters at the bar in Hotel Russie were always nice to talk to.

The patio was completely empty. In New York or Brussels or Los Angeles or Rome, I always felt a little bit more like an alcoholic when I was the only person drinking during hours when most people were probably working.

The evening was getting cooler and the heat lamps were on. The sky was purple with the onset of dusk. I took off my sweater and pretended it was summer. I pretended I was waiting for a large group of friends who would come to entertain me and smoke cigarettes and tell their funny stories. I had no friends in Rome—not one. I didn't know how to go about finding any. Americans, then, were not very popular in Italy. Most of the friends of friends I had enlisted as allies before I arrived had left Rome sooner than expected. Telephones had been disconnected, emails went unanswered. The war was not a very nice time to be living overseas.

The waiter brought bowls of potato chips and nuts and little squares of frittata. He smiled and called me *signorina* and leaned in very close to ask me how the writing had been coming along.

"Me la cavo." In fact, the writing had not been coming along at all. Despite numerous attempts and dozens of hours spent at the computer and in parks or cafés with my notebook, there was no writing to speak of.

Two nice-looking gentlemen sat down on the other side of the terrace and were joined by a woman who had been waiting inside for them. The men were tall and slender and one of them wore a very handsome brown pinstriped suit. The woman was blond and bored and spoke Italian with a heavy English accent. They were just the sort of people I had come to Hotel Russie to watch. They drank more than one round of cocktails. They spoke gently, without gesticulating. They smoked cigarette after cigarette and patted each other on the back when they laughed. They spoke too quickly for me to follow their conversation. I realized, slowly, watching them, that one of the men—the man not wearing the brown pinstriped suit—was Marco Fubini, the roguish MEP I had not so kindly profiled many months previous. In Brussels, Marco had been very generous and flirtatious and had gone far out of his way to include me in any goings-on that might have been of help to my article, and I had portrayed him as quite a shallow whore. Clearly I had been obliged to use "He's been through every woman in the Labour Party," and I could not have said it wasn't true.

The patio began to fill with people, and I was comforted that Marco would neither see me nor remember that we had ever met.

He saw me, though, and recognized me.

I ducked into my cocktail menu. I wasn't dressed to see Marco

Fubini. I was too forlorn, my charisma too tarnished. He came to my table, and I feigned my best surprise and pleasure. I tried, falteringly, to explain the mishap with that nasty article in the American magazine.

"But it is nothing, it is nothing," he said. "You have done nothing but help me. This is what people expect from the Italians. I found the portrayal very flattering. You have given me some excellent publicity. People know my name."

He put his hand on my wrist and on my forearm.

"Where is your *fidanzato*?" he asked.

"At work. Covering the hostage situation."

"Ah yes, it is very bad, this situation. It is the fault of the Americans."

I smiled. I was all out of arguments for the Americans. I was very upset about the war but very patriotic then and exhausted from the constant derision, which I was beginning to take personally.

He waved off his comment. "You must come with us," he said, "if your journalist has left you alone." He stood. He paid my check. "Can't you see?" he said. "This is the first evening of the summer."

We ate dinner at a sidewalk trattoria where the owner knew Marco and the waitresses adored him. "It's like this everywhere," his blond friend told me. She was Dutch, not English. "We can't go anywhere, we have to drink four rounds of limoncello before they give us the check."

Before the rounds of limoncello, we drank four liters of wine between us, and by the time I finally got in a taxi to go home, it was late and I was drunk.

"Out with all your friends?" Lucas asked when I opened the door. He had waited up for me. He was watching *Sex and the City* dubbed into Italian.

"You'll never guess who I ran into tonight at Hotel Russie."

"Trolling the hotel bars now?"

"Marco Fubini. And he was lovely to me."

"Good," Lucas said. "Maybe you can get him to put in a word for you at the mayor's office." He switched off the television and went in to bed.

I followed him. "Don't you want to hear my stories?"

"About your drunken evening out with Europe's biggest playboy? Not particularly."

"What happened to the hostages?"

"They shot one. I think Berlusconi will pay the ransom for the rest of them."

"They shot one?"

"The next time you have a rendezvous with one of your paramours, would you do me the courtesy of leaving a note?"

"I just went out for a walk."

"Anyway," he said, "it's gruesome business, you know, this hostage situation."

"I went to the hotel for a drink and I just ran into people and I didn't expect to be out so late."

"This one ripped the hood off his head right before they shot him. It's unpleasant to sit in the office and watch that by yourself."

"What happened?"

"I had to watch it and file a story is what happened."

"They shot him? Dead?"

He mimicked me. "Dead?" he said.

"Don't be angry with me."

"You could see his face. It's an unpleasant business."

I was uncertain, when Lucas went off to Iraq, whether he would come back upset with Americans and bored at the idea of the promises we had made to one another. He was not impressed with the American policies. He was not impressed with the American sense of right and wrong. But he liked the American soldiers and had found them full of an admirable conviction. These were loyal men, he thought, who wanted to do what they had been told was their duty, before getting out as quickly as possible. Lucas, too, had wanted to get out as quickly as possible. Iraq was a competitive post. Lucas had been very lucky to get it. But once he got there, he phoned nearly every night to tell me he wanted to come back home. Lucas came back with adventures and stories, glad he had gone, but said with energy, "I wouldn't want to do it again" and "Thank God I have you."

After the *Tribune* invested all the hostile-environment training in him, and after they had found someone willing and competent, they got the idea that they might continue to dispatch him to the most unsavory corners of the earth.

"I would go anywhere you want," I insisted. I meant it.

He was offered the bureau chief position in Nigeria. Bureau chief would have been an important promotion. Without discussing it with me, he declined the job, telling his supervisors he was no longer interested in hostile environments.

Summer came and no one could sleep. The heat was too much. The mosquitoes were ubiquitous, day and night. I was covered in explosive hives. I flinched when Lucas touched me.

"I hated Rome in the summer," my mother told me. "I sat in my hotel room ordering hamburgers."

"I love Rome in the summer." I was determined not to let on to my mother any sense of dissatisfaction.

"I don't think you do," she said. "Don't speak in hyperbole to me, Katherine. You love it indeed. Not one person loves Rome in the summer."

"I guess I'm just in love," I said.

"I guess," she said. "Do you need money?"

After the night I came home late, I avoided Marco Fubini's phone calls. I avoided the market next to the train station. I shopped only at the *supermercato*, where the tomatoes weren't so nice but I knew I could pick them myself. When people shoved me in line, I pretended I was dead and I shoved back as hard as I could. I sent my letters to work with Lucas to be weighed and mailed. I left the house as little as possible. I stopped trying to write anything at all, in the belief that if I stopped trying for a while, eventually a story would come to me.

In June, before the summer became too intense, but long after I had grown accustomed to the onslaught of mosquitoes, Marco Fubini sent me an email. A worthy politician friend needed a bit of help: he was young and rich and photogenic and couldn't get the press to look at him. "Potrei aiutare, cara? Per favore, un favore piccolo."

I phoned Marco immediately. "But can I say anything I like?" I asked.

"You must."

"But I can't seem to write anything nice," I warned him.

"Please phone him immediately."

Paolo was young and hedonistic and had serious political aspirations. It looked as if, due to party politics and the general apathy of his constituents, Paolo needn't do anything to get elected but stay out of the media. Nonetheless, he wanted attention. He was certain he would not get where he wanted to go without the appropriate attention of the international media, by which he meant the American media.

The piece I wrote was mean and funny and, somehow, packed

with a certain reluctant admiration for Paolo's bad behavior. I
liked him. I liked the honesty of his disrepute. It was a hatchet
job, and everyone would be pleased. The English and Italian and
EU papers would write it up and everyone would suddenly know
this previously obscure cad of an heir to a large Italian boxed
milk company.

In an effort to make friends and be social, Lucas and I went out
one evening with some of the people from his office: a California
girl called McKinley I had been looking forward to meeting and
two of the journalists from the Italian side.

The restaurant was the sort of place where Marco Fubini
would have been very popular: void of tourists, inside a nonde-
script storefront tucked into an alley off a quiet street, tables
crowded together in a disastrously fire-hazardous way, the whole
place thick with the heat of the kitchen and everyone shouting in
anger or love. It was McKinley's regular spot, but no one seemed
to recognize or like McKinley.

The waitress took a shine to Lucas. Bold, charismatic women
were always drawn to Lucas, and most of the women in Italy are
bold. Lucas was shy and introverted and admired the confidence
of demonstrative women. The waitress came to the table and
caught his eye immediately. "Cosa voi, biondo?"

"Cosa voi, biondino?" McKinley mocked, and interrupted Lucas's blushing stutter to order dinner on behalf of all of us.
"*Biondo mio,*" she cooed toward Lucas after the waitress had gone.
"I hope you all don't mind I ordered dinner, but I do know what's
best here and it didn't seem like Lucas was able to speak."

"It's fine," Lucas said. The Italians shrugged. McKinley was
the sort of girl who interrupted a lot and ordered for everyone.

"She's kind of a bully," I said later, to Lucas, after dinner and
after McKinley had beseeched me to phone any time I felt lonely.

"I sometimes feel like she puts me down a little."

"A little."

"I don't want to have a problem at work."

"She's the only person in Rome who's asked me to call her."

"She's not bad," Lucas said. "Call her."

In the following weeks, while the American president was in town and every byline of every article was McKinley's, I imagined her treading all over Lucas at work and decided not to call her.

"McKinley took your headline again," I said one of the five days the president was in town and Lucas had written nothing.

"Byline," he said.

"Your byline."

"We all write those things together."

"Yes, but she gets your headline."

"It's not my byline to get."

"You need to stand up for yourself."

His ears went red. I watched his jaw flex and release. "I have done just fine with my career until now without you," he said. He emphasized *you*.

He was standing right there, and I missed him so much I could hardly breathe. "I'm just trying to help."

"I'll do without your help," he said.

Berlusconi, it was rumored, did after all pay the ransom for the remaining three hostages, and they were returned to their small hometowns. McKinley covered their homecoming, with additional reporting by the bureau chief.

I got a phone call from a friend of Tom's, an editor he knew at a glossy women's magazine. She wanted that article about the shoe-designing heiress.

"What's she heiress to?" the editor asked.

"I don't know. Property, I think."

"Does she drink a lot?"

"The Italians don't really drink like that."

"Is she in with that whole Milan crowd?"

"More like the Rome crowd."

"Anyway," the editor said, "you just do your thing."

My thing, it turns out, was a very cruel and tender piece about a shoe designer who had the misfortune of inviting me out the one night in her life she threw up in the bathroom of a fancy nightclub in Rome and had to be escorted home by her ex-boyfriend. She was a naïve girl who never drank, and the night I came along she tried to impress too many people.

Contrary to what Lucas had promised, a bad reputation for being a ruthless reporter can be a great asset in magazine journalism.

"You get more bylines than I do," Lucas said one evening on the terrace, in between songs on his guitar. I hated when he played his guitar at me. It reminded me of insincere high school crooning, but I wanted very much to think it was romantic. The gay American couple downstairs thought it was romantic.

"Does that make you proud or sad?" I asked.

He smiled and strummed his guitar. The American boys downstairs shouted up requests.

I needed someone to help me select a wedding dress, and McKinley seemed to be my only option as a friend, but I decided I would rather be lonely. I bought a long, beige, silk-crêpe dress from Valentino, where the salesladies always helped me speak Italian. I bought the dress, but I had no vision of myself wearing it. I never felt love for it the way women talk about loving their wedding dresses, the way they store them with tenderness for their daughters to wear. It was a very stylish gown and very expensive. It transformed me completely into something beautiful; I looked almost like Grace Kelly, with my broad slender shoulders and light hair pulled back—even I thought so. Grace Kelly in *To Catch a Thief*. Clarissa would be breathless. Touching the fabric was like sweeping your hands through honey. I paid for the dress with a credit card my mother had sent, but something about buying it made me feel very, very alone.

TWENTY-TWO

The Funnel

There had been a lot of rain that year in Rome, and when the rain stopped, the heat began immediately. We took B vitamins before going to bed at night, but the mosquitoes attacked us anyway, and we were cowardly when it came to mosquitoes. We flinched and despaired over the bites as if we had severely broken bones. There were no screens on the windows, and the heat in the apartment was too intense to leave the windows shut overnight. In the apartment next door we could hear the arguments between our neighbor and her unemployed twenty-four-year-old son. "It's not bad when they argue," Lucas said. "What's bad is when they make up." If the neighbors next door were not arguing and making up, we could hear the American boys downstairs having sex.

When I hung our wash on the drying rack outside, the mosquitoes would land in families on the damp edges of our T-shirts and underwear. We consoled ourselves with lemon granita and cones and cones of gelati.

We saw a man run over by a car at the Ponte Sisto. Traffic had stopped for him to cross, but he didn't see the car that didn't see him. He flew into the air like a stick, and when he came bouncing down on the hood of the car and into the street, we heard his neck snap in two. There was no blood. That night I had worn the same blue silk wraparound dress I had worn to my grandmother's funeral. I felt very pretty. We were on our way to Trastevere, meeting a journalist friend of Lucas's in on leave from Baghdad. Just before the car accident, Lucas had taken a series of pictures of me smiling on the bridge. Later, I would send those pictures on to Clarissa and Ethan, relaying stories about the horrors we heard from Baghdad and begging them to come see me. Lucas and I couldn't be of any help to the man who had been hit by the car. Too many people had stopped to watch. Even if he had survived the hit, the crowd wasn't letting him breathe, so Lucas and I walked on to dinner, a little bit disconcerted and sad.

One afternoon, after I had finished writing and the writing had gone badly, the rain had stopped and I took the subway up to Corso d'Italia to meet Lucas for lunch. It was not a long walk from the subway stop to Lucas's office, but by the time I got off the train, the rain had started again. I arrived at his building soaked through to my scalp and my skin, embarrassed.

"Don't you have an umbrella?" he asked, ushering me out of the newsroom.

"I always lose umbrellas."

"Don't you have a hat?"

We had no extra space in our apartment, so I had sent my hats to my parents' house in California. I didn't want to tell Lucas. I didn't want him to feel so bad about the size of our apartment, which usually I liked just fine, but which had no space for luxuries like hats.

"I don't have a hat."

"You," he said. "Why did I think you had a dozen hats?"

"I don't know," I said.

"We have to find you a hat." Instead of eating lunch that day, we spent an hour in La Rinascente and the shops on Via Veneto, looking for a hat. It was romantic and generous of Lucas to want to buy me a hat, but we had no money then, so I pretended I didn't see any I liked.

"This one?" he would ask.

"Not quite."

"This one is nice. Yellow, it's nice."

"Not quite right," I said. The hats were beautiful, and my throat was full of appreciation and love. "It's silly to buy a rain hat now," I said. "This is probably the last rain of the year." By the end of his lunch hour, as we stepped out of the department store, the rain had stopped.

The wedding approached, and Lucas's friends in Brussels planned a bachelor party for him in Barcelona.

"Why Barcelona?" I asked.

"I don't know," he said. "I guess the boys want to go to Barcelona."

"The beach," I said.

He nodded. He nodded at nothing. "The beach," he agreed.

The night before he left for the bachelor party, Lucas woke up in the middle of the night vomiting. He woke up in pools of sweat, hyperventilating.

"What's happening?"

"I'm afraid, I think."

"Afraid of Barcelona?"

"Not that."

I was afraid, too. I had a feeling what was coming.

"I think I'm afraid of you," he said.

———

Lucas had begun to have fantasies of jumping out the sixth-story window of his office on Corso d'Italia. On the flight to Barcelona for his bachelor party, he told me later, he had prayed and prayed that his plane would go down. When the plane didn't crash, he told me, he had considered running away, never coming home.

Four weeks before Lucas and I were to be married, we took what we hoped would be a relaxing trip to see his parents in France, and Lucas had sweated profusely the entire two-day drive from Rome to Bergerac. By then, I was drugging him. It was for his own good. I told him to start taking Ativan with his cocktails or I would leave him, and either way his wedding nerves would be cured.

To make matters worse, when we stopped in a dusty bar just before arriving at his parents' small town, there was no ice in our gin and tonics.

"I guess we should have had beer," he said.

I tried not to crinkle my nose, but I crinkled my nose. "At least there's gin in it."

Lucas looked at me and shook his head. He drank the whole warm gin and tonic in two swigs.

One afternoon in Rome, while the rain came down so hard it leaked through the windows and beneath the door on the terrace and didn't let up, an afternoon I was so lonesome that I couldn't think of eating anything without feeling sick, I had taken a permanent marker, crossed out all the brand names in our house, and written "Lucas Peabody" on everything we owned. I wrote "Lucas Peabody" on the toothpaste and "Lucas Peabody" on my underwear and "Lucas Peabody" on all the containers in the kitchen. We had Lucas Peabody olive oil, Lucas Peabody pasta, and Lucas Peabody's Mark Kentucky bourbon. I thought this was clutch-your-stomach-and-fall-down-laughing hilarious. I had thought Lucas would find the "Lucas Peabody" rebranding effort thoroughly charming and postmodern and funny, but instead I got the impression he found it alarming.

He could have been alarmed, too, that although I had no job and little to do in Rome, I refused to iron his shirts, or that with my ample free time, I had made "I heart Lucas Peabody" T-shirts for the two of us and most everyone we knew. He could have been concerned that I balked at anything but cloth napkins with dinner, or that wool gave me a rash, or that when the shower door broke one morning, I started crying and couldn't stop.

He shook his head. He asked the bartender for a beer. I tried to rub the grease off the rim of my gin and tonic. I missed New York, where in the case of a greasy gin and tonic, I could return it to the bartender and smile and say, in the only language I really knew, "My glass isn't clean." In New York there are almost always clean glasses. In Rome and near Lucas's parents' house in France I had become accustomed to wiping a space in the grease where I could take a drink.

"You know what I'm afraid of?" he said, sitting on a wobbly wicker stool at the bar.

The Lucas Peabody replacement strings for your guitar, I thought. "What?"

"Well," he thought for a moment. "I am afraid, for example, that someday I might want to buy a farm in France, to raise geese and make foie gras, and you might not want to do that."

"You are afraid that you might want to raise geese?"

"And make foie gras."

"And you're afraid I wouldn't want to make foie gras?"

"I'm afraid you don't want the same things I might want."

"Like raising geese."

"Like the geese."

"Well, of course I would want to raise geese. I want to make you happy, I want to do what makes you happy." I was desperate. "We'll be geese farmers." I was ready to say anything.

"We will?"

"Yes, of course we will." I was horrified at myself. Of course I certainly would not ever, ever move to France to farm geese, not under any circumstances, but we would handle that situation later.

"There's a farm," he said, "where we can go tomorrow and see the geese being fed."

I opened my eyes very wide in an expression I hoped looked like happy anticipation. "Yes," I said. "I'd like that very much."

The proprietor spoke a rough, southern French to a patron at the other end of the bar. We looked down there. They looked back.

"Are they talking about my American accent?" I said.

Lucas looked well into his beer. "Not everyone is talking about you," he said.

I continued trying not to look down toward the end of the bar. The proprietor and the patron kissed each other three times and the patron left.

"It's empty this afternoon," Lucas said to the proprietor.

She shrugged. "It's only afternoon," she said.

I wondered if it were a comment on our drinking habits. Lucas looked at me, as if he heard everything I was thinking. "I know," I said.

"Not everything is a slight against you," he sighed.

I drank the gin and tonic quickly, and wished that it were only gin.

"What would you like to do?" Lucas asked.

"We'd better go home," I said.

"It's not home."

Lately I called every place home.

Lucas's mother had set the table on the terrace, the evening was warm, and as usual she had cooked all the things she knew I would eat: nothing with green beans or aubergines or chicken or beef. Lucas's mother never said things like *You're a difficult person to feed* or *My, aren't you a picky eater*. She made whole trout and broccoli with parsley sauce as if they were the foods everyone else liked, too. Though it was too warm for scarves, she wore the scarf I had knitted as a Christmas gift. Last Christmas, when she had opened the package, she touched the yarn and said, "I've never owned anything cashmere." I had felt a quick pang of anger that her sons and husband had never bought her a cheap, two-ply cashmere sweater.

"Tell me about your dress," she said. "Can I wear a hat?"

"I hope you will wear a hat," I said.

"And Dad wants to know what color tie."

"Any tie."

Lucas drank champagne before dinner and wine with. The more we talked about dresses and hats and ties, the more Lucas drank. His parents seemed to notice nothing. He did not speak all through dinner. Sweat soaked the back of his shirt.

After dinner, his father poured everyone ample glasses of cognac and we sat in the garden watching the stars.

"Your brother chose the color for the pool," his mother said.

"I paid for it," Lucas said, "and Des chose the color."

"Well, yes," his mother said.

Lucas kept his eyes on the pool. "I paid for the house in England and I paid for the pool, and Desmond chooses the colors."

We were all quiet enough, waiting for him to say everything he had to say.

The pine trees at the edge of the garden were a little bit silver in the night, and I tried to keep my eyes on the pine trees. I felt responsible for Lucas's anger. In Rome, there had rarely been an evening I hadn't reminded Lucas that his parents had cleaned out his savings to pay for their pool.

"You'll hear the rooster in the morning," his mother said.

"At dawn," his father said.

Lucas, looking at the pool, said, "Katherine wants to see the geese tomorrow."

His father grunted.

"Yes," said his mother. "Yes, Katherine, you'll like the geese."

He didn't sleep that night.

In the morning I asked, "How did you sleep?" and he sighed with such sorrow I felt dizzy.

"I had thirty nightmares last night," he said. "And in every one of them, I was trying to get out of marrying you."

"That's not very nice," I said.

"My back hurts." He turned to me. "Does it look okay?" His back was covered in wide red welts.

"I need to go home," I said.

"I don't feel the same way during the daytime."

"I knew this might happen when you went to Iraq."

"This has nothing to do with Iraq."

"It's not so exciting to be domestic and do the same thing every day, is it?"

"Oh, Kath," he said, "I have given up everything and moved to Rome."

I said, "I have given up everything and moved to Rome."

"Come on," he said, pulling on his clothes. "My parents want to get to the market this morning before it closes."

At breakfast, the clothesline was hung with towels. The first time I had visited Lucas's parents, the summer before, I had come down to breakfast to discover the clothesline hung with the bright, trashy rainbow of my underwear. Lucas had given the laundry from our trip around France to his mother, and the whole family had eaten breakfast beneath my thongs and bras. His father made a big deal of it at the time, exclaiming repeatedly, "What an invigorating breakfast!" and "Quite a fortifying meal, really!"

But this morning the clothesline was hung with towels. I left the croissants and jam uneaten in front of me. I listened to the rooster next door and the subtle rush of the breeze and thought, specifically, Remember the subtle rush of the breeze. I didn't want to speak to his parents; I didn't want to become closer to anyone than I already was.

His mother had plans to take us to her friend's bridal shop and past a kitchen store after the market and before the farm. Lucas and his father had their hair cut. I went with his mother to buy plants for the yard. We carried the plants back to the hot car, and I dreaded the afternoon, when surely we would find the flowers had wilted completely in the heat of the day.

"Isn't it a pretty shop?" she said in front of her friend's atelier.

"It's a pretty shop." It was a horrible shop under any circumstances, full of cheap lace and synthetic fabrics, and it was especially horrible that morning. "What a sweet little shop," I said.

"Let's see if they're all finished at the barber's." She walked with a bounce, with a bounce so happy that it almost became a limp.

Lucas's curls were soft on the floor of the barber's shop. He'd had everything clipped away, and he looked as masculine as a soldier. All those curls he'd let grow during the war so he wouldn't be mistaken for an American were limp on the linoleum floor of the barber in Bergerac.

"Look at that," I said.

"Do you like it?" he asked.

"Yes, darling," I said. "Oh yes, yes." I ran my hands over the sharp feel of his hair close to his scalp.

"What a boy!" his mother exclaimed. She looked at his father. "How did we end up with such a blond boy?" she said, happy like a teenager.

His father shrugged. "Not too much," he told the barber.

His mother stayed inside to watch Mr. Peabody have his hair

cut. Outside, during a moment alone, I asked Lucas quickly, "Would things be different if I had been writing my novel?"

"Yes," he said, without hesitation, as if the answer to that question should have been obvious. He looked away. "I can't be responsible for you," he said.

His mother bounded out of the barber's. "Let's get lunch!" she exclaimed. She wrapped her hand around mine. "Can't we please get lunch when Dad's done?"

"Lunch," Lucas said. "I'm hungry for lunch."

"Mmm," I smiled, "me, too."

They took us to lunch. I had a sort of feeling that if today could be over, tomorrow would be different, and today would be a short nightmare in the history of what would become our life.

Neither Lucas nor I could stomach lunch. "Just not hungry," I said.

"Just such a long travel day yesterday," Lucas said to his parents.

"You're going to like the farm," his mother said to me. She was so lovely, with those open blue eyes like paint, with her nicely done hair and her perfect rings and her happy, limping walk. "You're going to wish everywhere in the world was just farms and farm people. You'll see why all we English people want to be French," she said. "Or Californian. All English people want to be Californian, don't they, Arthur?"

His father grunted.

I knew farms and farm people. I had spent my childhood climbing up peach trees. I was the only girl in graduate school who knew how to eat a pomegranate. Climbing up peach trees had not reminded me, however, not to wear heels to a farm. Heels work very nicely at a small market in rural France, but not quite so well in the rich rural soil and wet depth that is every farm outside of Paris. I stuck in the mud and tried to pretend with each step that I wasn't sinking.

I had imagined that this would be a sort of farm for tourists, with fat Americans in shorts and white socks snapping photos of the peasant farmer stuffing grain down a goose's neck with a stick. It wasn't that sort of farm at all. We drove up the dusty road to Lucas's parents' house after lunch and knocked on the door of a neighboring farmer. Lucas's parents asked the nice gentleman if he wouldn't mind feeding the geese for us.

"Oh!" the farmer exclaimed. "You like the geese!" He took us round to the back, where goslings ran around in a cornfield, following the farmer as if he were the mother goose as he knocked down the mature stalks for them to feed. "They are funny little geese!" the farmer said with what seemed to me genuine affection. They quacked and squawked and made generally jubilant noises of pleasure, pecking at the corn and waddling after the farmer in an obedient line. "They think I am the mother!" the farmer said, delighted, laughing.

"Wonderful," Lucas said with more tenderness than I had seen in him in a long time.

The farmer's wife brought us paper cups full of sweet white wine.

The farmer explained the geese live on the corn for the first five months, after which time they're brought into what Lucas translated for me as "the feeding room."

"*Voilà.*" The feeding room was a long room of goose-sized cages, one for each bird. On the ceiling was an enormous mechanical funnel filled with two tons of grain. "This is how we feed them," the farmer said, grabbing a goose by the neck and very gently slipping the long funnel down its throat and into the bird's tummy. In the same way my grandmother had stuffed my brothers and me to completion, this farmer fed his reluctant geese until they groaned with the pain of food, relaxing in compliance and resignation.

Next to the feeding room was the throat-slicing room, six

funnels lined up on a wall. "The goose goes in neck first," said the farmer cheerfully, holding up a stun gun attached to the wall. "We stun them first, of course."

Lucas asked question after question. How much grain a year, he asked, and how to process all the parts of the animal, and at which temperature the foie gras is sterilized. How many geese a season, the length of the season, and with what substance do you wash the blood into the drain? Just plain water?

"Are you a producer?" the farmer asked suspiciously.

"No," Lucas said. "No, I'm a journalist."

The farmer didn't seem to like that much better.

We each bought a jar of foie gras and piled back into the car. I was quiet during the ride back to the house, not because the visit to the farm had disturbed me. In fact, I appreciated seeing how foie gras was made. If I were going to eat it, it was important that I see the process.

Lucas stared at me in the car, and yielded when I stared back.

In the afternoon, we all took naps. I slept but Lucas did not sleep. Welts appeared on his pale chest.

"You're all red," I said.

"I didn't want to have my hair all cut off," he said, "but I wanted very much for something to be different between us."

His new haircut was sharp and uncomfortable to touch.

I missed his soft curls. I missed the Lucas who looked at me with admiration and pride. I said, "I think I should never have written 'Lucas Peabody' all over everything."

"Let's not talk about the past like it's over."

Downstairs, his mother had set the table with bowls of cherries, because I was homesick for my parents' summer house in Michigan, which was something I had mentioned but not made a point of. Lucas's mother listened very closely to everything.

Lucas and I would be late for dinner. "I cannot go on living my whole life like it's one long audition," I said.

"Maybe I'm not as in love with you as I thought I was," he said casually, half turning to face me on the bed.

"I love you more every time I look at you," I said, and meant it, although I was beginning to doubt whether I could go on loving someone who seemed to love me less and less. "I don't know when this stopped being fun."

"Let's just postpone the wedding until I'm less anxious."

"I don't think you'll be less anxious. If we postpone the wedding, we'll both be anxious."

"I can't get married like this," he said, turning away from me.

"I had better go home as soon as possible."

"I don't want you to go anywhere," he said, facing the door.

I had to pretend I was dead.

He turned to me. "Listen. I don't want you to go anywhere."

"You'll have to call the airline," I said. "I don't think I can do it."

He bought me a ticket to leave the next morning from Bordeaux. I would go directly back to the United States, without stopping in Rome to get my things. He wanted to see if I would go; I wanted to see if he would let me go.

I spent that night without him, in a guest room down the hall. I didn't sleep. I listened to myself breathe, listened to the breeze between the silver pines. I repeated old conversations over and over and stared at the ceiling until the rooster crowed in the morning.

In the morning, he came in to see me. "I don't know how this happened," he said. He had not been crying.

"Did you sleep?" I asked.

"Yes," he said, and smiled.

"You must be enormously relieved."

He didn't say anything. I was in the bed and would not let him near the bed. My small bag was packed and his parents were waiting downstairs to take me to the airport.

We were quiet for a long time. He sat on the floor. Finally he said, "I'm afraid of the depth of your sadness."

I said, "This is as deep as it gets. Is this frightening you?"

Lucas and his flabbergasted parents drove me to the airport.

"Is this because we made you go to the farm to see the geese?" his mother asked. She had cried when Lucas told her last night before dinner that I would be leaving in the morning. "I thought Lucas would be happy," she had said, wiping her face with her open palm.

His father was full of platitudes: "It's better to have loved and lost," he said. "Maybe," he said, "maybe if you just wait. And hope. Wait and hope."

"You're driving too slowly," his mother said.

"I am not going to get another ticket on this road," Mr. Peabody snapped. He turned to us gently: "If this is true love, it will prevail."

Lucas had his hand on my knee, and I let him keep it there a while before moving away.

At Bordeaux, I vomited when I got out of the car, and vomited all the way across the parking lot to the terminal. "I'm a little bit carsick," I said. I heaved and heaved. Lucas held my hair back. I was very impressed with myself for making such a production.

I checked in for the flight and his parents left us alone to try to talk something out. We sat in the airport café and ordered colas neither of us drank. "Are you really going to let me leave?" I said.

"Are you really going to leave?" he said.

"Don't make me stay here waiting for you to decide whether or not you feel like being in love."

"I do love you. But I don't want to feel responsible for making you happy."

I looked at him blankly. "You were never responsible for that," I said. "Happiness just happened between us." I thought again of how I should not have tried so hard. I should not have written "I heart Lucas Peabody" on my underwear. "I refused a plastic hat in a storm because I wanted to make you happy," I said. I felt stunned and frightened, afraid that if I hadn't pleased Lucas, I would never be able to please anyone.

Going through security, I took off my belt and forgot to put it back on again. I made a phone call from the gate, to Clarissa in New York, where I would have to stay for a few nights before flying on to the summer house in Michigan.

"Are you sure this is what you want?" she asked through the long-distance delay. It was six a.m., New York time.

"No," I said and for the first time broke into unmitigated sobs. "No, it's what he wants."

"Come home," she said gently.

"How did this happen?"

"Come home. Just come back home."

An older Frenchwoman tapped me on the shoulder. I turned. I had imagined my tears were masked by my large sunglasses. "Are you all right?" she asked.

I looked at her. Tears were pooled in the rims of my sunglasses. I wondered if she'd like to hear about the geese and Lucas's nightmares. "Yes," I said. I hadn't realized yet I wasn't wearing my belt. "Yes, I think I have everything I need."

TWENTY-THREE

The Cure for Sadness

My father has an impressive collection of horrible books. He owns light biographies of ex-presidents and famous CEOs of various large companies. He owns every book written about the O. J. Simpson trial. He owns golf manuals, books full of golf essays that are not by George Plimpton or anyone else I have ever heard of, and golf biographies. He owns Greg Louganis's memoir. He has shelves and shelves of mystery novels and courtroom capers. He owns books by Donald Trump and by Howard Stern. Upon seeing that he had actually purchased *The Nicole Brown Simpson Diary,* I took the worst of his books and hid them underneath his bed.

"Why would you do that to my books?" he asked when he discovered them.

"Because it upsets me that you read this trash," I told him.

He paused. "It makes me forget other things," he said.

Getting depressed is not my father's specialty. We leave that to my mother. She is magnificent at depression: she can stay in bed for six months at a stretch, getting up only to use the toilet or to eat, which she will do exclusively when no one else is in the vicinity. My father's role is to call everyone "buddy" or "sweetheart" and to tell the same jokes over and over and over.

Unfortunately, my father thinks one of the great common denominators between him and me is our interest in books. Consequently, he and I often have nothing to talk about. He makes up for this by buying me things. In the months after I returned from Rome, he sent me an ionic air purifier, an electric bathroom heater, a Tempurpedic mattress, and a year's supply of spirulina. Occasionally he will phone, and the only thing I can interpret from the silence is a profound disappointment on both our parts that there is just not much to say. There is a lot of love there, but not so much conversation.

Every year at Christmas, disaster strikes. The boiler will explode or an old septic tank no one knew was buried in the backyard will spring a leak. These disasters will wait all year, until the entire family has come home on December 24, and as my mother cooks on every burner and in two ovens, as Ethan frantically wraps the gifts he bought that afternoon, as Richard complains and shouts and finds new reasons to be angry, something in the house will feel Christmas coming and explode. It has happened six years in a row. Dad gets so upset he stops breathing, locks himself in the bathroom, and won't respond to our calls. Every year I am afraid this year will be the year he breaks down. Every year, when the crisis has passed, I am enormously relieved that my father has not died of a heart attack.

When I called off my wedding with four weeks to go, he shouted at me. "I'm having a hard time," I said, which he does not like to hear. He wants me to be "mentally tough," which I assured him I am. "I can be mentally tough and still have a hard time," I said imperiously.

"You are not the only one having a hard time with this!" he shouted. "Do you think you are the only one who is upset about this?!" I had not imagined that canceling my wedding had upset anyone the way it had upset me, and I was surprised that he was shouting. I wanted him to be mentally tough.

"No," I said. "I am not the only one upset."

He hung up on me, which was the long-distance equivalent of locking himself in the bathroom.

I was alone in Harbor Springs with my mother. "That's not very nice," she said. She phoned him immediately. "You had better be nice to my daughter," she told him. "I mean it. Or else."

Several days after he had yelled at me on the telephone, he came to the summer house in Michigan, where my mother was helping me recuperate. The house was so new, it still smelled like hardwood and paint. Picking my father up from the airport, I saw he looked small, worn out from the flights, his posture collapsed. My father looked the way I felt, and neither of us matched the immaculate, bright, unspoiled house.

"Come on outside with me," he said early the first morning he was there. "Let's improve the view."

I had a hangover, because I had a hangover every morning that summer. He gave me a pair of loppers and we went to work on the smaller trees on top of the dune, just before the expanse of Lake Michigan.

"This is illegal," I told him.

"Look," he said, "I'm the one who pays your speeding tickets."

We began to thin the forest at the edge of the dune.

"Dean is going to see you," I said. Dean was the CIA agent who lived next door and Dean was a nature lover. I wondered often if Dean's cover was that he worked for the CIA, what did Dean *really* do?

"Dean this, Dean that," my father said. Dean was involved in litigation with every neighbor within a half-mile radius, except us. We had escaped Dean's wrath so far, and I thought we were courting danger with these loppers.

I lopped, and I figured Dad would be paying the lawyer's fees when Dean sued us for improving the view.

We improved the view for most of the morning in silence.

"You know I don't like to talk," Dad said, "but I want you to know I'm very proud of you."

I snapped a fledgling tree in two.

"A lot of other girls would have stayed," he said.

"So what," I said.

"If we lop all these twigs," he said, "we'll be able to see the sailboats this afternoon." He used a small electric chain saw and felled anything with a diameter of less than twelve inches. "Your mother likes to see the sailboats."

For all of July and August, I would sit on the porch with the telephone in one hand and a cocktail in the other. I would watch the lake go from blue to black and finally blend with the night sky. "You talk to everyone else a lot more than you talk to me," my father told me.

"I talked to you when we were chopping down trees."

"Shhh!" he warned. "Sound travels at night! We only cut down the sick trees," he said.

"We only cut down the weeds."

"I'd like to cut down the whole damn forest," my mother said. My mother liked to watch the sailboats.

One evening, Dad joined me on the porch with his own cocktail. "Your mother broke up with me plenty of times," he told me.

"I did not," my mother said from the door, shaking her head. "Only one time when I was crazy and decided I didn't want to marry you."

"I mean after we were married."

"Well," my mother said, "I was depressed."

———

My engagement had come almost as much of a surprise to me as it did to my family. The end of everything came as a surprise, too.

"I knew," Clarissa told me the weekend I spent at her house on my way back from Europe after everything fell apart. "Martin knew, too. When we visited you in April and the only thing Lucas talked about was mountain biking in South Africa."

"Is that all he talked about?"

"Darling, he needs the kind of girl who wears shorts, has thick ankles, and likes to ride around in the dirt."

"I have a bicycle."

"You have very slender ankles. He drank three cocktails before dinner. It was a work night. I knew there was trouble."

Lucas had bought a mountain bike for my birthday, which I used to ride around the parks in Rome but which I was much too afraid to use in traffic, and which I never intended to ride on an actual mountain. Riding around on my bicycle in the center of Rome, I was rained on unexpectedly and attacked by aggressive daytime mosquitoes and hurled hither and thither by the cobblestone streets. I couldn't begin to imagine what a mountain might do to me.

"He said he might want in the future to move to France and make foie gras," I confessed to Clarissa that first weekend back in the States. She was cooking a soft-boiled egg, which for two months after the breakup was all I could eat. I had come home just before the Fourth of July, and tickets from New York to my parents' little summer town were unavailable through the weekend. I slept on an air mattress in what would, three months on, be the baby's room. Clarissa was large and round and she soft-boiled egg after egg for me.

"He wanted to make foie gras?"

"I told him that would be wonderful, that of course I would move to France with him and live on a goose farm and we could make foie gras."

"A goose farm. Really."

"After I said it, I went to the bathroom and threw up."

"Did you?"

"I threw up repeatedly."

"The idea of farm life makes me want to throw up, too," she said.

"We went to see the geese fed."

"No. With a stick?"

"They don't use the stick anymore. They have a big mechanical funnel."

"The stick is for tourists."

"They keep the geese in small pens in a cold room so they store up fat. At feeding time, when those geese see that farmer coming toward them, they just sink their long necks deep into their squat little bodies and they back up into the corners of their cages." I wiggled back into the corner of my chair.

"How traumatic."

"It's not traumatic, but it's quite personal. The farmer sticks his hand back there and he grabs that goose by its neck and then the goose plays dead. It knows it's caught."

"Cooked."

"It knows what's coming. The farmer sticks this long funnel straight down into the goose's tummy. You can actually see the funnel moving straight down through the throat into its tummy."

Clarissa patted her tummy.

"And the farmer flips a switch and this enormous machine on the ceiling attached to the funnel grinds and grinds and just forces that corn right into that goose and the goose is completely still and when the farmer lets go, the stuffed goose sinks its neck way back into its body and puffs out all its feathers and groans a loud, long groan." I took a breath and imitated the groan. I was enjoying my own performance. Clarissa looked on in horror. "Those geese groan just like people, like people who've eaten too much turkey."

"You were going to marry a man who tried to drive you away with the threat of a funnel?"

"It's not as bad as it sounds."

"The funnel? The funnel is not so bad?"

"I ate the foie gras afterwards."

She stopped what she was doing in the kitchen. She peeked through to the dining area. "You ate foie gras?"

"Of course. I am not an idiot. We were in the Périgord."

"You won't even eat chicken."

"Chickens aren't cared for like those geese. Those geese think the farmer is their mother."

"Quite right!" Clarissa exclaimed. "What a horrible trick!"

"Well," I said. "They have very big cages. They get fed by hand." I drank my tea. "Anyway, foie gras tastes better than chicken."

"How could you think of marrying someone who fantasized about that?"

"I wanted him, Clarissa."

She put the soft-boiled egg in front of me. "Here," she said. She tapped the shell for me and lopped off the top. My soft-boiled eggs were always better when Clarissa lopped off the tops. "Now you'll probably have to marry Pierre."

I started to cry.

"I'm kidding," she said. "I'm joking, I'm joking."

I started to really cry, with hiccups and sobs that came from my whole body.

"Oh no!" she said. "It was a joke, a joke so absurd it was meant to make you laugh." Both Clarissa and I found Pierre physically repelling, though we liked him fine. His tea company had become quite successful in the past few years, and you couldn't go to any grocery store or coffee place without running into *The Adventure of Tea*. Pierre was generous and kind in very many ways, but he was awkward and familiar and not remotely sexual.

"Look. Look, poke my tummy," she said.

I cried.

She poked her tummy. "Watch, look, you can see it kick out the other side."

"I don't want to poke your tummy."

Clarissa poked at her big turgid tummy. "It moves around!" She looked at me. I stopped crying.

"I don't want to."

She said, "Martin hates it when I poke the baby."

My mother lost her diamond ring. She forgot to wear it out for the day and when we returned home, it was not where she was certain she'd left it. "Do you think that cleaning lady took it?"

"I don't know the cleaning lady."

"Plenty of the contractors have keys to this house."

"I don't think anyone took it."

"Of course someone took it!"

"I think you'll find it, Mother."

"I will not find it. I know where I left it. I left it here by the telephone. I left it out in the open here by the telephone and now it's gone."

After a four-hour search, I found the ring in a felt jewelry bag in the back of the china cabinet. "Why did I put it there?" Mother said.

There was another ring in the bag, a fifteen-carat aquamarine surrounded by diamonds, a ring I had never seen. "What's this one?"

"Oh. That's your wedding present."

"Wedding present." It was enormous. It was something blue.

"You can have it instead for not getting married." She kissed the top of my head. "Thank you for not getting married, darling." I knew my mother had not wanted me to get married. My mother wanted me all to herself.

Though I had never worn jewelry, not even an engagement ring, I wore that blue ring with diamonds all summer and into the fall to remind myself that a lot of girls would have stayed.

The weekend I was supposed to get married, a few close friends of my parents planned to use their tickets anyway and come out to Michigan for what would have been a week's worth of parties but would be, instead, a lot of sitting on the porch and a lot of gin and tonics. Clarissa had not planned to come to the wedding—she had been having an uncomfortable pregnancy and didn't want to travel—but as the weekend approached, she made plans to rent a car and drive out from New York.

"Pierre is coming, too," I told her.

"Of course he is. Pierre will miss no opportunity."

"And my parents' friends. Some people are enjoying this whole thing, you know."

"I think you'll need me around that weekend after all," she said.

"I always need you around."

"And I could use some time away from Martin."

"How's Martin?"

"Oh, Martin, you know," she said. "He hates me for being pregnant."

On my return to the United States, I carried nothing but clothes for a weekend trip to France: a pair of jeans, two T-shirts, my toothbrush, and a bathing suit. My belt was doubtless still at the security check in the Bordeaux airport.

"What are you supposed to wear to cocktail parties?" my mother said when she retrieved me from the one-room airport just outside of Harbor Springs.

"I'm not going to any cocktail parties."

"Not going," she chuckled. "What do you think we do all summer here in the backwoods of Michigan? This isn't France," she said.

We took an overnight trip to Detroit, four hours away, to buy underwear and a sweater and a flowy dress to wear to the various fundraisers and catered barbecues and country-club dinners I would frequent that summer to distract myself.

"Wear your new skirt," my mother said now. "There will be interesting people there."

We were going to "Dart for Art." This was Harbor Springs' own concept in fundraising, in which old people paid money to get drunk and then race all at once to grab paintings and sculptures and other donated items—like promises of dinners or pedicures—lined up along the walls.

"Why aren't you dressed?" I asked my mother.

"I'm not going, you go on by yourself."

"But I didn't want to go in the first place," I said.

"You must. I bought the tickets."

"These are your friends, Mother."

"They're certainly not my friends. I don't know any of those people."

"But you bought the tickets."

"It's what I'm supposed to do. I don't want to go."

"I'll be uncomfortable."

"You're skinny. Everyone will talk to you."

I was too skinny. Since the wedding had been canceled I had lost enough weight to be called, more than once, and accurately, emaciated. I didn't wear my glasses, so that I would not be able to see all the people not talking to me.

"It wasn't a fight," the grandfatherly man seated next to me at dinner told me before I could ask him about his two black eyes.

"What was it?"

"Deep-sea diving," he said. He had already told me that his name was Mr. Cabott and that his real hobby was big game hunting, and that he had a zebra and a leopard stuffed at home, but that the polar bear got away.

"You have unfinished business with that bear," I said.

"Anyway, it was deep-sea diving that did it to my eyes. I don't want you to think you're seated next to the violent type, my dear."

Later on, after an hour of gin and tonics and a long dinner full of wine, we all got up to race around and grab the best art we could. It was all local art and looked pretty bad to me, so I grabbed instead a certificate for four rounds of golf to a club my father didn't belong to.

"What did you get, my dear?"

"Golf."

"Golf?!" Mr. Cabott said with disdain, a bold American-flag painting propped against his chair. "Golf," he said and shook his head. "You need to learn about pictures, my dear."

Later on, Mr. Cabott invited me to a party on his boat. "I've got a nice friend in town and he's written a nice book, so we're going to throw him a good party. Why don't you come along?"

"Thank you, Mr. Cabott."

"You look like you could use an invitation." He winked at me. He leaned in. "Listen," he said. "Up early. Work till lunch. Eat. Work some more. Stop at three for suicidally intense sports.

A stiff drink or two before dinner, wine with. Off to bed early so
you can work the next day."

I nodded and smiled as pretty a vapid smile as I could
manage.

Later that evening I told my mother, "I was invited to Mr.
Cabott's party."

"I don't know any Mr. Cabott," she said.

"You must. He's one of your art people friends."

"I told you, those people aren't my friends."

"Anyway, he's got a writer friend and they're having a book
party on Mr. Cabott's boat."

My mother nodded. "If you're going to be social, you're going
to need more skirts," she said. She liked all excuses to go shopping.

Later that week, I went to Mr. Cabott's party on the dock
where the boat should have been.

"Darn boat sprung a leak," Mr. Cabott told each of the fifty
guests individually. "Somewhere between Lake Charlevoix and
Lake Michigan. Had to tug it back in."

I was disappointed.

He put his arm around me. "Don't want people drinking red
wine on the old boat, anyway," he whispered.

Political talk of any sort always made me nervous. Mr.
Cabott's guests and his book-writing friend were all wholeheart-
edly—socially and professionally—political. The president this
and the war that. I had had enough of politics while in Italy. I
stood at the bar and talked to the barman. At parties and gather-
ings, I am always more comfortable talking to the bartender. If
there is no bartender, I am more comfortable in the kitchen,
washing dishes.

"You know that Mr. Cabott is going to the arctic to find a polar bear he missed last time?" I asked the bartender.

"No," he said. "I just met Mr. Cabott tonight."

"Yes," I said, "but I get the impression that's what he tells people first."

"Oh no," said the bartender, "first I heard all about the details of how that little boat looked tugging in Mr. Cabott's big boat, and how he's afraid of people spilling their red wine."

I nodded. In Harbor Springs, like in Italy, strangers amplified my own feelings of strangeness. The men at Mr. Cabott's party wore straw hats and white pants and pastel-colored shirts. The women wore expensively frumpy dresses in simple shapes and elaborate prints. My mother and I had bought a light-pink tennis shirt and ribbon belt for me to wear with my jeans. I felt preppy and out of sorts and very lonesome. Suddenly, on that dock with an empty slip for Mr. Cabott's boat and all those cheerful political people, I wanted to walk right into the water. I began to feel very strongly, in fact, that if I did not leave I would have no choice but to walk into the water.

"Kate!" called Mr. Cabott. No adult acquaintance had called me Kate since prep school. "Come here, my dear. Jake here has written a book, I'd like you to meet Jake." I had been avoiding Jake. He was an older man with muscles and a tan and, I had been told, a string of political books that always landed on best-seller lists. He wrote the sort of books I imagined my father might read if my father were feeling particularly current. I was sweating into my pink tennis shirt. Jake was talking at me. He spoke in long sentences without breaks. It seemed everyone on the dock was laughing but me. I felt sick to my stomach. I had maybe drunk too much wine. Mr. Cabott had been kind and generous and I wanted to walk into the water.

"I'm on Italian time," I told Mr. Cabott as I left. I had not been on Italian time for two weeks. I had also not mentioned to Mr. Cabott or anyone else why I had been on Italian time in the first place and why I was back.

"You phone me if you need anything," Mr. Cabott told me.

"Life can be a difficult old game. Did you read about that man in Colorado who leveled the whole town with a bulldozer he built himself?"

"Thank you for the invitation."

He took my hand in both of his and smiled at me and winked.

"How was the party?" my mother asked.

"Good." I made myself a Manhattan and went to the porch to watch the last of the sky go black. She came to the door for a little while. "Did anyone call me?" I asked.

"Were you waiting for someone to call?"

"No one called?"

"How was the party?"

"The boat leaked," I said. "Had to be tugged back in. We had cocktails on the dock." I wondered what my mother would think if I took up smoking. I needed to do something to keep myself from walking into the water.

"I remember Mr. Cabott," my mother said then. "He's the one with the stuffed animals. Last summer he had his arm in a sling from a rifle with too much kickback."

I played tennis to keep myself from sleeping all day. I ate popcorn and soft-boiled eggs and not much else. I kept waiting for my hair to fall out. In the shower I would look for it between my fingers. I checked my pillows in the mornings and my sweaters at the end of the day, but my hair never fell out.

"Stop pulling out your hair," my mother said.

"I'm not pulling."

"You are."

"I'm checking to see if it's coming out."

"You're pulling it out," she whispered.

"I like to have my hair pulled," I told her.

Delia sent champagne and good books and ginseng to the

house in Michigan as a care package for the brokenhearted. I hadn't heard anything significant from her since her move back to Nashville. I knew she had gotten married because she sent announcements rather than invitations, and she had told twenty people in an email that she was trying to get pregnant, but Delia had evaporated from my day-to-day life. Receiving a care package from her compounded my desire to walk into the water.

"She's disenfranchised," Tom told me over the phone. "I know people, Kath. Do I not know people?"

"You know people, Tom."

"It's easy for people like that to turn and forget everything."

"Yes, Tom. It's good I have you."

"I don't mean it that way. You just have to watch out for people."

I had loved Delia's naughtiness, but since her move back home, it seemed to me she had divorced herself from her time in New York. She sent pictures of herself and her husband camping, soda bottles in hand. When I had written her an email from Rome reminding her of a nineteen-year-old stranger she had slept with for several days on end, she wrote back, "Why do you still bring these things up?" At the time, I felt embarrassed and ashamed, as if I were a pathetic old friend living in what had been the past.

Two years previous, Delia had taught me how to swear in normal conversation and how to inhale cocaine from the banisters in hotel stairwells. She taught me how to kiss boys whose names I didn't know. The few times we had been in contact since she left New York, she got very angry whenever I mentioned any of the reasons we got along so well.

Clarissa arrived at the Michigan house after the fourteen-hour drive from New York looking just as fresh and lovely as if she had taken a taxi fifteen blocks. Her clothes were straight and unwrinkled. She had her short hair pushed softly behind her ear. "What a view!" she told my father.

"We had to cut down some of the dead trees," he said, throwing his voice toward Dean's house. A sailboat floated by. The water was flat and glassy. A gentle wind hit the windows beside the porch.

My mother came shuffling out, carrying an Adirondack chair small enough to fit only a very tiny person. "We've bought a chair for wee Clarissa when she comes."

Clarissa absentmindedly patted her tummy. "Or wee Martin."

"No, no," my mother said. "I know you'll have a girl. Unplanned babies are always girls."

Later, on the porch, sipping from my drink, Clarissa said, "When I was driving here, I thought I'd make a big show of how miserable marriage is, so you'd realize you'd dodged a bullet."

"Thank you, Clari."

"And then I realized that I really am miserable."

"All pregnant people are miserable."

"Martin hates his job," she said. "You know. He feels trapped."

"Everyone is trapped. It's part of the food chain."

"It's no good being dependent on someone else for your entertainment, darling. I miss tutoring."

"You hated tutoring." I looked at her. She was holding my drink now. "You're going to have a child, Clari. You'll have a child for the rest of your life."

She looked at me and winced. "I'm afraid I'm going to be terrible at this."

"You're meant for it. The way you look after people. The way you've looked after me."

"Am I meant to be a housewife?"

"Don't knock housewives. There's an art."

She looked up from my drink. "I can't tell anymore when you're joking."

"Clari, you're going to be Clari no matter what." Two years previous, when the doctors had told her there would always be that shrunken piece of tumor in her brain, they told her also that pregnancy was out of the question.

"Yes," she said. "Too bad Martin doesn't see me as the same Clari you do. I think Martin sees me as a bit of an anchor, you know."

"He does not. Not the way he looks at you."

"The old ball and chain."

"Ball and chain. Where did you get that?"

"He looks at me differently now," she said. "You didn't get a good glimpse of him the last time you were in New York, you were crying too much."

"I have been crying an awful lot."

She put her head on my shoulder. "This whole marriage children thing is very *Revolutionary Road,* you know. The great nightmare for urban people, all this responsibility and commitment that should perhaps have been avoided."

Inside, my mother rolled a pound of chevre into strips of roasted pepper. In the next few days, no fewer than thirty guests would come through the house. My father read *The 48 Laws of Power* in the armchair on the screened porch.

"Everything changed very suddenly," Clarissa said. She looked at me, and then looked at me again, hoping she hadn't said the wrong thing.

"It's always surprising, the things that happen."

She smiled. "Don't let me drink this," she said, handing the cocktail back to me.

The next day, before everyone started arriving, before the maelstrom of guests and questions, before we went to fetch Pierre and my brother Ethan from the airport, Clarissa and I ate lunch on the pier. Mr. Cabott had driven his big boat into the bay and was lunching on the pier as well.

"The two loveliest girls!" he bellowed from one end of the dock. He came to our table and I saw his black eyes had almost healed. "How's your Italian time?" he asked me.

"I'm feeling well," I said.

He had a big tropical drink in his hand. Northern Michigan is not the sort of place a person drinks tropical drinks, even in the summer. Anything more exotic than a gin and tonic is generally considered a great sociopolitical risk in Harbor Springs.

"How have you been recovering?" he asked. Mr. Cabott had a talent for asking disarming questions.

"Recovering?"

"You know how it goes."

"I am the girl recovering," Clarissa offered.

"Are you, my dear? You're just preparing for the trauma that will require eighteen years of recovery."

Clarissa had that cigarette-starved look on her face.

"Did you see the boat, Kate?" asked Mr. Cabott, pointing toward the bay at what must have been a 140-foot yacht. There were several white-clad staff milling around on the deck. I wondered why Mr. Cabott bothered befriending me.

"I won't take my cabernet out there," I said.

He laughed and laughed. He nodded. "You, Kate," he said, "you are really top dog."

Clarissa was eyeing his tropical drink.

"It's fine for a pregnant woman to smoke," Clarissa assured me later, having a cigarette in the car on the way to fetch Pierre, "but not in front of one's parents' friends."

There are many cures for sadness. One is to get up early, work, eat, play suicidally intense sports, drink, eat, and go to bed early. Another is to level the whole town with a bulldozer you built yourself. My cure, which is not the best, is to drink and read and stare for months at the lake.

The Friday night before the morning I was meant to get married, Pierre and Clarissa and I went out drinking until very early in the morning. Until that evening, I hadn't known there existed in Harbor Springs places to drink past two a.m. Pierre and Clarissa and I managed to find the speakeasy in my parents' summer town.

"Don't let Kath kiss Pierre," Ethan warned Clarissa at the start of the evening. "She's feeling awfully vulnerable."

Pierre had brought an entirely new wardrobe for the weekend: soft cotton shirts from Pink and a new pair of loafers and casually pressed striped linen pants. Clearly he thought this weekend was his big chance.

In the last bar of the evening, in the basement of the restaurant on the pier, Pierre was distressed to notice my interest in the barman.

"She's always got a thing for the bartender," a very sober Clarissa sighed. Pierre's eagerness was tiresome for everyone.

"It's really unbecoming, Katherine," said Pierre.

"I'm going to talk to him."

"Oh, don't. Have some dignity."

"*You* have some dignity, Pierre."

"You're going to speak to the barman."

"No, Pierre, in order not to embarrass you, I will not speak to the barman." We were all silent for a moment. I said, "Pierre, you used to be fun."

"You used to be more sensitive," he said.

Clarissa went to the ladies' room. For a very pregnant woman,

Clarissa did not have to go to the ladies' room very often. "He's not the barman," she said when she returned.

"He's behind the bar," Pierre said.

"No. He lives in Los Angeles. He's here to see his parents. The owners let him tend bar a couple nights."

Pierre said, "You talked to the barman?"

"I'm going to live in Los Angeles!" I said. It was true. In the fall I would start on a freelance contract with Tom's magazine, writing celebrity profiles.

"You won't last in Los Angeles," Pierre said. He had said this before.

"You won't last," I said. I was exasperated with Pierre, but I felt tenderly toward him, with his smart new shirts and linen pants I knew he had chosen with me in mind.

"This is the most fun I've had in ages." Clarissa tapped and tapped a cigarette on the table and did not light it.

The next day we spent preparing what my mother kept calling "a casual barbeque," but which required an awful lot of work for a casual barbeque. Tables were rented and elaborately set with quaint gingham everything and African daisies in milk jugs. Ice was delivered. Because I adored it, Mother had ordered West-vleteren from a man I knew in Brussels who would drive the three hours north to purchase it for you from the hatch at the abbey door on Tuesdays or Thursdays, the only day the West-vleteren monks sell their beer, and would ship it to you overnight.

She put Pierre to work slicing buns, until Ethan noticed Pierre slicing the buns in half vertically rather than horizontally. "Pierre!" my mother shouted. "Do you do these things on purpose so you don't have to help?" I felt sorry for him suddenly.

Daddy kept kissing Mom, and it occurred to me how much

he must miss her all summer, alone in the house in Fresno, and wanting to have someone around to share all his gossip.

Clarissa and I squeezed limes for her special limey gin and tonics. One of Dad's fraternity brothers shucked fifty ears of corn. Ethan seasoned hamburger patties and my mother polished her silver and my Auntie Petra's, which had originally been sent east for the wedding.

I didn't know most of the guests. They were friends of my parents' from bridge or the club or generally around town. A few families had flown in from California, and children played freeze tag on the beach. I hid upstairs in my room with Clarissa, squatted behind my bed so no one would see us if they opened the door.

"The morning after Martin and I were married, I woke up and thought, well, we did it. Here we are. We have actually done it. That's all I felt."

"You were happy when I saw you in Rome."

"We were happy to be in Rome, of course."

I remembered an argument Martin and Clarissa had in Rome, walking past the hideous Vittoriano monument, about whether or not Clarissa planned to change her name. It was the standard exchange between a man and the woman who does not want to take his name, but it seemed to me charged with more hostility than necessary, and it also seemed to me this might have been a discussion that should have taken place before marriage.

"Anyway, Rome is horrible, we know now," I said.

"For a happy life, do not go to Rome."

"I know the way he looks at you," I said. "Martin admires you."

"You think he admires this tummy?"

"Yes," I said. "Even I admire your tummy."

"Poke it, then," she said.

I looked at her sideways.

She poked it herself, and we watched wee Clarissa get irritated. "Daddy's not here to protect you," she said to her stomach.

"I'm going to love Los Angeles."

"Of course you will." She laughed. "Writing celebrity hagiographies."

Ethan opened the door and came round to the other side of the bed. "I knew you were in here," he said. "Do you really think you're hiding?"

"Don't make us go down there."

"There's someone here who wants to say hello. One of Dad's golf friends."

Mr. Cabott had come to the party, and he had brought with him his son, whose friendliness and floppy hair I recognized—the bartender from last night, visiting from Los Angeles.

"Why didn't you tell me you knew Don Cabott?" my father asked with sincere joy and surprise as I came downstairs. "He says you two have become quite friendly this summer!"

Pierre sulked in an armchair in the corner.

I took an apartment on Beachwood Drive, just down the road from the Hollywood sign. I woke every morning to tourists parked in front of my bedroom, up early to snap photos of themselves in santa hats or bikinis or jumping up and down in ridiculous poses with HOLLYWOOD in the background. As it turned out, my new friend John Cabott and most of the celebrities I interviewed that fall lived within a half-mile radius of my apartment, so I walked most everywhere. Lucas never sent my bicycle from Rome. He sent my clothes and most of my books, but sometime in the fall he sent an email to Ethan informing everyone he had no intention of sending the bicycle, due to the cost of the shipping.

"It's better that way," Clarissa said, her newborn wailing in the background. "Let him be the person who kept your bicycle."

"Do you need to get the baby?"

"There there, lovey. There there, darling." When Clarissa spoke to her daughter, her voice was wonderful, adoring, a simple voice I had never heard before. The baby quieted. "How old does a child have to be before you can send it away to school?"

My conversations with Clarissa became very short that year. I tried to make up for it by sending favorite books from my childhood: one where a greedy, provincial farm town is completely flooded in oatmeal, and another in which a petulant little boy is eaten by a lion. Clarissa appreciated my fondness for catastrophic morality tales.

At the end of the summer, I went briefly to Fresno to return gifts that had been shipped to my parents' house. There was an entire storage closet full of new copper pans and bistro flatware and Royal Crown Derby china. There were sterling-silver wine coasters, clay roasting pans, platinum-rimmed crystal rocks glasses. There were shrimp forks and demitasse cups. I pulled everything out of storage and set it all up in my parents' foyer, labeling each box with the name of the giver and their address. This enterprise took the better part of one day, and when my father came home from work in the evening, he found me on the front stairs, batting a silicone spatula against a soup pot and trying to get up the courage to put the gifts in the car and make the returns.

"That's a lot of presents," he said. "Can't you mail them back?"

I shook my head. "Those pots are heavy," I said. There was no need to explain to my father the fear of returning those gifts, facing the gossips in my mother's bridge group and the wives of my father's golf friends. He knew exactly my hesitancy, my terror. This was a nightmare I had been dreading since I got on the plane in Bordeaux.

"Don't do it," he said.

I shook my head.

"Phone those shops and have gift cards sent instead." He reached into his sport coat for his wallet. "I don't want you to return those gifts."

"I have to return the gifts, Dad. I'll just drive around and pretend I'm dead."

"Don't do it that way." There was recognition in his voice; he knew clearly what it was to pretend you were dead, and when you would need to pretend you were dead. "Put those boxes in the car and take them to Los Angeles. I want you to have nice things you like." He gave me his credit card and refused to hear any more about it. "Take it, Kath. Let's just put an end to this whole ordeal," he said.

I saw my father much more often that fall and into the winter. My mother had always visited regularly, but now that both Ethan and I were a comfortable three-hour drive from their home in Fresno, she and my father made frequent trips.

Every night for close to a year I dreamt of Lucas, and almost every time he was somehow indistinguishable from the gentle blond actor I had lived with in college. I missed Lucas. I missed his earnest quality, and how thoroughly he had loved me at first. I missed the good espressos and very best gelato in Rome. I missed my Italian-language classes with all the tourists. Still, to improve your Italian is a very bad reason to get married. That year I dreamt of Lucas, every morning I woke in a panic, worried that the wedding had accidentally happened.

On these visits, Dad and Ethan and John Cabott would play

golf until sundown, and when my mother and I had finished shopping or gossiping or looking for houses we would never buy, we would meet them for cocktails. No jeans were allowed in the clubhouse, so I wore skirts and heels and swept my hair into a twist. I had lightened my hair, which the people Ethan and I knew in Los Angeles said made me look happier than I had ever been.

"It's not the blond," I told them. "It's the Hollywood sign. I am in love with the Hollywood sign."

"Rubbish," John said.

"It's being closer to Fresno that keeps you happy," my father said, and my mother put her head in her hands.

"I think you're right," Ethan said to me. "The Hollywood sign makes me unreasonably happy, too."

We had moved on from the club. We ate dinner at the top of a hotel on Sunset with a complete view of the city at twilight.

I held up my port to toast Los Angeles's happy blondes.

"Your ring," Dad said, taking my hand.

I nodded. I had stopped noticing it. I wore it now out of habit. I no longer needed to be reminded that a lot of girls would have stayed.